I0742794

BURNED BY FURY

AN EVERLEIGH COLE NOVEL

SHAY LAURENT

BOOKS BY SHAY LAURENT

Everleigh Cole Novels
Haunted By Legacy
Burned By Fury

The Shifters & Sorceresses Trilogy
Wolf of Choice

BURNED BY FURY

An Everleigh Cole Novel

SHAY LAURENT

First published by Midlothian Press in 2025

Copyright © 2025 by Shay Laurent

This book is a work of fiction created without the use of artificial intelligence (AI) technology. All names, characters, organizations, places, events, and incidents in this book are either products of the author's imagination or used fictitiously. Any resemblance to actual persons, living or dead, or actual events, are coincidental.

All rights reserved. No part of this book may be reproduced in any form or by any electronic or mechanical means, without written permission from the author.

Without limiting the author's exclusive rights under copyright, any use of this book to train AI technology to generate text and content is prohibited.

Editing by Becky Johnson at Hot Tree Editing

Cover design by Julie Nicholls

ISBN: 978-0-6487871-5-0 (paperback)

ISBN: 978-0-6487871-4-3 (ebook)

For all the friends that add joy to the journey.

CONTENTS

EXPECTATIONS

The monstrous building that hosts the Council of the Accords and all its workers looms above me, its shadow leeching coolness into my bones. The crisp morning air of autumn, which I usually find calming, makes me shiver.

Come on, Everleigh. It's just a building. Just a job.

I pull in a deep breath, grounding my feet into my shoes and allowing the pressure change to bring me back to the present moment. Without warning, an intense warmth replaces the chill, reigniting my heart. As it builds, I turn to find the source. One corner of my mouth pulls up as I spot Alaric coming to a stop by my side.

"Alaric," I say, heat rising within me at being caught unaware.

His deep blue eyes catch my own. I'm transfixed for a moment as a ray of sunlight hits his face, transforming the darkness of his gaze into a tranquil blue sky.

"Are you going to keep staring at the building, or are you coming inside?" he grumbles, brow furrowed.

I must be delusional. Tranquil indeed.

"Just waiting for you, *partner*."

My smile grows at his grimace. I'm sure he didn't want to be reminded that he's now stuck with me for the next half a century. The bargain I made with the Archangel Raphael to protect my friends was worth it though, even if Alaric doesn't really want me around. Hells, I might not even survive the whole fifty years trying to enforce the Accords; the mortality rate is pretty high.

Puh-lease, anyone who tries it will be annihilated.

Alaric huffs out an impatient breath, sending a small cloud of white into the chilly morning air. Without sparing me another glance, he strides towards the front doors of my new prison, which are guarded by a pair of shifters in their bear forms, and I wonder briefly if they're the same ones who were here the last time I came.

I shake my head slightly and roll my shoulders back, envisioning my white, gold-tinged wings stretching at the same time. Standing a little taller, I follow Alaric into the lobby. Out of habit, I approach the visitor's desk.

"You're not a visitor anymore, Everleigh. We sign in on our floor. This way," he says as he points towards the lift.

A small shiver trails down my spine at the slight rumble in his chest when he says my name. Instead of showing he has any effect on me, I simply nod and walk in the direction he gestured, then wait quietly for him to press the button.

Alaric shifts slightly, and I can't help but wonder how unhappy he really is about being tied to me. If the scowl he wears is a measure, then I can assume he's less than impressed, but I try to remain hopeful given the warmer interactions we've had more recently. Enough supes already resent me simply for my hybrid status—like I could change it even if I wanted to. Being forced into close proximity with someone like that would be torturous.

We ride the elevator up to the ninth floor, then step out into a modern corridor of oak floors and white walls. A reception desk sits directly opposite us and a petite blonde fae looks up at our arrival. She offers Alaric a saccharine smile, which quickly falls from her face as he promptly ignores her and heads to a door at the right end of the corridor. I press my lips together to avoid showing my amusement, sure that upsetting someone on my first day wouldn't be the wisest choice.

Alaric bends slightly towards a retinal scanner, causing his faded denim jeans to mold over his firm arse.

Ohh, yes please! Squeeze it!

I shake my head.

What in the hells has gotten into you, girl? You've barely looked at anyone in a hundred years. Focus.

The door clicks open, and Alaric turns back to me, his mouth open to speak. He stalls for a second and swallows when he catches me looking. I raise my brows at him in question and he shakes his head infinitesimally.

"We'll get your access set up this morning. We only got the scanners installed last week."

"We don't need to see the blonde fae for that?" At his confused look, I feel the left side of my lips pull up and I add, "The one at the reception desk back there?"

He doesn't miss a beat. "No, we'll see Tess for that. This way," he says and continues through the door.

I stop in my tracks as we enter the open area I've visited once before. It's filled with state-of-the-art technology. Everything is spotless, and screens line the room, each flashing different streams of information faster than I can take them in. I watch a map zoom in, seemingly on its own, until I'm distracted by a bright-red head of hair.

A small, powerhouse of a woman stands and rushes over to Alaric, pulling him into an embrace. I stiffen slightly, unsure what to make of the exchange, especially when Alaric's frosty demeanor breaks and his smile draws one of my own.

So this is what a happy Alaric looks like.

"Tess," he grumbles, "it hasn't been that long since you've seen me."

"Oh, please," she says. "You could have been killed. *Again.* Anyway," she turns to me, posture slightly more rigid, "Hello again, Everleigh, my name is Tessa, in case you forgot. Welcome to the team." She offers me her hand.

I step forward and shake it. "Thank you," I offer neutrally, unsure whether she's happy I'm here or not. It can be hard to tell with some supes, especially the ones working to uphold the Accords. Most of them seem to have a tendency to push down their feelings, whereas I prefer to deal with them.

She nods. "I'm not sure if you recall, but I'm responsible for all things tech here, and all of the team that uses it. You, Alaric, and the other enforcers will work directly with me unless you need something in particular from the people in my team. I'll introduce you to them later. Let's get you set up."

Without waiting for my confirmation, she flits across to a computer and begins typing away. By the time I make it over, she has me look into a retinal scanner like the one at the door, and after another few moments and some muttered words, grins up at me, forgetting her rigid posture. "Done. You'll be able to gain access without Alaric now. Speaking of." She turns and looks at the wolf in question, who's leaning against the wall as though he's holding it up instead of the other way around. "Are you going to show Everleigh around, or…?"

He pushes off the wall, muscles bunching and releasing. "I'll take her to her workspace."

My brows fly towards my hairline. "We aren't going out? I thought this job was mostly done on the streets."

I'd pick him up if I found him working the street corner.

He huffs out a grouchy breath. "I don't think that will be necessary. You can start at the desk. Your gifts were what dragged you into this job. I have some jewelry and other artifacts for you to check out from some of our cold cases. Maybe you'll get a vision and we'll have something to go off."

Surprise ripples across Tessa's face before she reins it in, and I can't help but wonder if this is unusual behavior for Alaric.

Not wanting to start the partnership off poorly, I pull my attention away from Tessa, and nod.

Alaric leads me into a large room down another hallway, which looks as though it has floor-to-ceiling glass, just like on the outside, but the image of a beach at sunset tells me it's a screen of some sort.

"We can't have windows here for safety. There is a layer of magically reinforced concrete between the glass you see on the outside of the building and in here. You can program the image to be whatever you like though. This will be your office for as long as you're here." His face twists into a scowl when he stops speaking, which makes me desperately want to wrap my wings around myself for comfort. "Wait here," he says, then stalks out of the room. The itch to stretch my wings worsens tenfold the instant he is out of sight.

He walks back in after a few moments, holding a wooden chest that looks like it weighs more than he does, yet he doesn't break a sweat. Typical wolf.

My eyes widen as he opens the chest. It's lined with about twenty small compartments lined with red velvet, and it appears to have space for a second layer beneath the first. "Just a *few* cold cases?" I ask wryly.

"Yes. When the cases have gone cold, we place a relic with the most psychic energy into this chest."

"Why did you do that when you've never had other angels on board?"

He shrugs. "We just do as we're told."

I tilt my head slightly to the left, unable to believe he'd blindly follow the rules.

When Alaric sucks his cheeks in slightly, attempting to maintain his straight face at my obvious disbelief, I smile.

A little less frosty. Good.

"I need to go and check on some cases with Tess. I'll leave you to it."

"You don't need my help out there?"

His posture stiffens and his voice regains a little more ice. "No. Working in here is better. I'll see you soon."

I push out a huge breath and go to the mahogany desk in the corner, checking the drawers until I find a notepad and pen. After I take a seat, I run my hand across the artifacts in the top layer of the chest, feeling only faint pulses of energy.

This is going to be a long day.

I walk into my apartment as the sky darkens and watch my magically imbued rose tattoo bloom as I get closer to Raine.

"Honey, I'm home!" I call and hear Raine chortle in response.

"I heard you coming from downstairs. An elephant would have been less obvious."

I snort, knowing she can't help but make jokes. Her vibrancy since being changed into a vampire has blossomed just like our roses each time we meet. The Council approving me as her supernatural guide, instead of her getting a vampire master, is the best thing that's happened to me in a long time.

"So, how was your first day at work? As horrible as you thought?"

I smile, unable to help it around her. "No, it wasn't that bad." My brows draw down. "Although, I get the feeling that Alaric is planning to keep me pinned to the desk—"

Her eyebrows reach towards her hairline, and she begins to waggle them, deliberately misunderstanding me. "Oh really? I wouldn't mind being pinned to the desk by that sexy wolf-man. Shame he's taken." She winks.

Another snort escapes me. "Well, he's not taken by me, if that's what you mean. And, you know that is definitely not what I meant."

Raine sighs longingly. "That's not the impression I get. The sexual tension between you two is enough for me to cut with my fang! Oh, what I wouldn't give for that kind of attention from such a handsome beast."

I laugh, unable to contain myself. "You make it sound like we have some kind of relationship. The only thing he seems interested in is keeping me at arm's length and stuck in the office. I have a bunch of artifacts to try and pull visions from. It seems I'm desk bound until then."

She smiles knowingly and shrugs.

Incorrigible!

A sharp pain pierces my throat and chest, and I rub them, distracted from our conversation.

"Is the pain back? You were doing that last week."

When I look back at my friend, worry mars her features. All traces of playfulness are gone.

"I'm okay. It's not like angels or demons get sick or anything. This has to do with some kind of danger coming for Clara."

Raine's mouth twists at the sound of my twin's name, and I wish again that Clara had been less demonic when they met and had made a better impression on my friend.

"Have you called the bar while she's at work to tell her?"

If only she carried a mobile phone like the rest of the population.

I shake my head. "No, not yet. My sister isn't the best at listening to advice, especially when it involves being careful—she thinks she's invincible. It's better if I have something more specific to give her; hopefully I get a vision about whatever it is soon, instead of just this annoying burning feeling. The pain is getting worse, though, which means the danger is getting closer. I'll need to tell her sooner rather than later."

She sighs and grumbles something under her breath before a cheeky grin relights her features. "Well until that happens, I think we should make some dinner plans. Maybe with Alaric and Henry?"

It's my turn to sigh. "Seeing Henry would be great. I didn't think about how much it would suck not getting to see him at the psychology office every day now that I'm not working with him like I used to. I hope he's managing the clients and everything without having someone to debrief with."

Raine twists her lips to one side. "Well, I have been chatting to him most days, and he seems to be doing okay. Though, I think he's mostly been interested in all things supernatural. He's been asking me six million questions each time he goes through a new training module to introduce him to the supernatural world. You know, the stuff the High Witch gave him."

"*Oh, really.*" I lean back against the kitchen bench. "And how is that going? Seems like you two spend quite a lot of time 'chatting.'"

She sticks her tongue out at me and wanders over to the fridge, pulling out a bag of AB negative. "If we can't talk about you and Alaric, I don't see why we should talk about me and any interest I *might* have in Henry."

I laugh and lean out to poke her playfully, but she ducks under my hand in a flash with an impressive spin and a wink.

As I shake my head, another pain radiates through my throat and chest and dread pools in my stomach, worse than before.

The message is clear: Something bad is coming for Clara, and soon.

REGRETS

I WANDER OUT OF the elevator at work the next morning, determined to do something useful with my time. The same petite blonde fae is sitting behind the desk. I smile and wave in greeting, but all she offers is a thin stretch of her lips in return. I sigh.

At the end of the hall, I approach the retinal scanner, a small bubble of excitement rising at being able to use it for the first time. Humans have made some fascinating discoveries over time, and technology seems equal parts exciting and terrifying. Especially when supes are trying to stay hidden. It seems inevitable this will change at some point.

I bend a little and place my right eye in front of the device, watching as a blue light scans over my iris. A small green light comes on and the door clicks, letting me know I can go in. Despite it only being 8:00 a.m., the office is a flurry of movement. Tess's red hair is blocking her face from view as she stares at a screen. The vampire twins, Oldin and Stella, who I saw briefly when Raine and Henry were kidnapped, are watching news clippings at a speed so fast my eyes can't keep up.

I wander closer until I'm in Tessa's line of sight. "Hey, Tessa. What's happening?"

She looks up and offers me a brief smile. "Morning, Everleigh. Just another case that has come up. A little time sensitive. Alaric has already gone out today, but he said to let you know he'd be back later. He said you should keep going on the cold cases for now."

The look on my face must be unimpressed, because she adds, "Sorry. Try not to shoot the messenger. You can bust his balls later. I really need to keep going on this one, but if you need anything, just let me know, yeah?"

I huff a breath out of my nose and resign myself to taking it up with Alaric later. I pull my mouth into the best smile I can dredge up and nod. "No worries. If you need me, I'll be in my office."

"Okay, great. Oh, and Everleigh, your new laptop is here and has been set up so you can access all of our databases. There are links there to the human servers, too, if you need them, but there are procedures you'll need to use to access them. I've popped a cheat sheet of sorts onto your desktop. Your login and password are on a Post-it note on top of the laptop. Happy hunting." She winks at me, then promptly returns to her work.

I wonder what she is exactly. Usually, I can get a fairly good sense of other supes. She seems like a witch, but I can't see a trace of her aura at all, so I can't be sure. Maybe I can ask my ball-and-chain later.

The chest is still resting on the table in my office where I left it yesterday. I leave it for a moment and go to my desk. My laptop is sleek. It has a case on it that looks a lot like my wings—white with gold running through it. I smile, wondering who might have done that.

I take the login and password and open my new device. Across the desktop are several shortcuts with simple names: MissingPersons, GridSearch, Genealogies, and more. As I keep scanning, I see a document called CheatSheet and open it up, grateful Tessa seems to label things in an easy-to-use kind of way.

Since the artifacts in the chest only seem to have a paper list, I open up an Excel sheet to start categorizing them in a way I can add notes about any visions I have. Once I have my headings and tabs the way I want them, including a simple color-coding system, I head over to the chest with the new laptop and get started.

First, I pull out the pieces I worked with yesterday—a gold ring with a diamond, a silver necklace with a teardrop sapphire, and a scarab beetle made of onyx. I itemize them, including names, dates, and case numbers, then quickly add the few impressions I got yesterday. None of which were enough to go off.

It's a new day, Ev. Come on. You can do this. You always have hope. Dig it up.

I ignore the sharp twinge in my chest reminding me of Clara, since no vision is accompanying the feeling, and reach into a red velvet compartment to pull out another artifact. The petite porcelain vase holds a large amount of psychic energy, signifying the importance and connection the owner has with it. It might just be enough to show me where she is or what has happened to her. Cautiously, I lift it out and hold it in both of my hands.

Relief fills me when my vision begins to turn white, indicating my powers are going to show me something, and I offer a little prayer to the big guy for helping whoever is related to the small white vase resting in my palms.

The air is putrid. Breathing hurts in here.

The cold is biting into my bones.

It's like a cave. So dark and dank. It's like I'm buried with corpses.

I look around, desperate to find a clue to where I am.

I can barely see anything, and the vision is fading.

I lean forward and see a reflection in a puddle of something.

A woman. A witch. Her aura is muted, the hue an orange umber—desperation.

"Help," she mouths.

I'm suddenly back in my office, the fake beach and tranquil blue sky once again filling my vision from the other side of my desk. I carefully place the vase back into its compartment and hurriedly write what I saw in my spreadsheet. Seeing a face doesn't always happen for me, and I need to do something about it quickly, while the memory is fresh.

I jump up from my desk and rush out to the Technical Division where Tessa is talking to a shifter I don't know, their warmth radiating a good meter away from them.

Hmm... it doesn't feel like the hot burn of Alaric.

"What's up, Everleigh?" Tessa asks.

Appreciating her no-nonsense attitude, I smile a little. "Do we have a sketch artist on retainer?"

She half nods and turns to the other side of the room. "Hey, Zeke! Come here."

A thin, gangly male rushes over to us at a speed befitting a vampire, but without their typical grace. He bumps into at least three desks and a chair on his short trip, pausing to fix them each time. I pull on my psychologist façade, careful not to show any judgment towards him, sure that he already gets shit from the other supes for it. Time and again, they've shown they're not the most accepting of creatures.

To my surprise, no one comments, and Tessa ignores the pale pink flush on his cheeks. "Zeke, this is Everleigh. She's a new enforcer on the team. Everleigh, this is Zeke. He's responsible for anything involving faces and identification."

"Nice to meet you, Zeke." I offer my hand but pull it back immediately when his eyes widen in panic.

"Good to meetcha," he says quietly. "What do you need?"

"A sketch please, if you can?"

He nods, and rushes back to his desk, bumping another couple of chairs on the way, and collects a digital tablet and pen. Within seconds, he's back.

I thank Tessa and lead the way back to my office.

Zeke stands awkwardly outside the door, his ebony hair falling over part of his face, making him look extra vulnerable. His hand falls to his wrist, where a black fidget bracelet—a tool I've seen often as a psychologist—wraps around his wrist. He twists the copper beads wrapped within the black cord round and round.

"You can come in," I offer gently. "Thank you for agreeing to help." Seeing him look a little unsure about where to go, I point to a chair at the meeting table. "Please, take a seat."

He walks to the table, moving a little slower, as though he feels self-conscious in my presence, and I feel a twinge of sadness at his worry. Once he sits, Zeke immediately opens an app with a blank drawing sheet and looks at me.

"If you just describe the person the best you can, and then tell me what needs fixing, that will work."

I nod, and begin describing the woman's oval face, thin nose and lips, and the almond shape of her eyes. As Zeke draws, his energy changes. His nervous, clumsy demeanor transforms until he's focused—in flow—and completely absorbed in his artform. I watch on in awe as he takes the vision from my mind and brings it to life on his screen. Thanks to his vampire speed, it takes him little more than ten minutes to finish.

"It's perfect," I say. "She looks exactly as she did in my vision. You're amazing. Thank you."

The pink flush comes back to Zeke's cheeks, and he bobs his head, the nervousness returning as soon as he moves out of his element, his hand wandering back to the bracelet. I can't help but wonder what happened in his past to make him so nervous.

"I've emailed it to you. Do you know how to run it through the databases we have on file to find out who it might be?"

I shake my head. "I'd love some help, if you don't mind?"

He nods and reaches towards my laptop, and I move out of his way. He immediately opens the SupeCentral shortcut on the desktop and loads the photo he shared again to my laptop via the Cloud. His movements are fast, but still slow enough for me to follow so I know what to do next time, and once again, I'm struck by the kindness of some of the supes I meet. They're so different from those who have ridiculed me in the past.

Maybe I stayed away for too long.

"Okay," he says, "the search is running now. It will ping if it finds a match. Sometimes it can be quick, and other times it takes a while."

"Thanks, Zeke. I appreciate your help on this."

"Anytime."

Before I can say anything else, he shoots out of my office, narrowly missing the door frame.

After ten minutes spent changing the image on my wall screen, which now shows the Milky Way galaxy, my computer dings.

The sketch Zeke drew is sitting alongside a painted image of the same woman with the name Delilah Shelldrake. I pull up the case file listed with the vase and barely stop myself from swearing.

Of course her name was already bloody here, Everleigh. Why didn't you open the damn case file first?

I feel the heat rushing to my cheeks in embarrassment for wasting Zeke's time. I try to shake it off and search the case file for details of Delilah's last known location during the case. Once I find it, I switch to something more useful: the map.

Thinking back to my vision, I recall the dank cave and the stench, then scour the map for locations that might be a match. The most obvious option seems to be some caves an hour or so down the coast.

Ignoring my chagrin, I place the vase in a small satchel I carry around, collect my keys, and head out. As I pass by the technical division, I wave to Tessa, and call out, "Just going to check something out from a cold case. I'll touch base if I find something."

Tessa looks like she's about to object, but then a few screens start beeping and she turns around, waving me away.

Well, that was lucky. Once I reach my destination a while later, I turn off the car engine, and get out. Immediately, I scrunch my nose at the revolting smell intertwined with the sea breeze. I've definitely made it to the right place. Something here feels...off. Dread pools in my stomach, knowing I didn't tell anyone where exactly I was going. With a sigh, I send Alaric a dropped pin and the case number.

That done, I place my phone on the seat and pull out the small vase. The warmth radiating from it gives me another clue that I'm close to where I need to be. I suck in a breath of putrid air and wish pointlessly that I could release my wings from the ether—having them free always brings me a measure of comfort. But the punishment for revealing myself to any potentially watching humans outweighs any solace they might bring me.

Since I'm looking for the caves, I make my way down to the beachfront and head towards the worst of the smell, convinced it will lead me to Delilah.

A magical cold begins to leach the warmth from inside me and I stop. Someone else is here and I've hit their wards. They're carelessly hidden but painfully strong. I take a moment to reinforce my internal shields, mentally pushing away the parasitic cold, like a blazing fire razes a grassy field. Once I feel back to myself again, I continue towards the cliff face ahead.

I sense the auras before I see them. Two of them up ahead. As I round the corner into a cavern, they come into my line of sight, and the heat I'd regained seeps away. The women in front of me are dressed in obsidian witch cloaks, their auras almost blending in with their surroundings, except for the deep crimson flowing through them. Blood witches.

The one closest to me, an older-looking hag with gray hair, sniffs the air, and spits onto the rocky ground. "Half-blood. Why are you in our territory?"

I swallow and wonder if saying I am an enforcer of the Accords will lead to more trouble or less.

"I'm here looking for someone. I mean no harm."

The second witch, the younger of the pair, sneers at me. "We're not here to help. Begone before we destroy you."

The first witch hisses in her coven-mate's direction and turns back to me. "And what is it you seek, half-blood?" A hungry look crosses her face, and she smiles, her rotting teeth making me want to gag. "And what will you offer in exchange?"

What in the hellish realms was I thinking coming down here without backup? I can't give them my blood, which is the only thing they'll want.

I weigh my options and take one step back. The hag immediately hisses a word of power and blue flames spring up behind me, taller than I am.

Well, I guess leaving is out.

Ugh. Just kill them.

Standing a little straighter, I ignore my inner-demon and look at the older witch, who is clearly in charge. "I am an enforcer for the Council of the Accords, and I am here for Delilah Shelldrake."

SAVED

The old hag spits on the ground in my direction. "Enforcer scum aren't welcome on our coven's land. You should already know that."

Shit.

"She must be new," the younger witch sneers. "Maybe we should teach her a lesson about making demands of the Blood Stone Coven."

I twist my lips to one side, replacing fear with bravado. "So the offer of an exchange is off the table then?"

"Not with—"

The younger witch is cut off abruptly when the hag elbows her roughly in the ribs.

Some discord. I can work with this.

"Hybrid blood is a rather rare delicacy. Especially blood from the light city and the hellish realms." She pauses for a moment, deception flooding her muted aura with a smoky gray. "A cup of your blood in exchange for the near-dead witch."

The young one looks ready to attack her superior but holds a tight lid on herself.

I just need to get close enough.

I nod. "A deal then."

Yes! Kill them!

"This is a terrible fucking idea," the inferior whispers none too quietly.

The hag ignores her, faded pink tongue running over what remains of her rotted teeth. "Well, come closer. No need to be shy."

I stroll towards them, looking for the talismans they wear to power their blood magic. As I draw near, the hag pulls a filthy, stained knife from her robes, and I reach for my own, immediately regretting leaving the house without it this morning.

Coming to a halt, I look pointedly at the knife. "I'd rather not be cut with that." Seeing the amount of old blood and guts covering the blade, I figure being cut with it would suck almost as badly as Alaric's anger if he finds me here hurt.

The second she turns to look at the young witch, I rush forward and grab the cord tied around her neck, ripping it free. The graying witch stumbles, her breath stolen for a moment. I toss the necklace into the blue fire, hoping like the hells it destroys it, before lunging for the younger witch.

Before I can identify her talisman, she grabs me by the wrist, and with a muttered word, I let loose a piercing scream. It feels like my blood is boiling. Like I'm being cooked from the inside out. As she reaches for me with her second hand, I release my wings from the ether, and smash one right into her, knocking her back to the rock with a thud.

An echoing snarl rips through the cavern, and by the time I turn to see whether I'm completely screwed, a giant, deep-gray wolf has ripped off the hag's head. When those icy eyes lock with mine, I recognize him. Alaric. He looks past my shoulder and huffs. I turn and see the younger witch running away.

I'm never going to hear the end of this. Oh well, I guess I'll go all in.

I look back and shrug, then saunter towards Alaric. I ruffle the fur on his head and whisper, "Thanks for the save."

He snarls a moment too late for me to be concerned. I continue past him towards the back of the cavern to find an entrance to the actual cave Delilah is being kept in.

We need to get out of here. That young witch may very well bring back reinforcements.

While I'm looking along the wall, I feel the energy shift behind me as Alaric changes back to his human form.

"What in all the flaming realms of hell do you think you're doing, Everleigh?" His voice sounds like a tightly wrapped explosive. "You could have been killed. You don't even have bloody weapons on you. Did you even read the case file or location files before you came traipsing down here?"

I freeze momentarily, melting a little at the protective undertone to his anger. Since he does seem to care, and did in fact save me, I try to take the path of least resistance. I glance over my left shoulder, pushing my now loose hair behind my ear to get a better look.

Ugh, those jeans. Couldn't he wear something less distracting, something that clings a little less to his chiseled muscles?

"Everleigh," he barks.

"What?" I snap my eyes to his mostly furious face. "Oh, sorry. Uh, yes, well maybe we could talk about it back at the office? I need to get into the caves behind this wall to find the missing lady from the file."

Alaric grinds his teeth a little and starts searching the wall. Grateful for the reprieve, and somewhat impressed by his self-control, I go back to the task as well.

Ah, there.

"Could you bring some of the witch's blood over here? It looks like we need it to break the spell and get through."

Without comment, Alaric bends down, picks up the hag's dripping head and stalks towards me, not so much as flinching when he wipes her gaping neck against the rocky wall. The demonic side of me purrs at his stoicism, and I try my best to push it down before I seem unhinged.

The section of the wall dissolves in front of us and I walk straight through before fear can get the better of me. I quickly pull the petite vase out of my satchel again, shocked it isn't broken, and let it pull me towards the witch, the rest of the cave fading from view as I narrow in on the psychic energy I can feel flowing through this place. After a few twists and turns, we arrive at what seems like a dead end, causing me to snap out of my almost trance-like state.

"Well, this is the place. Do you think it needs more blood or something?" I ask, doubt coloring my tone since there are no traces of blood on this wall.

Alaric looks around, sniffing the decaying scent more fully than I would ever consider. After a few moments, he pushes on a piece of rock, which looks no different to the rest of the wall to me. This time, a section of the cave wall slides open.

The force of the smell crashes into me and I gag, my eyes watering. I look into the room, barely able to see from the oil lantern the witches have hung along the wall. I glance briefly at Alaric and notice his expression is deadly. My heart flutters, wondering if I'm too late, despite the warmth from the vase.

"Is she... okay?"

He pauses for a moment, inhaling again more gently. "She's alive."

I push a deep breath out, trying to prepare myself for what's to come, given Alaric's bleak assessment of the situation. Quickly, I reach out, grab the oil lantern, and make my way into the cave proper.

As soon as I move past the entryway, the door slides shut, and my heart jumps into my throat. Thankfully, it opens almost immediately, and I see Alaric's eyes staring at me from the other side.

"I'll wait here in case it shuts again. No one else is in there. Or out here. But I don't know how long that is going to last."

"Right. Got it," I say, and venture further in until I find Delilah cowering against a wall. As I approach, I get lower to the floor and use a soft, calm voice. "Delilah, my name is Everleigh. I'm here to get you out of this place."

It's like she doesn't hear me.

I sidle a little closer and spot the puddle next to her that I saw her reflection in. A puddle of her own urine. My heart cracks and I breathe out a shaky breath before trying again.

I draw my angelic essence to my mind, thinking of the love and comfort my mother used to transfer to me through touch. This time, I reach out and gently touch Delilah, knowing if we weren't in a time crunch, I'd never force this on her. She whimpers quietly and squeezes her eyes tighter.

After a few moments, my angelic essence flows into her, as delicately as I can manage. I'm starting to worry that too long has passed when she finally takes a breath and opens her eyes to see me.

I smile gently. "Hi, Delilah, my name's Everleigh. I work with the Council. I'm here to help you get free. Do you think you can stand?"

Her eyes widen, filling with tears and she immediately tries to push herself to her feet.

"Can I help you up?" She looks too frail to stand on her own, but touching someone who has experienced so much trauma without their consent could trigger unwanted thoughts or memories. I don't want to make things any worse for her.

She nods after a long moment, and I move to help her to her feet. I do my best to ignore the horrible state she is in, because I can't do anything about that yet. I carefully pull her arm around my shoulder, and we make our way back to the door. As we get closer, I warn her about Alaric and explain that he's helping us. Delilah nods tightly and continues on, surprisingly steady despite her poor physical condition.

As we make it to the door, Alaric looks at the witch, the gentlest expression I've ever seen on him displayed on his features. "We need to hurry," he says quietly. "Delilah, do you think you could stand me carrying you?"

I tilt my head slightly as I take him in, wondering how often and how many beings he's seen like this in his time as an enforcer.

Maybe he just saves the emotion for these times.

Delilah looks down at herself, her dress tattered and worn, stained with her own urine and feces and what looks like blood. When she meets Alaric's eyes, she flinches and shakes her head.

He crouches down, holding out a hand to her. "Please," he asks quietly. "I'm not judging you. I know how long you've been trapped here. But they could be back any second, and we don't want to be here when they arrive."

Delilah trembles a little, but nods, untangling herself from me and reaching out to Alaric. I look at him, too, but he doesn't meet my eyes.

He picks her up quickly, doing his best to hold her in the nicest way he can and then gestures with his chin for me to lead the way. As we walk through the cavern, he's careful to block her view of the dead hag, before meeting me out on the beachfront, the fire no longer blocking the way.

When we make it up to my car without further incident, I breathe a sigh of relief. Without waiting for the instruction, I open the passenger side door for Alaric to place Delilah inside, which he does as gently as he can manage.

He meets my eyes, and I can see he looks bone-tired. Not on the outside, but on the inside. His voice sounds exhausted, and I'm surprised he's allowing me to see his vulnerability. "I rode my motorcycle. I'll need to meet you both back there. We'll take her straight to the underground parking area. There's a medical unit inside."

Unable to stop myself, I reach out and press my hand to his shoulder and squeeze gently. "Thank you," I whisper. "For saving her and me."

His deep blue gaze holds mine for a long moment, filled with words he doesn't let out. Then he dips his head ever so slightly, and moves to his black and chrome motorcycle, the helmet resting on the seat.

Inside the car, Delilah has fallen asleep. I do my best not to wake her as I travel back.

I pull up behind Alaric in the underground bay. Octavia, the High Witch, is standing at the door with a wheelchair. Her pale pink skin looks white in the underground light, and worry mars her features. Her barely visible aura is a mess of colors, telling me she's feeling a lot of things right now, and I wonder how well she knows Delilah.

When I get out, I whisper, "She's still asleep. Alaric, would you mind?"

He leans in without a word and pulls her from the car. "I'll just carry her to a bed, if you'll lead the way."

Octavia doesn't look away from the delicate woman, but she nods. "We can take her to my personal medical suite on the eighteenth floor."

When no one moves, I lead the way to the lift and hear them following me.

Once we arrive, Octavia leads us through several doors until we reach her medical suite and Alaric lays Delilah down.

"Thank you," the High Witch says quietly, catching my gaze, then Alaric's. "I didn't think we'd ever see her again. She's been missing for almost sixteen years."

My eyes widen and I try to stop my mouth from popping open.

I should have looked properly in the case file. No wonder she's in such a terrible condition.

I should go back and end the rest of that coven. Monsters.

I shake my head to refocus on the lady in front of me. "I'm glad we could help. But maybe we should go so Delilah can rest and you can catch up with her."

Octavia nods and I follow Alaric from the room.

We wander back through the Technical Division and as soon as Tessa sees me, she lets out a big exhale. "Thank the stars you're okay! I thought Alaric was going to eat me alive when I told him you'd left, but I couldn't tell him where you'd gone. I was so relieved when you sent him the dropped pin."

I pull my lips into my mouth to stop my amusement showing.

"Everybody here should know better than to leave without reporting where they're going." He turns on me, all gruffness once more. "And you need to have weapons on hand. Not that you should have even left. You were meant to stay here."

I bristle at the change in his demeanor. "I was just following a lead. Though obviously I'll be sure to take weapons next time."

He growls, the sound reverberating through me. "No. No next time. You need to stay here and aim for the visions where it's safe. You do not need to be in the field."

"You're kidding me, right? I didn't agree to spending fifty years sitting behind a desk." I feel the heat rise to my eyes and see the red glow emanating from them reflecting on computer screens nearby.

"You. Are. Staying. Put."

Bite him into submission.

I open my mouth to argue but he storms out. My blood boils, and I turn to Tessa, eyes and mood blazing.

32

BROKEN

Alarm flashes in Tessa's eyes for a split second, then she holds her hands up, palms forward. "No, no. Don't take that rage out here. Come with me." She walks past quickly and beckons for me to follow.

Seething, I trail behind her, trying to rein in my temper.

She leads me down a hall, past my office, and towards a service elevator. "Just a little further," she mutters. "It'll be worth it. I promise."

Tessa taps her pass on the scanner and presses to go to B5, which didn't even exist in the main elevators. I try to focus on my curiosity to abate some of my mood from Alaric's shitty attitude, but it doesn't work well.

When we get out, Tessa leads me down a hall to the right. There are five doors with lights above them. Three are red and two are green. She stops in front of a green door and buzzes us in.

I pause for a moment. It's like a miniature warehouse that doesn't look like it should fit beneath the building we're in. Lined all along the wall next to the door are shelves with ceramic plates and bowls. On the wall to the left are helmets, safety goggles, and a range of bats.

I look at Tessa, the confusion taking some of the sting from the anger and underlying hurt.

She grins wickedly. "I knew that look you had upstairs. You wanted to break something. I'm all too familiar." She shrugs. "Welcome to the smash rooms."

I smile, probably looking feral, and go and pull on the safety gear. When we're both ready, Tessa grabs a pile of plates. I pick up a hardwood bat, knowing it will be more of a workout for me than something lighter. And I definitely need to work some things out.

"Incoming!" She lobs a plate towards me.

I pull the bat up over my right shoulder, focus on my anger, and swing. The bat connects with the ceramic plate with a deafening crack. It shatters into a thousand little pieces that go flying in every direction. A small part of me imagines that it's Alaric. He has no right to be scolding me like that for one mistake.

A grin lights my features when I look at Tessa. "Again."

After what feels like forever smashing the kitchenware, my arms are finally starting to ache. The anger is dying down, but I want to be certain before I head back upstairs.

"One more," I say, "just to be sure."

She laughs and lobs a bowl towards me. My muscles contract as I pull back, and release as I swing through. The moment the bat connects with the bowl, everything goes white, and I freeze, unable to see anything around me as I'm sucked into a vision.

Fire fills my insides.
Pain ricochets down my throat.
Can't breathe.
Silk sheets. Too soft. Can't hold on.
Need help.
Blackness calls.
Need.
Air.
Need—

As the vision fades, my heartbeat slowly returns to normal, and I see Tessa waving her hand in front of my face to get my attention.

Her lips move a second before the sound comes back. "—okay, Everleigh?"

My throat feels raw, as if the vision was real and just happened to me. I try to clear it, wincing at the discomfort. "I'm all right, Tessa. Sorry to worry you. It was just a vision. I forgot to warn you it might happen."

"Ahh, right. Alaric mentioned you getting them, but he didn't share any detail on the 'how' part. Anything you need to act on?"

I said I'd make contact if things got worse or I got a vision. It feels like both.

A sigh escapes, knowing I'm in for an argument. "Yeah, I need to go see Clara."

Tessa's brow furrows, clearly unfamiliar with the name.

"I'm surprised Alaric didn't say anything." *Or that you didn't just know.* "Clara is my twin sister. I have a feeling danger is coming for her."

Embarrassment lights her features, and I imagine the little emoji with the teardrop on its head. "Sorry, I feel I should have known that anyway, given your hybrid status and all, but despite all my tech time, I actually don't tend to keep up to date with any non-witch goss. And honestly," she mutters, "I avoid that, too, if I can. Being part of a witch coven can be nightmarish at times."

Ahh, so I was right. She is a witch! She must be using a talisman to mask her aura.

"It's completely fine." I laugh, feeling a lightness in my chest. "On second thought, it's actually a nice change."

Her expression smooths out and she tilts her head slightly to the side. "It must be hard, huh? Supernaturals hate anything that's different. I imagine being an angel-demon hybrid didn't exactly make for a smooth upbringing in our world."

"No, not exactly. But I've mostly just stayed away from our world. I've spent the majority of my life amongst the humans, moving every ten years like the Accords demand. Clara, on the other hand—" I huff out a dry laugh. "—she's followed the ten-year-rule, but I wouldn't say she's tried to blend in. If you've ever been down to the Scandinavian supe bar in Redfern, you've probably seen her."

Tessa parts her lips, then pauses for a moment, looking thoughtful. I watch as recognition turns to shock. "No way." Her eyebrows arch into her hairline. "Not the bartender with the red eyes?"

I snort indelicately. "That's the one. How'd you pick it? We don't exactly look the same."

She ducks her head. "The eyes actually. I saw yours go the same shade of red when you were ready to murder Alaric upstairs."

I shrug. "Ahh, well, that makes sense. But anyway, yeah, that's Clara. I need to go and tell her about the vision I just had, although I know she isn't going to want to hear it."

Tessa bobs her head in understanding. "I know we don't know each other very well, but do you need some backup with your sister? It sounds like it's important for her to listen."

A warmth builds at her kindness, but I can't ignore the tinge of regret that colors the moment, wondering if I could have been a little more involved in the supernatural world after my parents were gone. All I experienced before Alaric, and Raine, and now Tessa, were supes who despised me and Clara simply for existing.

"I really appreciate it, but I think my best chance is trying to talk to her on my own."

"I get that, but the offer still stands."

"Thanks." A thought pops into my mind alongside some blossoming hope for me and Raine. "Any chance you might like to join Raine and me for a girls' night? Hells, maybe even with Clara as well. I don't really have many connections in the supe community."

Tessa grins. "Sounds great to me. I haven't been out for a girls' night in a hot minute."

"Awesome." I smile. "I'll tee it up with Raine, and we can pick a day and time. For now, I'm gonna go and see Clara. Thanks for today too. Smashing the never-loving hells out of some stuff really helped."

Should have just jumped Alaric so he knew he was a bad wolfy.

"Anytime," she offers, and takes my bat and helmet so I can leave.

A few hours later, I walk down the abandoned street to the bar where Clara works, hopeful it will be mostly deserted given the early hour. The wards on the street are the best I've ever seen—there are no humans in the area despite its proximity to the city. As I approach the nondescript wooden door, I hear a deep male voice nearby, swearing ferociously.

After a moment, the voice cuts off and I hear my sister. "—you conniving piece of shit."

I dash around the corner and walk into a blood-soaked nightmare. Pools of blackened crimson fill the depressions in the concrete alleyway. In the middle of the space, a ghastly looking male demon is sprawled beneath my sister, ichor-like blood gushing from slices on his torso while those on his arms are beginning to clot. Several of his limbs are bent at wrong angles, stopping him from moving.

At the sound of my steps, Clara looks up at me with pulsing red eyes narrowed to slits. Blood is painted all over her face. Her black skin-tight outfit is soaked and shiny from spilling the demon's insides. Her ebony hair is tied back in her demon-hunting braid, and her blades are clasped tightly in each hand, now poised to throw in my direction.

"You stupid fucking hybrid bitch. I will kill—"

Clara cuts off the demon's words by slicing into his throat all the way down through his vocal cords.

"I was really getting sick of listening to his useless drivel. He had no details about Father's death." She stands up, spins back to the demon on the ground, and steps through his head with the sharpened heel of her stiletto boot. Once it's in far enough, he disintegrates, being pulled back into whichever hellish realm he came from. She turns back to look at me as she sheaths her twin blades, the matching pair to my own. "What brings you here, Sister?"

How could anyone possibly best her?

"Clara...." I bite the inside of my lip for a moment, hesitating. "Are you well? I've been worried about you."

She tilts her head to the side and narrows her eyes for a moment before rolling her shoulders back and forcing herself to relax. "I'm fine, Everleigh. Why are you so worried? You know I can take care of myself." She waves her hands vaguely at the carnage around the alley.

I nod reluctantly. "I know. But I've had a vision, and I can't shake the intuitive feeling that something dangerous is coming for you. I wanted to make sure you knew. Maybe, keep an extra eye out or something."

Clara pinches her lips together and rolls her eyes at me, reminding me of the hundreds of training sessions with Father when he tried to tell her something she didn't want to hear. "Again. I can take care of myself." She begins walking towards the club's back door, then looks over her shoulder at me. "Are you coming?"

I peer around at the bloodbath for a moment, wondering how it's going to get cleaned up. The click of her boots draws my attention back to the fact that my sister has continued walking on without me. I huff out a sigh and follow.

Once inside, Clara walks into the employee bathroom, strips off her saturated clothing, and steps into the shower. "So, what happened in the vision, Sister?"

I relay the information and the feelings back to her, trying to provide as much of the limited details as I can, while also trying to convince her the danger is real and she needs to be concerned, despite her general badassness.

She doesn't respond as she washes the gore from her lithe, muscled figure, but I know she can hear me, especially in such close proximity. Once she is clean and I can see all of her tattoos again, she turns off the taps. I quickly pick up her towel and pass it to her as she steps out.

"I don't know what you want me to say. I will be fine as always. I can take care of myself."

"You don't have to be so stoic with me, Clara. I'm your family—your sister. I'm never going to stop looking out for you."

She nods once, choosing to say nothing further on the subject.

I sigh, content enough with the fact that I've warned her and hopeful she will at least keep a closer eye out for potential signs of danger. Though, considering her love of risk-taking behaviors, it's unlikely she'd ever run from it.

"Okay. Well, that's all I needed to tell you." I pause, remembering my chat with Tessa. "I'm not sure if you might be up for it, but I was planning to have a bit of a girls' night out this weekend with a couple of other supes. I thought maybe you'd like to join?"

"I've no interest in bonding with your pet vampire or anyone else."

I try hard to keep the disappointment from my features. Spending time with my sister happens so rarely these days.

"The offer is always open if you change your mind. I love you, Sister. Be careful, please. If not for you, for me."

Before she can dismiss my worries again, I leave.

REPRIEVE

IF SOMEBODY TOLD ME I was in the hellish realms, I might have believed them after the week I just had. I was fairly certain that being chained to my desk, scouring through computer programs, and trying to assess psychic energy from cold cases, was a punishment even Nicon wouldn't approve of. Add to it the fact that Mr. Grumpy kept preventing me from working on the streets with him, and I was ready to stab something.

Or someone.

I roll my shoulders back and take a deep breath, determined to free myself from the weight of dissatisfaction and focus on my plans for tonight. The music booming from the nightclub draws my attention, and when the beat slithers into my body, I can't help but shake my hips.

It's time!

An unexpected swell of excitement rises in my chest as I walk into the rowdy human bar with Raine. A girls' night isn't something I thought I would ever get to do, especially not with other supes. My former life as a social outcast meant friends were not on my agenda. I catch Raine moving too fast for a human in her excitement and hook my arm through hers to slow her down.

"I'm so pumped for tonight, Ev! I never even had a girls' night before I was—"

I yank her to a halt and give her a warning look as I cringe on the inside, thinking of the coals I would be hauled over by the Council if she outed us in a human bar.

She laughs, her carefree smile causing the skin around her eyes to crinkle. "Before I was living with you."

I roll my eyes indulgently, thanking the big guy again for putting Raine in my path. "Well, I can't say I've had one before living with you either."

Her eyes widen in surprise. "No way! Well, I guess we'd better make this one to remember. Where's Tessa?"

I scan the gyrating throng of people on the dance floor. When I don't spot her, I look over to the bar.

Tessa is waving at us, her long legs perched across the two seats next to hers. Her short emerald-colored dress, which brings out the deep red of her hair, is hanging loosely over her thighs.

I squeeze Raine's arm and point to our destination. "Looks like we're starting with drinks. Let's go."

Raine offers a squee of delight and begins ever-so-gently shoving humans out of our path to get to our new friend.

"Hey, Tessa!" I half yell over the music, knowing her hearing isn't as acute as mine or Raine's.

"Tess is good," she calls back. "I mean, we've smashed some shit together now, right?"

I grin. "Well, then you should call me Ev!"

"I don't really have a nickname," Raine exclaims, pouting.

"We'll come up with something," Tess yells as she stands up and abandons the seats and her empty glass. "This is way too loud. Let's head up to the rooftop bar so we can get some cocktails and catch up."

The sky looks clear, the stars sharp as they twinkle down at us when we reach the outside terrace. I get the strange feeling some of them are laughing at us. I tuck a few strands of my straightened hair behind my ear, trying to ignore the impression so I can enjoy my night.

Tess pulls my attention from the night sky. "How'd everything go with Clara?"

Raine returns with our Blue Lagoon cocktails and groans when she overhears the conversation.

Tess smiles wryly. "That good, huh?"

I smooth my black skirt over my thighs. "It could have gone better. But then, it could have gone worse too."

Raine makes a grumble, which sounds a lot like Alaric when he's in a bad mood. "She should just be more respectful of Ev. She's only trying to keep her sister safe."

I lean close and put an arm around my friend and squeeze her in for a hug. "Thank you," I say, feeling the words aren't doing my gratitude justice.

She smiles back. "Of course, never expect anything less from me. I've got your back." Raine takes another sip of her drink and then her face lights up with joy. "Okay, so I decided to make tonight even more awesome by keeping some news secret, although it's almost killed me, so I sure hope you appreciate it. I've been offered a job!"

"What?! That's amazing. What is it? How did it happen? I know you've been so worried about not being able to work since you... changed," I yell over the now thumping bass. "And how did you manage to keep it a secret?"

Tess leans closer to hear so we don't need to talk so loudly over the music.

Raine gives a little squeal and pumps her fist into the air. "Woo! I was sure you were going to figure it out because I kept getting so excited at home." She grins at me, her happiness infectious as always. "Anyway, I couldn't believe my luck, really. I was actually on the phone to Henry at the time, answering a question about... special food for people who like the woods, and then I got a call from Octavia—"

"Like, *Octavia*, Octavia. The boss lady?" Tess interjects.

Raine lets out another excited squee and I laugh happily in response.

"Yes! She totally did. A job came up as a teacher at a *special* school for youth with difficulties in regulating their emotions while they adapt to *changes*. It's just perfect. I actually get to help kids again."

Her double meaning is easily caught. She's been offered a job teaching supernatural kids.

I reach out and hug my friend again. "That's amazing. You're going to be perfect at that job."

Tess tips a little to the side in her chair as she leans closer to Raine, the alcohol starting to wear on her. "Just don't let those lil' shits get away with anything. You show them who's boss, or they'll eat you alive."

Raine looks horrified at Tess's suggestion, and I can't help but chuckle. "I'm sure there are other ways. It'll all be okay."

An hour and too many cocktails later, we're about to go and dance when Raine's phone dings and she pulls it out, frowning. "It's Henry."

I sit back in my chair, now needing to know what's going on. "How is Henry? I've barely been able to see him since he started his new learning program, and I haven't heard from him at all since I started my job this week."

"He's been good. Missing you as well though, Ev." She chuckles. "I've actually been speaking to him a lot for the last couple of weeks. He's full of questions about all the stuff he's learning."

Before she can say anything else, her phone dings a few times in a row. Confusion mars her delicate features as she looks at the texts.

"Uhh, I think Henry might be drunk... and coming here to find us. I can't quite understand his messages, but he sounds worried about something."

"No!" Tess half squeals before grabbing each of us and pulling us towards the dancing humans. "It's girls' night. We were about to dance. Quick, let's go!"

The need to find out what is going on with Henry is warring with enjoying this special night.

He'll be here soon. I can find out then. No harm in enjoying the night a little. Clara is always onto me about living a little more.

I stop resisting and join my friends, dancing and getting lost in the rhythm and heavy bass of the pop songs blasting from the speakers.

After a little dancing time, someone shoves into my back, causing me to trip into Raine. She catches me but is looking over my head. "Henry?"

I turn, my surge of anger fading as quickly as it arrived. He looks a little unsteady on his feet, but I reach out and pull him in for a hug anyway. "Henry, I've missed you!"

He squeezes me, then leans back, his eyes looking glassy from the booze. "Ev, I've missed you lots!" When he turns to look at Raine, his cheeks flush a little more and he holds onto his suspender straps, looking a little shy. "And you, hi," he yells to her.

"Is everything okay?" she calls out. "It sounded like something was wrong in your texts."

Tess leans into our little circle and shakes Henry's hand while giggling.

"This is Tess," I offer. "I work with her."

His face relaxes a little at her intrusion, but he's started wringing his hands. "Can you ladies come over where it's a little quieter? I need to show you something right now."

Concern makes my stomach feel unsteady alongside the cocktails as I follow along behind him.

Henry opens a video on a news site and holds it out to me, Raine, and Tess. My chest tightens dramatically as my eyes scan the headline: *Vampires are REAL: Woman attacked and left for dead.*

NEWS

THE WOMAN IN THE video is covered in double puncture wounds, is pale as a sheet, and is stained with her own blood. Fresh bruises cover most of her skin and are especially dark around her wrists and neck. There are so many bites on her that it seems as though more than one vampire is responsible.

When Henry hits Play, the camera zooms in on the woman's face. She looks completely dissociated, as though she's sitting there in the flesh, but no one is home inside her head. She twitches occasionally, seeing things that aren't there. Whimpers come every few moments when she squeezes her eyes shut. "Stop.... No more.... Please.... Stop...."

The camera man turns the camera to a reporter, who looks shocked and a little fearful. "You heard it here first. This lady said she's been attacked by vampires, and she sure as hell looks like she has. We'll have some experts analyze the footage and what appears to be fang marks. But in the meantime, keep your families and children safe. Lock your doors and don't invite anyone in. Maybe pick up some garlic or something. Stan Suntin for the *Daily Scoop*, out."

After a pause, the camera view moves back to the woman, who's now on the ground curled in on herself. The image speaks more than any words the newsperson could say.

Once the image fades away, there is silence amongst our group. The noise from the club surrounds us, but it feels as though it can't break the barrier of our shock.

I'm worried for my friends, but my eyes are drawn to Tess, who now seems completely sober, her mouth twisted in concern. When she locks her gaze to mine, guilt flashes across her features and my stomach feels as though a rock has landed in it.

"We can go in together," she offers as she looks meaningfully at the crowd nearby. "We can make a plan of attack. Alaric has already—" She cuts herself off with another apologetic glance at me, like she's said something she shouldn't have.

I nod slowly and release her from the intense eye contact by looking at Raine and Henry. "Will you guys be okay? I need to go into work with Tess and figure out what needs to be done." I'm dying to know what Alaric is hiding from me, but forcing the information out of Tess risks breaking our newfound friendship.

Raine squeezes my hand and pulls me into a brief hug. "Of course. Let me know if there is anything I can do to help."

Henry nods, chest puffed out as he tries to bring back his brave face. "Yeah. I'll make sure Raine gets home safe to your apartment."

I sneak a peek at Raine, who is also looking completely sober now that she has stopped the constant stream of drinks to stay intoxicated. She stays behind Henry to hide her amused grin and lightly flushed cheeks, clearly finding his drunk bravado to her liking.

They'll be okay.

"Okay. Well stay safe, and I'll check in with you both later. Thanks for coming to tell us Henry. It means a lot."

"I've always got your back, Ev. Just take care of yourself. Don't get into anything unsafe, okay?"

I smile gently at my human best friend, always amazed at the care and bravery of such vulnerable beings.

I follow Tess downstairs, through the sweat-slick crowd and out onto the street. We wander a short way along the footpath until we get to her sleek Mercedes. I slide inside after she unlocks the doors. Once she clicks her seat belt into place, she unclips a small vial from around her neck and tips it back like a shot. She looks over to me and explains, "It's a small potion to sober me up. It burns the alcohol from my system so I can drive in a pinch. It'll give me a hell of a headache later, though, so we better get going."

I nod, impressed by the resourcefulness of witches in addressing such things as a full supes gift (or curse) of burning away any alcohol in their system very quickly. Such musings don't keep my attention for long, though.

"So what is it Alaric decided I didn't need to know?"

Tess flinches at my words and looks at me for a moment. "To be clear, I was against this. We're all meant to be a team, and you two in particular are supposed to be working together, according to the boss."

Nicon's devilish smile takes over my vision for a moment as I'm drawn back to the decision he made with the Council that Alaric would be responsible for showing me the ropes and working with me. His motivation seemed double-edged at best.

"I appreciate you wanting me included," I acknowledge, "but what wasn't I told?"

Tess's brows draw down. "So, a few days ago, there was a really similar video, but it showed a human who was attacked by a werewolf. The guy was torn up pretty bad. Couldn't stop talking about the man who turned into a wolf in front of him and started taking chunks out of him." She swallows audibly. "It was pretty horrible."

A pit forms in my stomach, feeling terrible for yet more humans dragged into supernatural problems as nothing more than pawns and sacrifices for a game they have no understanding of.

"So have you guys found the victim?"

Tess nods, but her grave expression speaks volumes. "He was found this morning. *Dead.*"

I let a breath out through my nose. "I suppose it's too much to hope that he died peacefully in hospital while being treated for those wounds?"

"He was found in a public park with his head torn off. It looks like whoever attacked him came back a few days later and finished the job."

A pain builds behind my eyes, and I rub my head, trying to release some tension.

"And how is it I didn't hear about this, if not from you or Alaric or the team, then in the media?"

"We thankfully managed to find the video almost immediately after it was posted to the news page's website. We took it down and monitored the web for any new information popping up. Some of the team stayed at work around the clock to remove it while Alaric went and followed up the clues."

"I see. Well, it sounds like the team did a pretty amazing job." I pause, considering how to word my next thoughts. "Tess, it seems like you and Alaric are relatively close, right?"

She nods hesitantly. "Close-ish. I mean, he doesn't really let anyone in fully."

"Right, yeah, I see that. But... why do you think he keeps trying to freeze me out?"

Tess turns to look at me for a moment, an unreadable expression on her face, making me wonder again why I can't see her aura. I wish that wasn't the case. She turns her attention back to the road. "Honestly, I'm not really sure. He won't actually answer, but the impression I get is that he is being... protective or something."

My face scrunches. "But I can take care of myself. He's seen that plenty of times in the past."

"I know," she offers quietly, "but I'm not sure that's the issue. It's almost like he... doesn't want you to. Like he doesn't want you to be in any danger at all."

An unexpected warmth fills my chest, confusing me, as it's paired with my frustration at being frozen out. After being isolated away from supes for most of my life, being cared about is such a strange feeling.

Why does he care, though? He can't be interested in me. He barely speaks with me.

I can't help but sit in silence and ponder over the memories of our brief time together in Paris, then more recently, thinking over his actions and decisions. He does seem different this time around, but I can't put my finger on why.

Maybe he does just want to keep me safe. Maybe it's just because he doesn't want to lose anyone else.

Tess clears her throat. "We're here, Ev. Look, I know you're frustrated by Alaric's decisions, but... I don't know, just, try and be as understanding as you can. I honestly don't think it's coming from a bad place, and it's certainly not something I've ever seen him do before."

I take in her concerned expression and bob my head in acknowledgment.

I'll try.

Tess leads the way into our workspace. I trail behind her, only half in the present. When we enter the main room with the computers, I see the twins, Zeke, and a few others madly working on their devices, before my eyes zero in on Alaric. He's sitting in a chair, glaring at something on a screen.

"Hey, Alaric," Tess calls.

He looks up at Tess, his face softening for a moment before he sees me and a frown settles.

"Tess. What are you doing here, Everleigh?"

Tess stands a little straighter. "I brought her in. I'm not sure why you didn't call us after that latest video was posted online."

He purses his lips, looking broody—and a little irresistible.

What in the hells are you thinking, Everleigh? He's your work partner.

Stuff that, bite his lip!

"You never take nights off, Tess. I wasn't going to interrupt. The rest of the crew is working on it. How'd you find out?"

I shake my head, determined not to be distracted by my demonic side. "Henry came and showed us the video," I interject, not content to be ignored or frozen out of the conversation. If Alaric wants to push me out of the team, he'll have to try a lot harder than that.

His stormy eyes find mine, darkening at the mention of Henry's name. Within a second, an almost silent rumble echoes around the room, so quiet I wonder if I imagined it. Tess's slightly raised brows indicate I didn't.

"Right. Of course. Well, it seems more damage control is needed." He looks back to Tess, dismissing me. "If you're staying, we could use your help."

She nods and goes over to the team without another word.

When Alaric's eyes return to his own computer, I speak again. "What can I do to help?"

He's silent for a moment, and I watch his shoulders stiffen before he looks back at me. "Nothing. You should go home. There's nothing you can do."

The softening and interest towards him burns away inside me. "I'm sure there's *something* I can do to help with this case."

Alaric's head shakes roughly from side to side. "I disagree. We're focusing on damage control right now. Tech is not your strong suit. We've got this."

Heated breath comes from my nose as I try to draw on the patience I would use with difficult psychology clients. "There's no reason I can't help in another way. Maybe I can examine the body and possessions of the man attacked by the werewolf? It could lead to a vision."

His nostrils flare and his head whips around to Tess. I see the tension build in her back, although she remains stoic, refusing to look at him.

"Don't blame Tess. You should have told me in the first place. I'm supposed to be your partner here. Shutting me out and hiding me away with the cold case relics isn't going to help."

He narrows those dark, stormy eyes at me. "Fine. Go ahead to the morgue and see the first victim. There's no concrete evidence these cases are connected, though."

Surprise wells inside me. "You really think they're not?"

Alaric shrugs. "There's no conclusive evidence yet. Two cases could be an unlikely coincidence. It seems more likely than a vampire and a werewolf working together like this. Everyone knows how rarely their motives align."

I purse my lips, the feeling inside me telling me these cases are in fact connected. "It's not the impression that I am getting," I offer. "I am fairly sure there's some kind of connection."

He nods slowly at me, acknowledging that my angelic intuition may be telling us something. "Well, if you get anything, don't just leave. Come back here and tell us first."

Relieved at having a small opportunity to participate, I agree quickly before heading out to go to the morgue. The corridor is dark and deserted—along with the desk usually attended by the petite blonde fae. I hit the elevator button and wait, wondering if the man downstairs is going to give us any clues about what is going on—whether the big guy, or whoever these visions come from, will deign to show me anything helpful. A part of me hopes He does. Being useful to the team could go a long way towards them accepting me. We're going to be stuck working together for a long time. I'd rather get on with everyone.

The morgue is frosty, stopping the bodies within from deteriorating too quickly while being worked on. The walls are lined with metal compartments, acting as storage for the corpses while they await inspection. Since I didn't take the time to ask where the newest victim might be, I make my way over to the section Alaric showed me the last time I was here, hoping a filing system is being used by the coroner.

When I get close to the small doors, I see there are labels near the handles. I approach the first door and read the description.

Declan Jones, 44
Cause of death: Decapitation
Autopsy status: Complete

Somewhat relieved I found the correct victim, I unlatch the door and slide the metal table out from within. Once it's fully exposed, I pull back the white sheet and look at the man. My stomach feels a little queasy at the mess the wolf left behind. The meaty stump of neck is jagged around the edges where the head was ripped off by the wolf's teeth, and the rest of his body is missing chunks.

I send a prayer to the big guy that the human soul is now resting peacefully with him, despite the lack of an afterlife for us supes. I'm always hopeful he will accept prayers for others, even if he doesn't care for me.

I place my hand a couple of inches above the man's forehead and close my eyes. I breathe in through my nose and gently exhale as I push my feet into the floor, grounding myself into the present. Releasing all thoughts and judgments allows me to connect with my angelic intuition and be open to visions—should they choose to reveal themselves.

After a few moments, I run my hand down his body, trying to remain calm and open, to not rush. When I reach what's left of his throat, my own begins to burn. I raise my left hand up and rest it in the same spot on my own body.

The pain worsens, familiar in its feeling, and my eyes flash open.

This is just like the pain in Clara's vision. Her attack can't be related to this, it can't.

Just breathe, Everleigh. Just breathe.

I take a few moments to recenter myself, trying desperately to let my worries about Clara go. To stop clinging to my fear for my sister so I can be open to helping with this case. With a lot of concentrated effort, I return to my task.

As I run my hands over the wounds, flashes of agony are mirrored in my own limbs. I hiss at the sensation, fluttering my eyelids to check I haven't ended up with the same tears in my skin. *Nothing.* I continue down, but no vision comes. I feel more pain, then I begin to hear whimpers. Whimpers of the man, begging, begging the wolf to stop. The responding laugh makes my insides turn cold, and the rumble... it feels wrong. I can't put my finger on it, but it doesn't sound right. It's like listening to a recording of your own voice. It sounds distorted. Uncanny.

When nothing further comes, I huff out a breath.

Why can't I just get normal visions? Why do I have to be so damned different from the other angels? I snort out a laugh. If I was no different to them, I wouldn't be here helping like I am. Hells, I wouldn't be who I am at all.

Reluctant gratitude washes over me for the hellish life that led me to this point: to actually being interested in helping other supes and humans.

When the door bursts open, I turn quickly, startled to find Tess in the entryway, the clock above the door showing it's already the next day. I've been here much longer than I thought.

"We've got something. Come back upstairs!"

That's all I need to hear to race after her.

TENSION

"Tess, what did you need to get?" Alaric grumbles the second she takes a step through the door. Once he sees me enter behind her, the energy becomes intense enough I could cut through it with a blade. His gaze whips back to Tess. "Why?"

She stands stubbornly with her shoulders back, staring him down. "I told you I was against not telling Ev in the first place. I'm not going to stand by idly while you freeze her out, especially when she now knows."

Alaric looks like he's going to burst a vein in his forehead. He appears to be visibly forcing himself to keep his mouth shut while he pulls himself together.

The room is frozen for a solid thirty seconds until Zeke crashes into a table. The tension thaws, and everyone looks at him. A light flush fills his cheeks, and his hand immediately drops back to his bracelet. "Uh, sorry. I've confirmed the location. Should I...?" He looks hesitantly between Tess and Alaric, clearly unsure whether to speak it or not.

"Just send it to *everyone's* phone, Zeke," Tess says.

He nods, relieved, and speeds back to his table.

Tess turns to both Alaric and me. "We need you both to get to the scene and see if we can get the woman—"

"No *we* don't. I can go and retrieve her on my own. It's safer."

Heat rises within me, my insides churning at his controlling nature, protective or not.

Tess shakes her head before I can formulate anything to say. "No. Ev needs to go as well, Alaric. If you get there and the girl is gone, Ev is the best chance we have to get any clues about what happened."

He growls low in his throat but says nothing. Tess narrows her eyes back at him, holding the silence.

"Fine." He looks at me and a devious grin lights his features. "We're taking my motorcycle. Let's go."

Tess parts her lips, likely to object, but I smile at her and shake my head. He clearly doesn't know me as well as he thinks.

She shrugs and gestures for me to follow the already retreating Alaric.

As I get close enough to pass her, I whisper, "Thanks. I hope I can help find the woman before it's too late."

Down in the garage, Alaric is already on his motorcycle. If I wasn't trying to play it cool, I'm fairly sure I would drool. The demon in me *loves* this look—the black leather jacket and dark jeans showing the finely tuned muscles straddling the powerful beast beneath him. I ignore the pulsing feeling in my core and approach the wolf in front of me to take the helmet he's offering.

Don't worry about the helmet. He looks like an invitation for a good time to me. Take a ride!

I bite down on my lip to get out of my head, then pull the helmet on and fasten it before slipping onto the bike behind him. Once he turns the bike on, I slide my arms around his abs, which I can feel tighten through the jacket, tense beneath my touch. When he takes off, I lean against him, soaking in his heat.

Alaric tries to scare me—taking corners overly fast, tipping the bike further to the side than necessary. I meld into him, my breasts pushing against his back, but I don't hold on any tighter. He seems to take it as a challenge, and pops a wheelie, trying harder to catch me out. Instead, I laugh and enjoy the thrill of the ride, letting my inner demon free to enjoy the simple pleasure of being on a bike but not in control of it. Trusting the wolfman in front of me to keep us safe. I focus on the feeling of being alive instead of the shitshow we're about to walk into. This is the closest I can get to flying right now—the wind, the speed.

It ends all too soon.

I step off the motorcycle once we stop and remove my helmet ready to give to Alaric. I can't help the grin still on my face from the wild ride, certain things didn't go as he'd planned.

When he approaches, the left corner of his mouth is pulled up in a slight curve, and when his eyes lock with mine, their usual stormy appearance seems to have flecks of lightning spreading from their centers.

My mouth dries a little at the heat in his gaze, and I hand the helmet over wordlessly, staring into his eyes a little too long. After placing it down on the bike, he approaches me again, standing so close I feel his heat melding with mine all over again. Being this near to him is like standing in the heat of the sun on a cool day. I feel drawn in.

He seems to step closer without touching me, the smirk gone. The heated look in his eyes has turned hungry. I want to taste him too. I guess Alaric likes me on his bike as much as I do.

I lean closer, wanting more.

He mirrors me, those hungry eyes making me feel like being devoured by him could be a good thing—that I should let it happen.

I begin to close my eyes, sure his lips on mine are the next right thing in the world.

A shrill tone comes from Alaric's phone, startling us both so completely, he gasps, and I jump back.

He picks up the phone and checks it as he rubs a hand on the back of his neck. His eyes lose their warmth when he hears whatever is said on the other end, and he turns away. All hope for the moment coming to fruition now lost.

I try to slow my racing heart and cool my heated core. I shake my head and tuck my hair behind my ears.

What in the hells were you thinking, Everleigh? We're here to find a woman who's been attacked. Not to make out with each other.

Alaric ends the call and turns back to look at me, his stormy blue eyes back to their usual shade. He clears his throat and sticks his hands in his pockets, showing me he's not completely back to normal.

"They've had some luck getting the footage—and all its shares—down, but it was harder than last time. Let's go down to the scene."

"So, you do think they're connected after all?" I ask as I fall into step with him.

"I have a gut feeling they are," he rumbles. "If this is turning into a pattern, we only have about two more days before this woman is dead and the next video is released."

"I didn't really get much at all from our first victim, but there was something...off? I don't know how to describe it, really. The attack didn't feel right coming from a wolf." I frown and turn my gaze to Alaric. "Does that make any sense?"

His mouth bunches up in thought. "I think I get it, but it looked similar to attacks I've seen from my kind in the past, so I don't know. Let's see if the pattern holds and go from there."

I nod, relieved he's not dismissing my angelic intuition, especially when it's related to another werewolf.

Hells, he's even being kind of nice; a far cry from his behavior in the office around everyone else.

We both come to a halt outside a closed down video rental store, the same one from the clip online. The area appears disturbingly vacant, despite the high-density population.

"I wonder if all of the neighbors know what happened here, if they've all seen the woman?"

"It's possible." Alaric takes a deep breath that seems to last forever before he releases it and continues quietly, "We may need to send a team out here to take stock of the situation. We can't have this many people aware. The Council hasn't approved widespread knowledge. If this pattern continues, there will be an uproar across the factions."

Tightness pulls at my chest, and the intense urge to release my wings to ease the tension in my back overwhelms me for a moment. The comfort of curling up within my wings like I used to do with my mother calls to me even after all this time.

"Do you think that's what the attacker wants? That could be their reason for doing it?"

He shrugs, a slight lift to his defined shoulders. "It could be. It's too hard to tell. Attacks from two *different* species following a pattern like this is highly unusual. You know we don't work together unless forced." *Like us* are the words he doesn't need to add to that sentence.

I nod, nothing left to say, and then make my way closer to the scene, looking around.

"There's some blood here," I say as I point to a stain on the ground close to the store entry where the woman sat. I reach down and wave my hand over it, focusing, but there's no signature, nothing for me to draw on. When Alaric meets my eyes, I shake my head, feeling defeated.

"It's not your fault," he offers gruffly. "I didn't expect we'd really find anything here. I can't even pick up a scent of which way she went, despite the blood. She was likely moved from here by car."

A small portion of relief washes over me that Alaric isn't angry and trying to use my lack of finding something as a reason to kick me off the investigation again.

"Thank you," I say in a low voice, "for not blaming me."

He huffs and pulls his hand back up behind his neck, rubbing it. "I'm sorry, Everleigh. I... I know I haven't been so great to work with. I haven't had a partner in a long time, and I just don't want you to get hurt."

"You know I'm not made of glass, right? I can take care of myself." When I see I'm starting to lose him, I hasten to add, "I do appreciate that you care, Alaric. I want you to know that, okay? And I promise I'm not trying to run off on my own to solve all the world's problems or anything stupid like that. I just... I want to *be* your partner. I want to be included. You understand that, right?"

Lightning crackles in his gaze once more. "I understand. I'll even try to remember it, Everleigh. But remember this: No one is allowed to hurt you."

Warmth tingles through me, excited by the idea of Alaric caring about me and my safety in a way no one really has since my parents were killed. The thought of them makes tears well up in my eyes, and I pounce on Alaric, hugging him tightly to me.

He stiffens for a second, but then melts into the hug, our bodies pressed fully into each other. I can't help but inhale his rich scent, shivering with need. He might be my work partner, but a part of me recognizes the call of his wolf, the need to protect, and I can't help but want that too. After so long being isolated, it feels too good to have Alaric truly care.

He whispers quietly in my ear, "We should get back. Maybe the others will have found something using the footage from this area."

I nod in agreement, reluctant to move from the warmth of his comforting embrace. I take another deep breath, and step back, feeling his heat leach away inch by inch until it's gone, until he's looking at me from a distance.

We walk back to his motorbike, and when we arrive, I pause, considering. I turn to recapture his stormy blue gaze. "How about I do the steering this time?"

His eyes heat and a rare smile lights his features. "You can ride?" He *definitely* loves the thought of me on his bike.

A grin builds on my face. "I can."

"Well, that explains a lot," he grumbles playfully, his smile still in place. After an extended moment, he hands me his key.

Alaric's arms around my waist make concentrating more difficult, and I can't help but wonder if I distracted him as well. Determined not to make a fool of myself, I pull my attention from the butterflies now wreaking havoc in my stomach and start the bike.

I take a few turns slowly, getting used to the feel of a pillion on the bike with Alaric's build, then I give it my all. Just as he did, I lean the bike more than I need to around bends, and I go so fast, my hair flies free of my jacket.

It's like flying.

I'm lost in the moment.

Until I feel Alaric's cock harden behind me.

I can't help but wriggle back in the seat, wanting to feel closer, spurred on by a desire that's been absent in over a century. His hands tightening around my waist force me to stop.

"Focus on the road. You might be unbreakable, but my bike isn't!"

Unsure, I halt my movements and try my hardest to ignore the swirling storm inside my stomach, the pulsing in my core, the desire melting away logic.

Hells, I need to get laid. And not by my partner.

When we pull into the garage, I wait for Alaric to withdraw, then quickly get off his bike. I hand back the key, avoiding his gaze, uncertain what I might find in it—matching heat or his usual hard indifference? The first could be a problem. The second would hurt too much. Instead, I head straight to the door, my inner demon raging at me to go and take him for a ride, while my angelic reasoning keeps me moving.

Chicken.

I allow my inner selves to argue with one another while I make my way to the office. I lean down and look into the retinal scanner to get inside, and a rumbled purr sounds from behind me. I feel the red flash into my eyes as I look over at Alaric, my hungry gaze meeting his.

Transfixed, I prowl towards him, my inner demon winning the primal fight, wanting to indulge in the beast in front of me. One step to go and the door behind me bursts open.

"There you two are..." Tess starts before trailing off.

I'm frozen, my crimson eyes locked onto Alaric's, devouring him from a foot away.

His eyes look gray, the storm darkening, a hunger matching my own.

"Uh—guys?" Tess adds, and I hear a hesitant step forward. "Is everything all right?"

Alaric bares his teeth and growls as those footsteps get closer, finally ripping his attention away to look at the incoming threat.

As soon as his attention is elsewhere, his growl stops immediately, and he grumbles something unintelligible to our friend about his bike and my recklessness before walking briskly into the room. It's a convenient excuse to cover up what we were about to do, and the look in both our eyes.

I close my eyes and breathe. One in. One out.

Down, girl.

After a moment, I'm sure my eyes are back to their usual golden hue, and I turn to look at my friend. "Sorry about that,"

I mutter. "We uh...." Heat rises into my cheeks, and I pull my lips between my teeth, nervous and unsure what to tell Tessa.

Hells, I don't even know what to tell myself yet.

VISION

Awareness suddenly lights Tess's face and the tension bleeds from her posture. "I knew it was coming. He's far too protective not to be interested," she half whispers, so the team doesn't hear us. "Come on. We've got something."

Wordlessly, I follow her into the room, trying to convince my aching need to settle down so I can refocus on the case.

Everyone is standing around a single computer when Tess and I enter. When I'm close enough, I see the twins have put together a mash-up of different videos following cars seen near the victim at the time of the broadcast.

Zeke looks at me and says, "We've narrowed it down to about ten cars that were in the area. Unfortunately, we've only been able to follow them so far before the footage cuts off. We've sent some scouts out to the registered addresses, but for now, all we can do is wait."

When Zeke rubs his throat, I'm pulled from the room and into my vision so roughly that had I not seen it before, I might not know what it was.

Fire fills my insides.
Pain ricochets down my throat.
Can't breathe.
Silk sheets. Too soft. Can't hold on.
Need help.
Blackness calls.
Need.
Air.
Need—

My vision fades in a blink, sharper than normal, and I'm stuck wondering again if the danger Clara is facing is related to this case.

A soft, warm hand is on my arm, and I turn to look at Tess. "Something about the case?"

I shake my head. "Clara. The danger is nearer."

Alaric's gaze pierces my own as he says, "Do you think whoever is involved here is also after your sister?" echoing my thoughts.

"My vision doesn't match our pattern, but I can't help feeling there is some kind of link."

He nods brusquely and turns to the twins. "Include Everleigh's twin, Clara, into our surveillance watch, just in case."

Heat builds behind my eyes, grateful again for his protective nature, even if it grates at times.

Tess clears her throat gently. "Everleigh, I've popped Declan's belongings in your office. I was hoping you could get a read on something there to give us another avenue to go down." She raises her voice. "Everyone else, let's get back to following down leads."

The team murmurs their agreements and departs to follow her orders.

Declan's belongings give me nothing.

The leads for the woman go nowhere.

This case is nothing but torture, death, and dead ends.

When I step into the office three days after the last body was dumped, it's with a lump in my stomach the size of an asteroid. I know what's coming. The room is dead silent. The team, except Alaric, are all standing around one of the large screens. A new video is playing from a different broadcasting service. A teenage girl is screeching about the fae as blood drips from her torn-out eyes, her fingertips bloodied from ripping them out herself. Trying to unsee.

My heart breaks all over again for the damage supernaturals deal out to unsuspecting humans. And after the sadness, the anger follows as always, my eyes pulsing red, ready to rip apart whoever is responsible for this senseless attack.

The girl's screech pulls my attention back from my mind to the video playing live. She yells of fae, of a secret world, of horns and magic. Of those who look too beautiful to be real. Of treachery when the beauty turned to horror and the world rotted before her eyes.

Her screeches turn to yells, her voice becoming hoarse, morphing into whimpers. She collapses on the ground, still.

The camera drops to the ground, landing on its side. A man runs over to the girl, checking for a pulse. I don't realize I'm holding my breath until I see him relax and call emergency services, telling them she's breathing but bleeding badly.

My mouth opens in disbelief when he leaves the girl to run back to his camera and grab it. "This is not a joke, folks. Vampires, werewolves, fae... they're all real! Even if the videos keep disappearing off the web." Recognition lights up his face. "Hell, *because* they keep being removed. Something fishy is going on here! Watch your backs. It seems like humans are the targets of these supernatural tyrants."

The sirens sound in the background, and the man pales in the camera. "Shit. How am I going to explain this? I gotta go." He looks back at the girl still collapsed on the ground, but ultimately decides his need to escape is more important, and the screen goes black.

The silence of the room echoes so loudly, it's deafening.

My angelic intuition warns me a second before the door opens. Things are about to get worse, not better.

Alaric charges in, his usual stormy, emotive eyes like voids. And I know. I know before he says anything. *The second victim is dead.*

The team all turn to look. Alaric shakes his head, a sharp, final movement. Still, somehow, it feels unfinished. Like I'm waiting for the other shoe to drop, a bomb to hit.

It comes in the form of a demon. The Ruler of Demons to be precise.

Nicon stalks into the room, his charcoal suit ironed to perfection, his expression livid. He takes in the group of us with a single glance. "Update," he demands of the team.

Tess steps forward in front of the twins and Zeke. "The pattern is confirmed. A video, then three days later the victim is killed and dumped in a public place. Then a new video. The newly released victim appears to have been attacked by the fae."

The demon ruler's eyes deepen to a red so dark, they look black, a rare loss of control for the usually curious and playful Lord of the Realms.

"We may have one advantage this time," I offer.

He turns those black holes to me. "And what is that?"

"This time the victim, the girl, was picked up by paramedics. We may be able to get to her before she is killed like the others."

Nicon stills for a moment, like a predator ready to pounce and devour his prey. The beings in the room around me seem to take a collective breath and hold it, waiting for the Ruler of Demons to make his decree.

"Very well. We may have a chance. Go and get her."

Alaric steps forward immediately, partially blocking my view of Nicon. Irritated and a little chuffed, I step to the side so I can still see.

"I will go and get her. We don't know how many of them there are. Surely whoever it is will be watching, biding their time for the kill. Everleigh can stay here."

"Alaric," I mutter, "you promised."

He stills immediately at my words but keeps his focus on Nicon since he's made the demand.

The Ruler of Demons stares down my werewolf. "No. You've kept her locked up long enough. She will go too."

Alaric stiffens, tension radiating so hard through his muscles, they appear to be quivering.

Nicon holds his gaze, waiting for an act of defiance or of acceptance. Alaric bows his head by half an inch, teetering on the edge of insubordination, but accepting the order from our boss.

The little bit of control Nicon obtained from Alaric seems to have put some water on his fire, and his eyes begin to fade back to their usual crimson shade. "Good. Report back when you're done."

I take a step towards the door, ready to get out of the room, but Alaric still isn't moving.

Come on, Wolfman.

I move closer to Alaric and place my hand on his lower back—high enough that I'm not touching his chiseled arse, but low enough to draw his attention, especially after the moment we had outside. I know Nicon spots the movement when his eyes flick down to my hand, and then back up, amusement bleeding into his expression.

Alaric's muscles bunch and then release beneath my fingers, and I huff out a sigh of relief when he gets moving.

At the door, I turn briefly back to look at Tess, but her eyes are all for Nicon, who's now grilling her with more questions about the video footage. I offer up a little prayer to Him, that my new friend manages to leave the conversation unscathed. The Council members seem to be rather temperamental.

The car trip is quiet, the atmosphere tense compared to our previous ride on the motorbike. I can practically hear Alaric cussing Nicon out in his head. He pulls up outside the Sydney hospital Zeke sent him the address for but doesn't move immediately.

Silence holds us in place for another minute before I crack. "Do you want to talk about it?"

He looks at me with his deep bluish-gray eyes, and I decide I much prefer this to the dead, drained look he came into the room with earlier.

"There's nothing to talk about. We'll get some weapons out of the boot and try to stay under the radar. I imagine there will be some kind of security around her room, but there could be parents, and whoever in the hells is behind this looking for their chance as well." He looks over me, a tinge of concern shading his features. "Keep your eyes peeled."

"Okay. Sounds like a plan to me. Let's go then."

I turn to open the car door but feel the heat of Alaric's wolf beside me a second before his hand touches my arm.

"Everleigh, I know you need to be here, but...." A vibration rumbles from his chest, an echo of his wolf sharing the same worry. It pulls on my heart in a way I can't ever recall. I sense a softening in me that I don't understand—and don't have time to ponder. Instead, unsure what to say, I nod in gentle acceptance of his care.

He releases my arm, holds my gaze for a few more heartbeats, then climbs from the vehicle.

At the back of the car, I smile to see he's included my favorite pair of blades. We catch each other's eyes for just a moment, a small sliver of joy and appreciation in each other and our love of weapons before we strap them on.

As I place my blades in their sheaths, Clara's vision floods me once more, and I'm struck into stillness, waiting for it to pass. When I'm able, I quiet my fast heart and shake my head, sighing deeply.

"Clara again?" Alaric asks, frowning.

"Yes. Come on. Let's just go and see if we can find this girl."

In the hospital, we find the intensive care unit, and sure enough, there are security present. I look to Alaric, unsure how he would usually approach such a situation as an enforcer. He doesn't hesitate, continuing his path directly to one of the guards, and I'm forced to wonder if they're ours.

"We're here from the Bureau of Investigative Affairs to see the girl who came in earlier without her eyes." His voice is smooth steel, offering no give, no sense of uncertainty.

The guard he approached asks for identification, which Alaric flashes for a moment. He then nods to us and steps aside, leaving his partner looking rather confused.

He's not the only one. Where do I get an ID like that?

Alaric moves straight into the room, me following in his wake, trying to keep my expression neutral at the turn of events. I need to look like we belong here, or Alaric's ID won't be enough to save us from being kicked out.

I suppose I should have asked before we came inside.

We reach the bed and stop. The girl's eye sockets are completely covered with bandages, and she's connected to several monitors. The whiteboard above the girl's bed reads:

Jane Doe

Induced Coma

The information, or lack of it, gives me pause. On the one hand, no identification means no family and less complication for us, but on the other, she's all alone. Deserted during a time when comfort might be needed the most.

I wander closer and sit in the chair next to her bed, then reach out and take her hand in my own. Her fingertips are covered in white gauze that has been taped on, but her palms are simply soft. The softness only afforded by a life not yet lived.

For several minutes, I just sit with the girl. I brush her hair back from her cheeks, knowing if my hair was sitting like hers, it would drive me insane. Trying to give her a small measure of reassurance that *someone* is here. Someone cares.

Alaric's soft voice breaks the silence. "It doesn't seem like it, but are you getting anything from her that might help us to find whoever did this?"

I look up, a sense of hollowness filling me. "Nothing immediate, but I'll try." I stand and release the girl's hand, placing it down beside her. After a moment of grounding, I lay my hands in the air above her face and open myself to the possibility of a vision.

The woods around me are dark.
The world smells of decay.
A man with antler-like horns looks down at me, laughing, the sound as beautiful as it is terrifying.
I back away, hitting a tree.
It's soft and rotting. I get stuck.
I try desperately to get away.
Still the man who calls himself fae laughs.
His warm hands touch my temples.
Death. There is only death. My loved ones rot before my eyes.
I reach out. I scream. Nothing works.
Wrong. It feels so wrong.
Still he laughs.
Beautiful.
Terrifying.
Deadly.

My eyes fly open. I'm locked in Alaric's grip, his front pushed into my back, one hand over my mouth, the other locked around my middle, pinning both my arms to my sides. My breathing is rapid. I try to pull my mind away from the young girl's—to separate myself from the torturous images she tried so hard to unsee. Sound slowly comes back in the form of steady machine beeps and gentle words.

"Shh, Everleigh. Shh. It's okay. You're okay," Alaric croons into my ear, trying to calm me. "You're safe here. You're safe with me."

I realize with horror that I had been trying to claw my own eyes out, just like the girl. The sting of the light scratches on one cheek is enough to make my heart skip a beat.

Thank goodness Alaric was here.

I shudder, just considering what might have happened had I been alone. Breath by breath, I begin to relax, to let go of the vision, to let go of the horror the girl witnessed.

When Alaric feels me become more limp, he takes his hand from my mouth and loosens his grip. He continues to hold me still, not completely letting go.

Breathe, Everleigh. In. Out. In. Out. This will pass. It always does.

I give Alaric more of my weight, feeling relaxed but drained. "It was—" I swallow, trying to clear my throat. "It was terrible. She was tortured with those visions the fae gave her."

His warm breath against my neck makes me shiver. "Is there anything you think might help us? Could you see any faces we might be able to match?"

I shake my head. "Nothing clear enough. But, Alaric, I'm getting the feeling again that something is *wrong*. These don't feel like normal attacks."

He steps back and turns me gently to look at him. "What do you mean?"

Eyes closed, I try to review the visions I've seen, but explaining the impression feels too difficult. I huff out a frustrated breath. "I'm sorry. I don't know how to explain it to you, especially when it's not clear to me yet. All I can tell you is that the attacks feel *wrong* to me. They look right, from those I've seen in the past, but they *feel* wrong."

"Okay," he says, voice gruff. "It's a start. I've arranged for some people from the office to be on watch here for the girl." A buzz sounds from his pocket. He pulls out his mobile phone and his eyes scan the message. Alaric sighs. "But I'm afraid we've been summoned before the Council. They don't like to be kept waiting. We need to go, now."

CONFLICT

BEING CALLED BEFORE THE Council of the Accords again is not my idea of a good time.

After being ushered into the room by the mages on guard duty, I'm dragged back to a day that changed the course of my life—the one that landed me with my new job as an enforcer.

The room looks much the same as the last time I saw it—thick carpet in midnight blue that looks soft enough to nap on, and seven expensive leather chairs with small hardwood tables at their sides. One chair for the leader of each species of supernatural.

The recent attack has me turning to look first at Iridessa, Queen of the Fae. Her ruby-spun hair is curled into fine ringlets, pinned back at the front by a glistening sapphire tiara. The hairstyle paired with her porcelain skin makes her look impossibly young, perhaps in her early teens, despite being the most ancient in the room. The pale white gown she dons looks pearlescent in the light of the room. Today, her usual smile of secrets looks more strained, less playful.

A prowling black cat draws my attention, stalking silently back to its mistress. The High Witch moves her hands from her lap to allow her familiar to climb onto her deep purple coat, where it curls up and proceeds to watch us with intelligent eyes. Octavia smiles slightly at me and Alaric before settling back into her more neutral look. Her graying hair and wrinkled features remind me of the Fates, the Crone in particular.

Solomon Trite, the Arch Mage, is adorned in expensive mage garb befitting his station as their leader. His cerulean blue and gold cloak are held together once again with a golden talisman, which glows the shades of his attire, interspersed with black. His features look untroubled, and an air of superiority emanates strongly from him. My intuition tells me this is because mages are not under investigation right now, but were that to change, he gives the impression of one quick to anger.

Nicon, Ruler of Demons, stands tall at our arrival, straightening his designer suit jacket back into place before addressing the room. "Council, I have called this meeting so that we can get some updated information from the enforcers and determine our next actions." He stares at us, a warning in his red eyes. "Tell us what you know so far."

What in all of the Hellish realms are we supposed to not say? He could have warned us first. Maybe he warned Alaric.

I turn and look hopefully at my partner, but his low-level glare forces it to die fairly quickly.

Perfect. It's like trying to avoid stepping in invisible dog shit.

When it appears Alaric isn't going to talk, just remain close to my side, I step in to offer a summary of what I know.

As if the powers that be don't already know it all.

"Thus far, there have been three victims, which appear to be forming a pattern. A human is abducted or attacked by a supernatural in their native form, dumped somewhere publicly in a state of trauma—which is recorded by a news broadcasting service—then after three days that person is kidnapped, killed, and dumped. The very same day a victim is killed, another is dumped after being traumatized. I think that covers it."

All the members of the Council shift uncomfortably in their seats except for the Archangel Raphael. The Archangel to whom I owe my allegiance for the next fifty years, thanks to me calling on the Raphillian Rite to help Henry and Raine. While others fidget, the angelic leader in the Earthly realm sits impossibly still, his white-blond hair gleaming with a metallic sheen. His golden eyes lock with mine a second before he speaks.

"Tell us, Everleigh, what do we know about the attackers so far? Have you been able to glean anything from your visions?"

I shift a little, wishing I could maintain his level of smooth confidence. "So far it... appears... there has been an attack by a werewolf, a vampire, and a fae."

Orpheus Kildare, the Vampire King, leans forward in his chair so fast he blurs out of focus. His long inky hair draws light from the room around him and he shoves it roughly from his face in his haste to ask his question. "Why do you say 'appears' in such a way? Is there doubt about the attacks?"

I pause, unsure about voicing my hunch so openly when it's under the scrutiny of the entire Council.

Oh Hells, this better not be what Nicon was trying to warn us off. Thanks, Raphael.

Avoiding glancing at the Ruler of Demons, since I've been called out by another member of the Council, I roll my shoulders back and envision releasing my white and golden wings from the ether. I visualize wrapping them around myself. I let the image fade alongside my exhale.

"There is no physical evidence at this point, Orpheus, that the attacks are anything other than what they appear. However, some of my visions have left me with the impression that there is something 'wrong' or 'unusual' about these situations. Physically, they look right, but they *feel* wrong to me." I shrug and look briefly along the line of council members without truly seeing them. "I'm afraid I don't have any further insight at this point."

The Werewolf and Shifter King, Conall Wiven, lounges back more comfortably in his leather chair after I speak, a thoughtful look clouding his ice-blue gaze. "Perhaps this is something we should keep in mind in our discussions. The blame may not lay where we originally thought."

Solomon sits straighter, smugness pouring from his tone. "Oh no, don't try and weasel out of your guilt on this, Conall. A *werewolf* was the first to attack. You can't avoid the investigation into your kind."

Conall turns his now icy stare to the Arch Mage. "I did not suggest we stop trying to locate the traitors to the Accords, merely that we may need to extend the search."

"Oh yes, I quite agree," the ancient fae queen suggests in her girlish voice. "After all, this impacts all supernaturals should our enforcement team not be able to manage the slippage in the media." She turns to Octavia, her voice sweet—like poison covered in honey. "How *is* your little program going?"

I wince as Octavia pets her familiar, an unusual fire in her eyes.

"I am not sure what you are suggesting, Iridessa. The trial goes well, but as I stated at the last meeting, it is not my recommendation to increase to a larger scale at this moment in time. More research is needed on less agreeable subjects first, because those are what we will come across in the population as a whole. So far, those who've been in the trial have been open to the supernatural world—interested in it—the data is hardly a true representation."

Nicon watches the other Council members' interactions as avidly as if he were in a movie theatre eating popcorn. His irregular bout of seriousness seems to have disappeared in favor of his usual love of conflict. A true demon at heart, his need for chaos unending. When he sees me looking at him, he simply winks at me before returning to the "show".

Alaric, apparently sick of being here, risks a baptism of fire by interrupting our leaders. "If you wouldn't mind, Council members, our next instructions would be most helpful in allowing us to resume our duties. There is very limited time before we expect a new case and another victim should we not act."

The Arch Mage looks as though he's going to lose it at being redirected by a subordinate, his pride showing as his mightiest flaw. Much like the rest of his brethren.

Thankfully, Raphael interjects once more. "That is a wise thought. We can continue to consider the motivations and players who may be involved without you both. Your efforts are certainly needed to conduct the case. Nicon, do you have any additional directions for your team?"

The Ruler of Demons ponders the Archangel's suggestion for a moment, before agreeing. "No additional instructions. Continue to provide any information so that we can make the most suitable decisions. You are both dismissed."

We both bow to the room, and then again to our respective leaders, a hierarchical sign of respect in the supernatural world.

Relief and anticipation fill me once we escape to the hallway, glad to be rid of the Council for now, and anxious to consider my visions more fully with a little space.

At the elevator, Alaric looks at his phone, a deep furrow to his brows. "Tess has called five times," he mutters before answering.

"Is everything all right, Tess? We were in with—"

Tess's fast, loud speech comes through the phone, a jumbled mess to my ears.

Alaric lets out a growl that draws the attention of the mages from the other end of the hallway. They take half a step towards us, but when the elevator doors open, Alaric steps in, pulling me with him.

"We'll be down in a moment." He hangs up abruptly.

"God, what's wrong now?" I ask quietly, not sure how much more negativity the day can take without imploding on itself.

Alaric impatiently hits the Close Door button repeatedly until they shut. "The two officers I sent into the hospital to watch the girl have been killed. The girl is missing. And the entire security system was offline while it happened."

My stomach sinks. The security system being offline changes this from a random, opportunistic attack to a carefully calculated one. Whoever this killer is, they're dangerous. And they obviously have no intention of letting any of their victims survive to tell their tale.

We exit the elevator in a silence that makes me want to reach out to Alaric—to offer some comfort for his lost men. I keep my hands to myself, unsure if he'd truly welcome my touch right now. Once we make it down the hall and into the morgue, I look at the bodies of the two men—both shifters—lying on the tables. There are no clues left behind, no way to track their killers down with supernatural traces. Their heads were removed. Taken in one fell swoop each.

The callousness and uncaring of some supernaturals in their bid to get what they want, to reach their goals, is loathsome. My demon eyes take over in my fury, and the pulsing red reflects off the metallic compartments around the room.

"Do they have families?" I ask Alaric in a quiet, clipped voice.

He meets my fiery gaze with an exhaustion so complete, I don't know how he's still standing.

"Collins had only the pack, but Severil had a wife and two young cubs. I'll need to tell them." His voice fades out as he turns back to his brothers, regret tinging his exhausted features.

I step forward wordlessly and put my arms around my partner from behind, resting my head against his shoulder. A hug—a small piece of comfort—will barely dent the pain, but it's something. With little thought, I release my wings from the ether and encompass Alaric.

He stiffens for a moment, making me unsure, and then relaxes. We stand like this for minutes, hours, eons, until it's time to move. Until Alaric feels he has enough energy to keep going. He turns his head, still in my embrace, and kisses me ever so softly on the cheek. "Thank you," he whispers. Gratitude and a sign that it's time to let go.

"Of course," I murmur, surprised and heartened by his lips and his thanks. I unfurl my golden-white wings, stretching them once to relieve the tension of stillness before withdrawing them into the ether once more. "Are you ready to go? Would you like company to talk to Severil's family?"

Alaric shakes his head softly. "It's best if I go alone. This is pack news, and we prefer to grieve amongst ourselves."

I nod. "I understand, but if they do need someone to talk to, please let them know I'm here and offering support. Grief is something I'm all too familiar with personally and as a psychologist."

He pauses for a moment before answering, "I'll let them know, Everleigh. I'll be back in the office tomorrow. We can figure out our next move then."

Stillness engulfs me at his change, at his choice to include me in this case without being pushed. I watch silently as he leaves the morgue, wondering if the comfort I offered was the cause, or if there's more to it.

I'm jolted from my vision-turned-nightmare by Raine's voice. "Ev. Hey, Ev. Wake up. You're dreaming."

I groan and pull my wings away from where I'd unconsciously wrapped them in my sleep as I try to blink myself back to reality, to get my racing heart to slow, to breathe again properly. I feel Raine sit back as I pull my hand away from my aching throat once more.

Her deep brown eyes are full of concern. She takes one of my hands and squeezes it carefully. "Clara again? This is like the fourth time in the last couple of days. Have you called her at the club again?"

"Yeah, I called last night. I told her it's getting worse, but she wasn't really interested as usual." I sit up, feeling only half rested from my weekly sleep. It's always worse when it gets disturbed by visions and nightmares. I lean forwards and stretch my back and wings out, luxuriating in the feeling after being curled up. When I look back at my friend, her expression is simultaneously worried and frustrated, mirroring my own feelings about Clara's dismissive attitude.

"She still doesn't need any help, I assume?" she grumbles, rolling her eyes.

"Yeah. That's about the size of it. Alaric does have some people watching out for her in case there *is* a connection between her and the humans showing up on the news broadcasts."

She draws her brows down. "Henry has been watching out for any more videos and showing me before they get taken down. It looks like it's getting harder to keep things under wraps."

"It is. The moment videos show up on the internet, it's basically impossible to get them to disappear completely. People will have copies and then rerelease them. Three videos isn't so bad, and I guess whoever is behind this doesn't realize they'd get more credibility with repeated attacks from the same species instead of trying to convince the humans they all exist at once."

Raine smiles softly at me. "Well, lucky for us they aren't as smart as you, whoever they are."

I feel my cheeks lift and my eyes crinkle, a lightness filling my chest. I sit up and draw my friend into a hug, grateful all over again that she was put in my path by God or whoever allows me to see my visions.

She squeezes me back—just a little too hard—until I squeak and she laughs. I shake my head at my friend, causing her grin to turn mischievous as she releases me and darts back from the bed before I can try and get her back.

Her smile slips from her porcelain face after a moment. "I have to go to work. It seems like one of the other teachers has gone missing. I think she's pretty high up in the local witches' coven. They need me to take her place for the day."

Missing. I tense at the possible connection this might have to our case.

I tilt my head slightly, brow furrowed. "When did that happen?"

"From what they told me this morning, maybe a couple of days ago. I think on the first day they just assumed she was unwell or something, but on the second day with no response, they tried to scry for her. They couldn't get a read." She pinches her lips together for a moment. "Ev, you don't think this could be related to the case, too, do you? Like... she's not involved or... or been taken or something?"

Raine's words stir my angelic intuition into a tizzy, giving me the distinct impression that she might be onto something. The feeling sits heavily in my chest, wondering how this situation could possibly be getting any worse.

I rub my fingertips in a circular motion over my temples, trying to soothe the ache there. "I'll let the team know, okay. But be careful, Raine. If supes are being taken, too, that's more beings in danger we need to watch out for."

What in all the hellish realms is going on?

I need to speak with Alaric.

TAKEN

"Good morning, Tess. How are you?"

She turns to me, her red hair somewhat disheveled, with puffy bags and red rims around her eyes.

Alarmed, I move closer. "What's happened? What's going on?"

She waves a hand, brushing my concern away. "I'm all right. A witch from my coven has been confirmed missing. I spent a lot of time with her growing up. She was one of the matrons."

My body tenses, a hum of fear vibrating through me. "Is this the same witch who works at the supe school that Raine attends?"

"Yeah, that's her. Her name is Dorothea Altain. She's in the upper levels of our coven. Did Raine tell you about it?"

A little tension leaves my body, glad we're dealing with one missing witch, not two at least. "She did. The school asked her to fill in today. I was hoping to check in with you and Alaric about it this morning."

Tess straightens her posture, and a shred of fear enters her voice, making it sound strained. "Is that just because she is missing, or...?"

I reach out and squeeze her hand as I shake my head. "I think it might be related to this case we're working on."

She slumps into her chair, breaking contact with my hand. "Gods, surely this case can't get any worse. Besides," she adds with a modicum of hope, "she was taken too early to fit the pattern, so maybe it isn't related."

I look at Tess with sympathy, not wanting to push her too hard, but knowing that I need to back my intuition. When a familiar heat washes over me, I turn to see Alaric approaching from the hallway with our offices, already frowning, already looking tired.

We're all so exhausted. I wonder if it's always going to be like this.

"How much did you hear?" I ask him.

He grimaces. "Something about a missing witch you think might be related to this case. Can you tell us anything else?" He walks past me to Tess, squeezing her shoulder lightly, and adds, "We'll find her, Tess, don't worry."

She looks up at him, teary-eyed, seeming to have already given up trying to argue about this being related to our case. "Yeah, but in what state, Alaric?"

He offers her another squeeze but looks at me, waiting for an answer to his previous question.

"I can't tell you a lot, only that when Raine asked about whether this disappearance might be involved in our case, my angelic intuition kicked off to tell me it was. Unfortunately, I really can't say whether she's been taken, or—" I flinch as I meet Tess's gaze. "—if she might be involved in a different way."

Tess shoots from her chair, a fire back in her eyes. "Of course she's been taken! Dorothea would never be involved in something like this."

"Easy, Tess." Alaric soothes. "You know the Council is going to ask the same thing. Better we have an answer for them than be blindsided by the question when they ask. Let's try and get an audience with Octavia. Announcing this information to the High Witch in front of the Council would be a good way to make an enemy we don't need."

Tess deflates again and nods. "I have her number. I'll ask."

I turn to Alaric, an idea occurring to me about this case. "If there is a pattern of attacks, could there also be a pattern of supes going missing that coincide with it? Do we know of any shifters or vampires going missing that line up with our timeline?"

He freezes, shock lighting his face for a split second. "Zeke!" Alaric calls to the far side of the room, trying to get the attention of our resident vamp who has his head buried between three screens and noise-cancelling headphones covering his ears. He grunts in annoyance, picks up a piece of paper, which he scrunches into a ball, and lobs it across the room with disturbing accuracy.

Zeke snaps to attention as though he's been shocked by a zap of electricity. He pulls his headphones down. "Yeah?"

"Do you know of any high-up vampires who went missing around the time our second victim would have?"

He frowns. "Not from my coven, but it's unlikely that kind of information would be shared outside of the coven they're from. I'll need to ask around." He's already reaching for his phone, used to following orders.

Alaric nods. "Do it, please. We need to know as soon as possible." He looks back at Tess and me. "I'm going to check in with Conall since there has been no one in my pack go missing in the timeline."

Tess stands slowly. "Octavia is coming down. Ev, how about we meet her in your office? It's best to give a little privacy for something like this if we can."

I squeeze her hand, then turn back to Alaric. "Okay, so we'll all meet back here once we have this figured out?"

"Yes. I'll see you both soon."

I look over to Zeke and see he's already moving to one of the private spaces. It sounds as though he's on his phone, following up on a potentially missing vampire.

I sigh deeply. *Why do the clues have to come in the form of bodies?*

I change the screens in my office to a simple garden, feeling it's not time for a beautiful sunset at the beach. A storm might be more appropriate really, but it feels too much like a bad omen to put one on. Neutral will do.

Octavia walks in, her cloak a deep purple with silver trim embroidery today. Her expression looks grave.

Tess closes the door behind her, while I offer Octavia a seat at the table. Once we're all sitting, I look at my friend, wondering if she is going to speak. When she looks back at me with an uncharacteristically pleading look, I offer a tight smile and turn to the High Witch.

"Octavia, thank you for coming down. I am assuming you know that Dorothea Altain is currently missing?"

She sighs, weariness weighing her down. "Yes. I have been told. I have witches looking for her, but the efforts are proving rather fruitless thus far. Why is it you and Tessa have asked me down here for a witch-related matter?"

While she's too proper to put the emphasis on me, I understand the implication. Supernaturals tend to deal with their own species' issues. We don't involve others unless the case needs to include enforcers. And usually, a missing witch wouldn't warrant this.

I bow my head respectfully before I continue. "It has come to my attention that there is a potential connection between Dorothea and this case."

"What are you implying?" she asks in a cutting tone.

I refuse to flinch, but I do soften my voice. Like Alaric said, making an enemy of a member of the Council is a bad idea.

"The team is currently looking into the possibility that a high level supernatural has gone missing around the same time as the human victims in our current case. Alaric is inquiring with Conall, and Zeke is speaking with the vampire covens."

Octavia remains guarded. "And is it your thought that Dorothea is *involved*, or another victim here?"

I look at my friend for a moment and smile softly. "My angelic intuition has made no indication either way, but Tess assures me that Dorothea would not be involved in a situation such as this."

The High Witch relaxes infinitesimally. "I would agree with this. Dorothea has been a part of the trial with humans since the beginning and has shown no inclination to expose us sooner than when we are ready. Which means we need to consider that she has been targeted. Has there been any confirmation outside of your intuition that shifters or vampires have gone missing as well?"

"No, not yet. As I mentioned, the team is checking in with their own about it. We're hoping to reconvene later today and have some more answers."

She nods and stands. "Very well. I thank you both for addressing me individually about this. I will continue my inquiries and searches. If you are right about this, it stands to reason that the next victim will be attacked by a witch."

Once I'm alone, I realize that since there were no fae in our office this morning, no one has gone to check with them. I pick up the phone and dial reception.

"Good morning, Council of the Accords office, Errol speaking. How may I direct your call?"

"Hello, Errol, this is Everleigh Cole, an enforcer. Could you please connect me with Iridessa, Queen of the Fae's rooms?"

He pauses for a moment, and I wonder if he's going to refuse, but then the line rings.

A sweet, tinkling voice answers my call. "Greetings, you have reached the rooms of Iridessa, most splendid queen of the fae. My name is Nettle. How may I help you?"

Gee, could she lay it on any thicker?

"Hi, this is Everleigh Cole. I am an enforcer. I was hoping to arrange a meeting with Iridessa."

The fae hisses without warning. "That would be *Queen* Iridessa to you, enforcer. What do you need with our monarch?"

I sit back in my chair, shocked at the feral change in the sweet sounding fae. I choose to ignore her suggestion that I acknowledge Iridessa as Queen. "I need to speak with her regarding the current case about a topic she will be very interested in indeed."

"I will pass on the message, but do not expect a response."

The phone immediately beeps in my ear, and I pull it from my face, staring at it for a moment.

Such treacherous, temperamental creatures, the fae.

After only a few minutes my phone rings. "Everleigh Cole speaking."

"Miss Cole, this is Nettle. I do *so* apologize for my rudeness. Iridessa, Queen of the Fae, requests that you join her on the seventeenth floor immediately."

Her voice is back to the tone of sweet nothings a lover might whisper in your ear. I find myself smiling and have to shake my head to clear it.

"Thank you, Nettle. I'll be up shortly."

"Very well," she trills. "I shall see you presently."

Stepping onto the fae's floor is like stepping into another world. There are trees. *In the hallway.* A deep green moss covers the ground, flowers springing up sporadically. When I step out, a bird flies towards me and lands on my shoulder. A blue robin. I laugh, unable to help myself. Magic seems to sparkle in the canopy above me and it takes a few moments to locate the desk.

Behind the table made from a tree, which has grown sideways, sits Nettle. She looks as sweet and innocent as she sounded on the phone. Her deep brown hair is styled into a pixie-cut with a flower crown threaded through it, complimenting her dark skin. She's wearing a forest green dress, so similar to the foliage that she almost blends into the room.

"Greetings, Everleigh. Our splendid Queen will see you now. Please go through the door at the end of the hall."

I didn't see a door when I entered, but I nod and make my way further down the hall in the direction Nettle pointed. As I near the end, I begin to wonder if she is playing some kind of trick. There is no door.

A wide tree with draping fronds sits on the left side of the hall. With no other options, I wander underneath, and around the trunk. Vines begin to grow from the ground, snaking into the shape of an arch. Once it is in place, clovers sprout up all over it, followed by small white flowers. Entranced, I continue to watch, trying hard not to blink and miss the magic.

After all the greenery and flowers still, a wooden door appears, looking to be made of a deep oak wood. There is no handle, but the door opens on its own, welcoming me in.

It's no wonder humans are drawn in by the fae so willingly.

I step through and find a room much the same as the hall, except here, Iridessa is perched on a throne carved from a tree made of white wood. Her gown today is one of lilac silk, twinkling and glowing from an unknown source. Her deep red hair is curled once more, retaining her very youthful look.

Two fae guards stand stoically on each side of her in charcoal-colored pants, no shirts to be seen. Their defined abdominals would gain one's attention, if their eyes were not the yellow of an owl's. A maiden also sits at her feet, dressed in a simple blue dress, holding a tray up to her queen, laden with treats.

"Would you care for a bite to eat, Everleigh Cole?" Iridessa asks with a knowing smile.

Of course she'd bring up the way my clients were destroyed by her kind sixty years ago. Sadistic bitch.

I should have sent someone else to have this conversation.

I draw in a deep breath, trying not to be dragged into the pool of sorrow that comes when I think about those lost souls.

"No. Thank you." I say after a moment. "I need to make an inquiry regarding our case. Perhaps alone, should you wish others not to hear it."

She pouts prettily at me for a moment, then tilts her head to the side, reminding me of a bird stalking its prey.

I say nothing. Waiting for her to make her own decision, face purposefully neutral.

"Very well," she says. "Leave us."

Her servant immediately withdraws from the room, but her guards hesitate. In a heartbeat, she transforms from a beautiful child-like being to a skeletal glowing wraith. "I said, leave!"

Her wail is so high-pitched, I cover my ears with my hands.

As soon as they leave the room through more hidden doorways, she returns to the only form I had seen before today.

"I'm ever so sorry about that," she trills. "Sometimes they simply need a reminder that I am not a defenseless child."

I rest my hands by my side once more, surprised at her openness and at being able to relate to the ancient being in front of me so well. "Yes, I can understand that feeling."

Iridessa nods. "Now, what is it you needed to ask of me?"

I outline our current theory about missing supernaturals being related to the case we are trying to deal with at the moment. Her stillness tells me everything I need to know.

"Maveric went missing in that timeline. I have had fae looking, but we have found no trace of him. Do you believe him to be involved?"

"Do you think he could be? Is he someone that would like the humans to know we exist?"

She frowns. "I could not say with any certainty, I'm afraid. Maveric is old and keeps his opinions to himself."

I breathe deeply in and out, hopes dashed of a simple answer that supes are being kidnapped rather than willingly joining or forming the group trying to expose us to the humans.

"Very well. I will return to the others and see what else has been learned."

"And I, Miss Cole, will look into Maveric's life and see if he is a victim or traitor to this plot." Iridessa flashes into her wraith-like form, and then simply disappears. For Maveric's sake, I hope he's not involved either way—that his disappearance can be explained by something far less sinister.

I'm left with a racing heart, more questions than answers, and a suffocating sense of dread.

TIME

Tess sits with me at my meeting table, nursing her cup of coffee as we wait for Alaric and Zeke. She begins to stir it absentmindedly with a stainless steel teaspoon. I sit quietly and leave her with her thoughts while I rub my sore throat. If I wasn't an immortal, I'd think I was getting a terrible cold. I know it's about Clara, though. Now neither the pain nor the impending dread will go away.

"Sorry, Ev, I know I'm a bit out of it. Are you all right? I can tell things with Clara are getting more stressful for you."

"It's okay, Tess. You've got a lot on your plate right now, and things are complicated all around. The visions are getting more frequent, and I can't get rid of this damned sore throat, but I know it's about her. What about you? Are you doing okay? I can tell this is rough for you."

"Yeah, I guess. I know we were expecting the humans to be missing, but I wasn't expecting supes to be missing as well. I *know* Dorothea hasn't turned to the wrong side. She's so honorable. She's been there for me my whole life. I just... I need her to come back, you know?"

I reach out and squeeze her hand. "We'll find her, okay? We're going to get her back."

She offers me a small smile before leaning back in her chair. "I really hope so, Ev. She's too important to me, and to our coven, to be gone."

Tess goes back to stirring, mulling things over in her head.

When Alaric walks in, closely followed by Zeke, they both take a seat at the table. The tension in the room becomes palpable.

"What did you find out, Alaric?" I ask, unable to wait, needing to focus on something besides the painful emotional storm warring inside me and worrying over Tess.

"Conall said one of the betas from the east coast pack disappeared in our timeline. He was positive this particular werewolf was not in support of exposing us to the humans, though. What did the vampires say, Zeke?"

"I couldn't get a lot of information, but a higher up has gone missing. It fits the timeline."

"Did they think he could be involved?" Alaric shoots back.

"They thought it could be possible. They mentioned something about him enjoying power a little too much."

Tess nods, then says, "Octavia was in agreement with me that Dorothea would unlikely be involved, despite fitting the timeline."

Alaric bobs his head in recognition. "So just the fae to be confirmed. Perhaps their answer will give more clarity about whether the supe disappearances are willing or unwilling as we're each suspecting." When Alaric reaches for his phone, I know he's about to request a meeting. A meeting I've already had.

I clear my throat, trying to ease the pain and get everyone's attention at the same time. "Actually, I already spoke with Iridessa."

"You what!?" Alaric and Tess call out, sitting forward in their chairs. Zeke looks mildly impressed.

"What's the issue? Everything went fine."

Tess laughs, the first sound of amusement I've heard since she found out about Dorothea. "Girl, you are a badass. No one talks to Iridessa, especially on their own. How did you even get an audience?"

Alaric grumbles something unintelligible but obviously disapproving.

Hmph. He's cute when he's pouting. At least he's not stating his overprotective opinion to the room.

"I just used the phone. You know, called reception and got put through to her desk chick. After Nettle went a little crazy, I got a call back saying Iridessa would see me. Then I just rode the elevator. Why can't anyone see her alone?"

Alaric grits his teeth. "Because she is conniving and gets supes caught up in deals worse than the devil would make. Next time would you please just take someone with you?" I can hear a hint of betrayal in his voice. I *did* promise him after the incident with the two witches in the cave that I would stop going out alone.

Please, it didn't even involve leaving the damned building. So precious.

I shrug, ignoring my inner conflict. "Sure, if everyone is that worried about it."

"So," Zeke says into the loaded silence, his hand finding his bracelet, "what did she say? Does the pattern hold?"

I push my hand into my upper chest, trying to soothe the burning sensation. "Yeah, it does. One of her fae went missing. Maveric, she called him. Unfortunately, he's also like our vampire and could be in on it. Right now, there seems to be an even chance either way—kidnapped or involved." I frown. "Or even some of both. I suppose they don't necessarily *have* to all be the same."

Tess sighs, stirring her probably cold coffee again. "This case is killing us. They're ten steps in front of us at all times. How can there be no whispers about this? Someone has to know something. They're obviously really organized."

"I know what you mean. It doesn't make any sense. We're missing something," I add.

Alaric stands up. "We need to get back to searching for the girl. In another day, she's going to turn up dead, and the next victim is going to appear."

"Attacked by a witch, based on our pattern," Tessa adds, rising from the table. "Not that it's helpful information, really. We don't know anything about how they're picking victims, where the supes are being taken, or anything else. Just the inevitability of more torture and death."

The heaviness in the air is fraught with hopelessness, and the knowledge we don't know enough yet to make a difference. To stop what's coming.

"Hey," Zeke says quietly to the others, "we'll solve this. Don't give up now. We've already found their pattern. The bad guys *will* stuff up eventually. We'll catch a clue. Everleigh will get a vision. *Something*. Just don't give up, okay? Or we really will have lost."

Tess's mouth is gaping a little at the speech from Zeke, who rarely says anything unless spoken to. She quickly pulls it shut and gives him a quick hug. "You're right, Zeke. Let's go track these guys down."

His cheeks flush tomato red for a moment and he bumps into the table and two chairs in his haste to get out the door.

Tess smiles lightly and follows behind him, taking her coffee with her. She pauses by me and squeezes my arm. "I'll let you know if anything turns up about Clara. She's still being watched by some of the guys on the team."

"Thanks, Tess. The signs are getting more intense. I don't know how long she has left before this danger comes to pass. I've warned her all I can. She's stopped taking my calls now."

With another squeeze she leaves, and I turn to look at Alaric, still standing, but not moving. He looks as though he wants to say something, but nothing is coming out.

"Is everything all right?"

He rubs the back of his neck, still thinking about what to say or how to say it. "I....It doesn't matter. We can talk about it later. I need to get back."

I part my lips to speak, but Alaric rushes from the room and I'm left sitting, my thoughts pulled between whatever he might have said, my worry for Tess, and my building fear about Clara.

I see the black net canopy of my bed, then my vision is gone.
Fire fills my insides.
Pain ricochets down my throat.
Can't breathe.
Silk sheets. Too soft. Can't hold on.
Need help.
Blackness calls.
Need.
Air.
Need—

I tear myself free from Clara's head, sure this is happening right now. I need to get to my sister.

Thank goodness I saw her bed. At least I know where she is.

But fuck. I can't fly there.

Who gives a shit. Just fly!

It's still broad daylight.
Fuck, fuck, fuck!
I rip my drawer open to get my car keys and immediately panic about the traffic.

Take the beast's motorbike.

I run into my partner's office a couple of doors down and yank his bike key off the wolf plaque on his wall. I hastily replace it with my own keys, almost dropping them on the floor in rush.
He's gonna kill me. This had better work.
I charge to the elevator and press the button repeatedly.
Come on, you stupid thing. Let's go.
As soon as the doors begin to open, I squeeze in, select the basement level carpark and stab the Close button, wishing I could just fly to my sister.
"Everleigh!" Alaric yells at me from the end of the hallway, his voice appearing out of nowhere but coming closer.
I have no time to stop. "Sorry, it's Clara," I yell as the door slides shut.
I bounce up and down on my toes. *He really is going to kill me.*

The doors slide open, infuriatingly slowly. I rush to his bike, take the helmet off the throttle, and yank it over my head. I mount the bike, turn the key, lift the kickstand, and speed the hell out of there.

I barely look as I pull into the traffic.

I know I'm being erratic. Unsafe. Weaving between cars.

Come on, Clara. Hold on for me. Hold on.

Tears threaten to spill over and I suck in a ragged breath.

No, this is not happening. She's going to be fine.

"Come on!" I yell at the traffic moving far too slowly.

Accelerate. Brake. Swear. It's a vicious cycle I can't stop.

My throat feels tighter as I am pulled back towards my twin's fading consciousness.

No!

Faster!

I clench my legs into the bike, forcing myself back into my own head. Crashing now might mean I don't make it to my sister. That's not an option. If I fail here, that's it. *The end.* After so much heartbreak in our family, in Clara, there wouldn't even be an afterlife for her to find some semblance of peace in.

I won't lose her like that.

I pull to an illegal stop outside Clara's studio loft apartment, release the kickstand, and ditch the helmet.

I race to the back door and punch through the glass, unlocking the door from within.

Inside, I feel my sister fading.

"Clara!"

I run to the top of the stairs in the loft, to her bedroom. Clara looks dead. She's as pale as hospital sheets.

I know she's not. I feel her.

I rush to her side. Her pulse is slight. Her veins are tinted black in her neck and in her chest.

"Clara," I murmur. "I've got you."

I unleash my wings as I pull my sister into my lap and tuck them tight around us.

Okay, think, Everleigh. Think. What did Mom say?

I squeeze my eyes tight, forcing myself to think back.

With my eyes still closed, I envision the golden waves of my angelic aura. I drag in a deep breath and then push my aura outwards.

Thoughts of love and connection flood me. Of Clara. Of Mom. Of Dad.

I keep pushing, straining against my aura that wants to cling to me.

Breathe.

Push.

Breathe.

Push.

Breathe.

Push.

The moment Clara is inside, I can feel her. Her lifeforce is joined with my own.

"I've got you, Sister. You're safe. I love you," I whisper.

A loud crash downstairs jolts me out of my metaphysical bubble with Clara, though I still feel my aura wrapped around us both. I withdraw my wings to see who is coming, cursing myself for not bringing my blades.

Alaric, and Blake—Clara's demon boyfriend—appear on the stairs simultaneously.

"Are you okay?" Alaric booms as he skids to a halt next to the bed.

"What in the hells is wrong with Clara?" Blake demands, fire in his eyes. "What's going on?"

He reaches out for her, but I smack his hand away roughly. "Don't touch her!"

I look at Alaric, breathing in the comfort of his heat, trying to draw some energy to explain. "She's been poisoned. I've placed her into a magical stasis, but—" My voice cracks as the tears finally spill over. "—it's not a permanent solution. It will just give us time to find one. I can feel the poison in her. If we don't find a way to treat it soon, she's going to die."

DECISIONS

I VAGUELY HEAR BLAKE and Alaric arguing, but the words don't make any sense. Clara is the only thing that matters now. I need to find somewhere safe for her to be.

Perhaps I could ask the Scandinavian werewolf pack who did the wards for their bar after all. Surely they want Clara to be safe. They could reinforce the wards at home.

As soon as I think of home, I realize that's what I want and need. Clara will come home with me. I rise up from the bed, lifting my sister with me, causing a break in the fight going on at the base of the stairs.

"You aren't taking her anywhere," Blake deadpans. "She's staying with me."

My head is moving from side to side before I register that I'm doing it. "No, Blake. Clara is my family. My blood. She's all I have left, and she'll be coming with me."

Fire begins to build in Blake's hands along with the rage in his eyes, his muscles tense, ready to attack, to fight me for my sister.

Alaric moves towards Blake, a threatening growl emanating from him, and looking ready to rip the demon's head off with his bare hands. Before he makes contact, I unleash my wings from the ether. Their gold and pearlescent white illuminates the room in an instant. It's a threat, and both men know it.

Blake hisses and covers his eyes. "You're going to regret this, you stupid bitch. Clara's mine. She chose to be with me."

My eyes begin to glow, this time making the golden hue brighter. "She belongs with me. Over my dead body will you be taking her away."

Burn his eyes out.

With my glow brightening and Blake's fire raging hotter, Alaric tries to defuse the situation." Look, Blake, there is no reason Clara shouldn't go with her sister. I'm also damned sure she'd burn your demonic arse to a crisp if she knew this is how you were behaving towards Everleigh." He pauses to look at me over his shoulder and then back to the demon in front of him. "She'd also fry you both for burning her apartment down, which will happen any second if you both don't rein it in. Put this shit aside and think about the person you're supposedly here for."

Blake's flames disintegrate immediately, along with all the steam that was keeping him going. "Fine. Someone keep me up to date on how she's going. *Often.*" He turns on his heel and leaves through her front door.

My shoulders tense, waiting for a slam that doesn't come. I sigh, exhausted but grateful as Alaric turns back to look at me.

"Thank you for helping me. It means so much more than you know."

He nods to me, a deep sadness dulling his eyes. "I'm just sorry this even happened in the first place. The team was supposed to be watching her, but no one saw her even leave the club after she finished working."

I hum quietly in acknowledgment. "Clara has some mage-inked tattoos. It's quite possible she used the one that shows a hologram of herself doing a simple task to escape for the weekend."

"Well that would come in handy," he says gruffly. "Would you like some help carrying her down to your car?"

"I've got her, thank you. Although, do you know if my car is actually still there? I assume you parked it illegally in your rush to get up here."

"It's fine. I've got some guys watching it downstairs. I had them follow me here, just in case we ran into any more trouble. Let's take her back to your place. I assume that's where you want to go, right?"

My lips pull up a little at the corners. "That's right. You go ahead and lead the way."

He pauses for a second and lifts one hand towards me. "Uh, you might need to retract your wings first, Everleigh."

"Oh. Yeah. Right. Thanks, Alaric." I pull them back into their place in the ether, then follow Alaric with Clara back to my home.

When we arrive, he leads the way up the steps to my apartment and knocks.

Raine rips the door open as Alaric is lowering his hand and then steps aside to allow us in. Her eyes immediately well with pink tears and she wraps an arm around me briefly, trying to offer comfort.

"I fixed the guest bedroom for her, Ev, so you can take her straight in."

I must look a little puzzled because Alaric pipes up from beside me. "I sent Raine a text, telling her a brief version of what happened and what you might need."

"Ah, okay, of course. Thank you. Again."

"Come on, Ev. Let's go and lay her down so you can rest," she says in the soft voice she usually reserves for scared children.

Perhaps I'm looking a little fragile. Hells, I feel it right now.

Raine pulls back the covers of the king-single bed and then steps away to make room. I lower Clara onto the bed and pull the light-weight cover up over her.

"She looks like she's in a coma," Raine says quietly as I go to the recliner in the corner and collapse into it.

"That's a pretty accurate description really. I'm holding her in a magical stasis using my own aura. It will work for a little while until we figure out what has poisoned her."

"Gosh, you're amazing, Ev. Clara is so lucky to have you as her sister. Where can we find out about the poison?"

I'm quiet for a moment, then look over to Alaric as I recall my earlier thought. "I'm thinking we could speak with some witches, but first, Alaric, I was wondering if we could go and see the Scandinavian werewolf pack leader who owns the club? I'm hoping they can help me to connect with whoever did their wards so I can strengthen ours."

He stands taller, keeping whatever thoughts or feelings he's having right now on the inside. "Of course. I'll take you over to the club now."

I turn back to Raine and hold her hands. "I know you didn't sign up for this, but would you mind staying with Clara, at least at home until I can come back? I'm thinking we might need to enlist some help so she's not alone. Just in case the poison—" I suck in a deep breath and the sob trying to escape with it. "In case it spreads."

Raine drops my hands and pulls me into a big hug, squeezing me enough to feel it, but not so hard it hurts. The pressure is just the right amount to feel comforted and cared for. To feel loved by my friend. "Of course."

"Thank you," I whisper. "We'll be back soon."

The door to the usually closed bar is cracked open and it sounds like small explosions are happening inside.

"What in the hells?" I say to Alaric.

He shakes his head, a frown marring his handsome face. He steps closer slowly to try and figure out what is going on.

Yells and growls sound alongside banging.

My mouth pops open when I recognize the voice. "Alaric, that's *Blake*. Come on, we better get in there before he gets killed. If Clara wakes up and he's gone, she'll be homicidal."

"Fine," he grumbles. "But I'm going in first. Be careful."

I suck my teeth in to stop from smiling, his protectiveness growing on me again. I gesture grandly towards the door, enjoying the slight distraction from the current chaos. "Lead the way, warrior wolf."

A rumble sounds in his chest and a fire heats his gaze when he looks at me. Then he turns and enters the bar.

I follow close behind him and suck in a deep breath when I see the state of the bar. "Hells! We need to stop him, Alaric."

We quickly head down the stairs and into the back room where two giant wolves are cornering Blake, who has just blown up a table with his demonic fire. Smoke is rising from the ashy piece of wood left behind, the smell a bad mix of fire and wood stain.

"Blake!" I call out, pulling everyone's attention. "Stop. What in all the hellish realms are you doing?"

"I want fucking information about Clara, and they won't fucking give it to me. They deserve to burn for this. Them *and* the fucking bar."

"Blake, seriously, there's a better way to do this. It's certainly not helping Clara. How pissed do you think she's going to be when we save her and you've destroyed the place where she works?"

The wolf guards shift back to their human form, both familiar from my previous visits. The taller of the two looks at me, ignoring Blake now that he isn't blowing up the furniture. "What do you mean *when you save her*? What happened to Clara?"

My jaw completely drops as I turn to look at Blake in shock.

"Didn't you explain before you started asking your questions and destroying the bar?" Alaric asks in a deadly quiet, contained tone.

Blake sneers. "I don't owe them an explanation. It's none of their business."

I rub my temples, tempted to release my wings and blind him a little for his stupidity. I know it won't help, though. Bloody self-centered demons.

Turning back to the wolves, I explain, "Someone has poisoned Clara. I've placed her into a magical stasis to stop the spread. Without it, she'll die."

The guard who always seems to flirt looks pale. "But she's basically immortal. Surely poison shouldn't be able to kill her."

I nod, the gaping pit of despair I'd been ignoring reminds me of its existence. "Yes, I would have thought so. I don't know what's going on yet. I've just taken her somewhere safe for now.

Then we came down here to get some help." I turn pointedly back to Blake.

"What help can they possibly give you? How do you know one of them didn't do it?"

I pause for a moment, unsure what to say. I honestly have no idea who is responsible.

Alaric comes to my side and rests a hand on my shoulder. "If wolves attacked, it would not be in such a cowardly way. As the guard says, I'm not convinced most would even suspect something like poison would be effective on one such as Clara."

"That makes sense. Either way," I turn back to Blake, "I'm not here to ask them to solve the crime. I'm here simply to talk with their boss." I gesture around the room. "How are you going to fix this?"

Blake laughs, a hollow sound. "In my opinion, they should have protected her better. They deserve the inconvenience."

The wolves both growl at him in return, somehow still as menacing as if they were in their wolf form.

The taller one addresses him. "Blake, you are hereby banned for life. Leave this place now and expect you will hear from the Alpha for damage payments. If you inflict any further destruction of the property, we will be forced to kill on sight."

Blake's eyes become a fiery, orange haze for a moment, and he takes a step forward. If he goes ahead with the attack, we'll be forced to drag him into a trial we really don't have time for.

"Blake! Stop! You need to leave. Clara does not want you dead. Just think of her for a minute."

He turns those fiery eyes on me, and I ready myself to be attacked.

Alaric steps in between us, his voice and words both filled with warning when he says, "You are severely outnumbered right now, Blake. I suggest you take their offer to leave. Not that I would allow you to lay a hand or spell on Everleigh, but if you did try, I imagine Clara would kill you also. Blood runs thicker than whatever it is the pair of you share. Leave. Now. While you still can."

For a change, I say nothing and keep my place behind Alaric, glad someone else is stepping in and that I don't have to manage one more thing right now.

After a tense moment, I hear movement. Alaric shifts his position to keep me protected, but I still see Blake stalk out of the bar. I heave a sigh, glad no one else is going to be dying or attacked today.

Once he's gone, everyone seems to relax a little.

I look around the room. "He's done some damage. Are you guys going to be able to get this fixed before you open?"

The shorter wolf follows my gaze, then says, "Believe it or not, it isn't the worst damage we've had. We have spare furniture out the back. But we'll deal with that. What did you need for Clara?"

"Of course, that makes sense. We'd like an audience with your Alpha. I want to try and find out who did the wards here in hopes they can add some to protect Clara better."

The wolves look at each other, before the taller one walks away to the bar. He stops there for a moment to do something, returning quickly.

He hands me a small piece of paper folded in half. "For Clara. We love that crazy bitch. Keep her safe and bring her back." He looks down at the paper. "Tell her Raulin and Osco sent you."

Tears well in my eyes. "Thank you. Both of you. I'll do my best to save her. This will hopefully help keep her safe until I can do that."

Once Alaric and I are outside, I open the paper and read the name.

Delilah Shelldrake

Shocked, I show the paper to my partner.

He locks eyes with mine, equally surprised. "She's the one you rescued from the cave in our cold case."

"Do you have any idea how to find her again?"

"We can check our system, but I imagine there isn't going to be a listing. We're probably going to need to request an audience with the High Witch to find her."

I sigh, tired already. "Okay, let's do this."

HELP

Since Alaric and I couldn't get an appointment with Octavia until the next morning, I went home. After a night sitting by Clara's bed, and with a million thoughts dragging me down, I'm itching to go and do something that actually might help.

At around 9:00 a.m. I meet Alaric in the foyer, and we head into the elevator for our appointment together. As I press the button, my mobile buzzes in my pocket.

Henry: Spoke to Raine, she told me about Clara. You holding up okay?

I smile softly and text him back that I am managing okay for now before slipping it back into my pocket.

I look over to Alaric. "Do you think she'll give us the details?"

He's still for a moment, his expression neutral. "I'm not sure. Octavia is generally reasonable, but her friend had been missing for almost sixteen years. It might depend on what her friend has requested and what shape she's in. Considering we helped her, she may respond in kind though."

I exhale and close my eyes, hoping something will go right in a way that nothing else seems to have since this case began.

When the elevator dings to signal our arrival to the eighteenth floor, I open my eyes and see Alaric looking at me from the other side of the space. He looks...concerned, but before I can ask, he shoots outside, leaving me to follow.

I watch his fine arse walk up the hallway ahead of me, and I'm suddenly glad he decided to rush off instead of staying to speak his mind again. The last thing I need right now is another complication, but looking at his firm, sexy rear-end will always be a win.

A young witch dressed in a simple long jade-green skirt and a white singlet leads us to Octavia's office.

Inside, the High Witch is sitting behind her solid wooden desk, the wall behind her lined with ancient-looking books. Her purplish-black cloak makes her stand out from the myriad of tomes behind her. When she raises her head, her hazel eyes meet mine, and she beckons us in to take a seat.

We move closer to the two chairs, but I notice her black cat is curled up in one of the seats. Not wanting to disturb the little furball, I remain standing while Alaric sits.

Octavia looks at me with a confused expression.

"Your cat is curled up. I wouldn't dare disturb him. He looks far too comfortable."

Her mouth moves into a small *O* of surprise before settling into a smile. "Ah, I see. Well, I'm surprised he has stayed sleeping with a werewolf next to him, but perhaps he's not fearful of you, Alaric."

My partner seems at a loss for words and slight color rises in his cheeks. I can't help but grin at his reaction.

Octavia winks at me as she walks around and collects her cat so I can sit. The world feels completely off balance for a moment, given her usually serious and contained demeanor.

Once she is sitting back on her seat, her familiar in her lap, she looks back to me with a more neutral expression. "Alaric briefly told me what happened to your sister. I understand this is a very difficult and troubling time for you and for us all with this case. What is it you would have of me?"

I roll my shoulders back, sitting a little straighter in the chair. "I came to request a connection, if possible. I am told Delilah Shelldrake, the witch Alaric and I pulled from the cave and brought back to you, may be able to help me to reinforce the wards to protect my sister."

At the mention of Delilah, Octavia stiffens, her lips pinching together infinitesimally. When she next speaks, her tone is jagged. "And how did you come by such knowledge? Delilah's powers are a well-kept secret." This explains the hesitation in both men before they gave me the paper. They would have been weighing the consequences of revealing her name to me.

I push my nails into my palms, forcing myself not to squirm under her fierce gaze. "No one is just passing out her name without thought. I do promise you that. Some associates of Clara's from the club where she works shared it with me directly, in the hopes they might aid me in keeping her safe while I try to find a cure."

The room falls into silence, like that period of time in a human funeral when the casket is lowered into the ground. Neither I, nor Alaric, say anything, simply waiting for the powerful witch to cast her judgment on the situation. On us. My heart is racing, feeling so loud I begin to worry the others might hear it.

When Octavia frowns and parts her lips to speak, Alaric startles me by saying, "If I may, I do hope you know that neither of us would compromise the safety of Delilah should you share her information with us, but I understand you would also not want to betray her trust. Perhaps you might pass on Everleigh's details and let Delilah decide on her own?"

The High Witch's cat suddenly leaps off her lap and onto the desk, giving us a terrible view while looking at his mistress. He makes a chirping kind of noise, then proceeds to almost headbutt Octavia's cheek before jumping back on her lap with a purr.

"Yes, okay, Maximus," she murmurs affirmatively, petting her fluffy black beast before looking back at us. "Very well. I shall pass on your information to my friend, and she can decide what to do."

"Thank you, Octavia. I appreciate you doing this so that I can help my sister. Do you have access to my number to pass on to her?" I want to ask her if she knows anyone who might be skilled in poisons, but my angelic intuition—a kind of niggling feeling—is telling me now is not the time to bring it up. Knowing nothing good comes from ignoring that feeling, I decide to leave it alone.

She nods. "You are welcome. I do have your phone number to pass on, and I hope you are able to save your sister. On a different note, though, while you are both here." She turns to my partner once more. "Alaric, have you any updates on Dorothea? We have not been able to find any trace of her."

My gut sinks. I've been so focused on my sister that I haven't put any thought into Tess's witch mentor being taken.

"Unfortunately there haven't been any updates, even with the twins working through the night trying to track her movements. There's been no trace of the latest victim, and now we're running out of time for the girl."

I press my hand to my stomach, trying to soothe the sick feeling taking over as I refocus on the timeline for the case. It's been three days since the girl appeared, that means tomorrow we will have another body on our hands.

"Very well," Octavia murmurs. With reluctance, she asks, "Has there been any word about the supernaturals who have disappeared? Have any returned or been found deceased?"

Alaric shakes his head. "No, nothing. We'll send word as soon as we have any news of either."

I stand watching the sun rise from the window in my guest room where Clara lies, wings curled around me, leaving just enough space to see through. I can't recall feeling so somber watching the light bring a new day. Today though, my mood is justified. The entrance of the hazy yellows and pinks means a new dead girl, another victim starting their countdown to death, and my sister's poison spreading further.

"Ev?" Raine calls hesitantly from the door.

I turn around and see she's holding a tray with my favorite teacup and saucer, one made of rich golds, and pinks, and yellows, and some cookies. My tears well up.

Come on, Everleigh. You can't just keep crying. It's not going to help anyone.

I pull my wings back into their space in the ether and wipe the escaping tears from my face. "Thanks, Raine. I really appreciate it."

"I know it's not much, but tea always seems to make things feel a little more manageable for you."

"You're right. I always fall back on my tea. Will you sit with us?"

She nods. "Of course. Just a sec."

Raine flashes out of the room and returns a few seconds later with one of the soft cushions from the lounge chair and her thermal cup of blood. She places the pillow down on the floor and sits with her legs crossed, leaning against the wall.

I sit down with my tea and biscuits, unable to stop the sigh that rushes from me as I lean back. My sister is paler than usual, trapped in stasis. The black marks running down her throat are jarring to see, especially when the darkness has seeped from her veins into the skin above them. I pull the tea to my lips, close my eyes, and take a sip. I focus on the feeling of the slightly sugary heat sliding down my throat and making its way to my stomach. After a big exhale of warm breath, I open my eyes and look back at Raine.

Her expression is full of sorrow. "Have you heard anything from Delilah yet?"

I take another sip of the life-preserving elixir and draw in some strength. "Nothing yet. But she's been gone for a long time, and I don't know when Octavia was going to ask. Hopefully we'll hear something today. Are you working?"

"I hope so too, Ev. I'm supposed to be, but if you want me to stay home with Clara, I can cancel."

"You're so sweet, Raine. I appreciate you so much. It's all right, though. Tess and Alaric arranged for some of the team to keep guard outside and in the building until we have the wards upgraded. I also installed a monitoring system so we can see anyone who might arrive."

Raine turns her head towards the door. "Someone is knocking."

I sit up, quickly place my tea down, then pull out my phone. In the security system app, I can see a woman standing at the door and I recognize her immediately.

"It's Delilah!"

"I'll wait here for now," Raine murmurs.

I stand and nod to Raine, before rushing up the stairs to meet the woman who might be able to help me keep Clara safe. When I open the door, Delilah is standing tall, though her loose clothes show she is far from being her previous weight. Her almond eyes blink in recognition when she meets my gaze.

"Well met, Everleigh Cole. May I come in?"

"Of course, thank you for coming here. I appreciate it more than you know." I usher her inside before closing the door, then lead her to the lounge room. "Would you like tea or coffee?"

"A tea would be lovely, dear. Milk, please, no sugar. I'm afraid my stomach is not used to anything overly sweet again just yet." She pauses before taking a seat. "Is there someone else here, besides you, your sister, and I?"

"Yes, sorry, I wanted to offer tea before introductions. My friend, Raine, is sitting down with Clara. She's a vampire."

"Ahh, that makes sense. Well, she's very welcome to join us."

In a blink, Raine is at the top of the stairs with my teacup, her thermal mug, and a radiant smile. "It's a pleasure to meet you, Delilah. I'm so glad you're here."

The witch doesn't miss a beat as she says hello to Raine, who is busy placing our drinks on the table.

"I'll make the tea for Delilah, Ev. You go sit. Milk with no sugar, right?"

"You got it. Thanks, Raine."

I sit across from our new house guest, my nerves begin to kick in and my words stick in my throat. Asking means she might say no to my request.

Surely she wouldn't have come if she was going to say no.

"I was told you needed my warding skills for your apartment, to help protect your sister. Is that right?"

I nod, still mute, blood rushing through me with such force I'm sure Raine would be noticing the difference.

"Could you tell me, since Octavia didn't know specifically, who it was that gave you my name?"

My stomach feels queasy. I don't want to get the werewolves into any trouble, but they did tell me to share their names. "Raulin and Osco told me about you when I asked for help at the bar. Your wards there are the best I've ever seen, and my sister worked with them before...."

Delilah smiles widely enough that it reaches her eyes. "Ahh, those two scoundrels. It's been an age since I saw them last. Though I'm sure they still get into just as much mischief now as they did when I first laid those wards."

Raine places the tea down and sits next to me, giving my hand a squeeze before collecting her mug.

The still-smiling witch takes a sip of her tea and groans in delight. "Oh, I have missed this so very much. Okay, I won't waste your time, Everleigh, especially not after you saved my life. I am very willing to do your wards, though I will need another day to collect and prepare some ingredients."

I sag into the chair, full of relief at one thing going right. "Thank you so, so much. Please just let me know your fees so I can arrange payment."

She shakes her head. "No. You've made payment enough, Everleigh. I would have continued to waste away in that cave in my own filth if you didn't find me and get me to safety. Some wards are the least I can do. And speaking of, there maybe something else. Although, please, do not get your hopes up. I also have strong healing abilities. I don't know if I can help, but I can try to assess what the poison might be."

"I—Really? You would do that?"

Delilah smiles gently at me. "Of course, dear girl. Although, again, I will need to do so tomorrow. That will also require some particular herbs and materials I do not have after so long away."

Raine moves close and wraps her arm around me, stilling the slight shake that was beginning to build from the emotional overload of Delilah's offer. "Thank you," I whisper to her before looking back at the generous witch. "Of course. Tomorrow would be wonderful. Do you need me to source any ingredients, or anything, really?"

"No, that will be quite all right, dear. I will go to those I know I can trust for quality materials, then I will prepare them this evening and return on the morrow."

We all sit together with a relative measure of peacefulness to have our drinks. A small sliver of hope snakes through my aching heart.

After we are done, Delilah excuses herself so she can prepare. We follow her to the door to bid her farewell.

"Blessed be, Everleigh and Raine. I will be back when the sun rises once more."

As soon as the door closes behind her, my phone begins to buzz. I pull it from my pocket and check who it is.

Alaric Calling

My insides become a mess of hope and dread as I swipe to answer the call. "Hi, Alaric, what's happening?"

"The young girl is dead, Everleigh. And another video has been released. We need you to come in."

I squeeze my eyes shut as the small shred of hope I was holding onto plummets.

STEPS

THE TECHNICAL DIVISION TEAM is already gathered around the main screen talking when I arrive.

Tess sees me and comes right over, drawing me into a tight hug before moving back so she can see me better. "I'm so sorry about Clara, Ev. I'm sorry we needed you to come in when you should be with her as well."

I lean in and hug my new friend right back, sharing and taking comfort from the gesture. "Thanks, Tess. It's not your fault. It's whoever is behind this hellish case. Besides, I've got someone working on the wards at home for Clara as well as trying to identify the poison. You guys arranged for the temporary security as well. I can't do anything else at home right now. What can I do here to help?"

She nods, understanding my need to be helpful. "Okay, well, come over here. Have you seen the video yet? It's been made by a different news crew, so tracking them down will likely lead us nowhere again."

When I shake my head, she turns and nods to one of the twins to hit Play, and I settle down on a desk right by Alaric.

He reaches out to me, meeting my golden eyes with his deep blues, and squeezes my hand gently. The look in his eyes makes me feel warm and safe, and I feel the edges of my lips curl up, unable to turn away.

The video begins playing and Alaric lets go of my hand, his gaze leaving me last. I turn away from the safety and warmth of his body and eyes, and look at the latest the hells have to offer.

A man sits in the center of the screen, only half seeing, his shirt removed. A pentagram has been cut into his chest, the blood smeared across his body as clots begin to form over the actual shape. It looks as though it's the worst witch-kind might have to offer, like a blood witch has gotten hold of him. Tears roll down his face, stained by the blood already painted over it.

"I... it... a witch took me. From my home, I think? She cut me up and-and-and... she killed my wife right in front of me. My beautiful—" The man's sobs cut off his words for a moment. He looks lost and distraught. *"She laid her out on some big pentagram on the floor and forced some kind of potion down her throat so she couldn't move. She-she-she gave me one first so I could only watch."* The man's breath sucks in and out rapidly for a full minute before he manages to calm himself enough to continue. *"Then the witch slit my wife's throat. There was blood everywhere, so much blood. It just poured out of her. She-she choked on it for a moment, but then she was gone. But the blood, it kept coming. So much blood. And I just—I couldn't move."*

The video continues like this, talking of the witch who stole his wife from the world and said words of power that made a breeze in the room when all of the windows were closed. His shock stems more from despair at losing his wife than his own physical wounds—a testimony to his love for her. He slips in and out of a dissociated state throughout the video, his mind trying to save him from the horror he witnessed, while his heart draws him back into the grief and loss.

When it finally stops, everyone looks over to me, waiting, though I don't know what they're waiting for. The torture of this case seems never-ending.

When I don't speak, I feel Alaric's warm hand on my shoulder. I turn and look at him askance.

What can I do?

He applies pressure where his hand is, drawing me a little from the sorrow and back to the here and now. Out of the pain of the human. The pawn in this supernatural game.

Tess draws my attention, and I turn to look at her. "There have already been a couple of different videos rising online. It seems the victim was wandering around somewhere this time, as opposed to the same video just being reshared. We're attempting to track him using IP addresses and some geographic measures. We were hoping you could look at our young victim. Perhaps a vision will appear. Do you think you're up for it?"

"Of course," I murmur. "I'll head down. I was wondering, though... You know Dorothea well. Do you think this is something she would ever do? Assuming these cases are connected."

Tears well in Tess's eyes. "*Never*. She is the most caring, nurturing witch in our coven. Something isn't right here."

I nod. "Right, I thought not from what you said. I imagine if a vision comes, I will get the same feeling. Something isn't right. Something is not adding up in these cases."

Walking away from Alaric and Tess this morning feels more effortful. I've always gone it alone, but since letting some supes into my life, it almost seems harder to manage without their presence. Especially when my sister is lying on a bed in stasis.

It seems I've opened myself to both a gift and curse.

In the morgue, I go to the section with the new bodies and look for the girl. When I pull her out and lift the sheet back, I freeze. She looks even younger than the seventeen years written on the tag on the outside of the compartment.

You poor, sweet girl. I'm so sorry.

I take a moment to offer a prayer, hoping as always that the big guy is listening for the girl's sake, if not for mine. I ground myself into the present moment and try to visualize my thoughts and feelings floating away on clouds, letting each one go, so I can be open to my visions.

Once I feel more solid within myself, connected to my inner essence—a place of peacefulness—I open my eyes. This time I start simply by taking her hand and waiting, letting the psychic energy pull me in. Within a few deep breaths, my vision begins to change, a whiteness taking over, which morphs into another place.

I'm surrounded by trees dripping blood.
The branches are moving. Coming closer.
I scream.
I try to run.
Then he's there. The man too beautiful to be real.
I hit him full in the chest.
He laughs, a tone so alluring it makes me want to curl up in it.
I can't see his eyes.
"Help me, please," I whisper.
That laugh again.
He grabs me by the hair and drags me back.
Blood covers my legs as rocks and twigs cut them open.
My blood soaks into the ground.
"Stay still now, little girl. We aren't finished yet."
He transforms in front of me.
A giant hawk.
He flies away then loops back to me.
I throw my hands up and he tears my skin open.
"Let me go!" I scream. "Mom! Help me!"

The morgue comes back into view, but I can barely see or feel anything through the terror riding me. The girl's fear is now my own. I drop to the ground, releasing my wings to pull around myself. I hum the tune my mother used to sing to me, trying to remember that good exists in the world as well. It's difficult to do when all I can think about is the poor girl screaming for her mom as she died.

A familiar warmth draws me from my cocoon, and I withdraw one wing to see Alaric in front of me. As he moves to sit on the floor by my side, I return my wings to the ether. He pulls me in to rest my head on his shoulder. I breathe in his rich scent of forest and cinnamon. One breath, then another. Continuing until my world has returned to normal, until the girl's fear is a horrific memory.

"Thank you," I murmur into his shirt. "The poor girl was so terrified."

"I can imagine," he rumbles, "I don't think I've ever seen you look that way before. I came to check on you and it's as if you weren't here. The fear looked so real. Like you couldn't see what was in front of you."

I nod, agreeing with his assessment. "It definitely appeared she was attacked by a male fae. He had deep brown hair, and was beautiful of course. He also had antlers. He turned into a hawk and tore the skin from her arms. It's more than I saw in the last vision, and I think it will be enough to confirm with Iridessa if it was indeed Maveric."

"Yes. It will be enough to check. Did you get an impression of anything else? Anything similar or different from the others?"

I shake my head. "No, there was still a sense of something being wrong... or off, somehow. And I couldn't see his eyes. They were shrouded in the vision. But from where he stood, I should have been able to see them. Maybe some kind of clue?"

"Hmm. It could be. I can't think of another reason for the fae's eyes to be blocked from you. Usually they're the clearest feature on the bastards."

I snort, appreciating his brusqueness as it places me more firmly in the here and now.

"Come, let's go and reconvene upstairs. We're trying to connect some geographical dots to see if we can narrow down our search area."

Reluctantly, I pull away from Alaric and stand on my feet. Before I can do anything, he's already covered the young girl's face with a gentleness that speaks volumes. When he slides the compartment closed and snaps the latch, it rings with a metaphysical finality that tells me I won't get anything more from the young girl. That it's time to leave her in peace.

Back on our floor, I allow Alaric to lead the way and sign us in with the retinal scanner, my mind seemingly content to admire his perfectly shaped, muscular arse rather than drown in the worries I know are coming.

Tess and the twins turn to look at us when the door snaps closed. "Any luck?" Tess asks.

"Enough to identify whether the fae was Maveric. But his eyes were shrouded in the vision when I should have been able to clearly see them. It's adding to the theme of something being off about these attacks. I just don't know what it is yet."

"Well, at the very least, perhaps there is some hope that those disappearing aren't willingly involved?"

Alaric interjects, his voice a curious rumble, "What makes you say that?"

Tess turns to him. "I suppose I was thinking that if anything could tell us they weren't doing this willingly, it would probably be the eyes? Like you know, they'd probably look regretful or something if their loved ones are being threatened. It's just a thought, of course. I don't really know."

I move forward and pull her into my side for a squeeze. "That sounds like a good theory, Tess. I certainly don't have a better one right now."

I feel her slump a little in relief, knowing my agreement provides her a small measure of hope that Dorothea is not willingly involved in this mess. Especially when blood magic was clearly described in the video that went live this morning.

"Yes, I think the theory could have merit also," Stella, the female vampire twin, adds.

Oldin murmurs his agreement, while Alaric continues to look thoughtful—appearing to be replaying the scenario out in his mind.

A crash to our right has us all turning to see Zeke, who has just accidentally shoved a table into a wall with such force, they both fracture. He cringes and heat lights his cheeks, his chagrin bare for all to see. "Sorry, sorry! I've got the map ready."

I feel Tess shake her head ever-so-slightly and a small smile lights her face at Zeke being Zeke. "Pop it up on the screen for us, please."

He mumbles something so fast, it makes no sense to me, but he does as he's asked. After a few clicks of a keyboard, a map of the city comes up, showing Darling Harbour in the center. Another couple of taps, and a series of dots appear in different colors.

"Right. So," Zeke says, "the red dots show where the bodies of our victims in each case have been dumped, the yellow dots show where the original videos were taken, and then the smaller blue dots show the physical location of where each piece of footage was uploaded. I didn't bother with all the video copies on this map, because they appear more randomly dispersed. We can look at them separately afterwards, if you like."

It always amazes me the way Zeke can bump into things and seem so awkward, but if he starts talking about something that fascinates him, or that he's worked hard on, he's like a different vampire. He grows confidence within moments.

Alaric's brows rise. "This is actually a fairly limited area now that there are enough sites to map them properly." He turns from the image to Zeke. "Have you run any algorithms to show patterns, location proximities, and the like? Has there been any connection found between the victims using the data?"

The gangly vampire nods, suddenly nervous again. "The algorithm seems to like the idea that these drop sites are beginning to make a shape of some kind, but with the limited number of cases, it is still not able to predict the next area with a great deal of accuracy. We definitely have something a little more specific for the scout teams, though. As for the humans, the data hasn't shown a single connection unfortunately."

"Amazing, Zeke," Tess says to him, her voice full of warmth. "This is really helpful, thank you."

He blushes again before rushing back to his work area, only bumping into one table this time.

I see the twins watching him, shaking their heads simultaneously. Their movement makes me curious, but I decide to leave my question unasked, since Zeke would hear it.

Alaric and I decide to spend the warm afternoon scouting one of the predicted areas around Darling Harbour for any trace of the man who was attacked by the witch. We wander together down by the water in an unexpectedly companionable silence.

Rather than asking unsuspecting humans, we simply listen for any whispers of strangeness, any talk of the distraught man.

The warmth of the day paired with my partner's comforting heat makes time disappear rather quickly, and the next thing I know, I'm watching the orange and pinks of the sunset over the water. On occasion, I catch Alaric looking at me, and sometimes he catches me peeking at him, but mostly we look and listen.

When his stomach makes an almighty grumble, I can't help but laugh. "When was the last time you ate? I'm assuming that wolf of yours has quite the appetite."

"He's not the only one with an appetite," Alaric mutters before jerking himself to a halt, his expression one of mild shock. "Uh, sorry. Yeah, we need some food. Let's head back."

My stomach does a little flip at his unintentional confession.

Ask him out already!

Yes, girl. Be brave!

"How about we get a bite to eat together instead?"

WARDS

Alaric and I find our way to a fancier than planned steak restaurant not too far from the border of our search zone. I can't help but wonder if I was mad to invite him to join me for dinner.

Hells, is this a date? No. It can't be a date. Just a work dinner.

Alaric for dinner sounds like a good option.

Be cool, girl, be cool.

The host takes one look at Alaric's finely chiseled features and basically starts to drool. I can't exactly blame her, but I certainly didn't envision the staff trying to sit in his lap.

It's not like you'd mind if that happened though either, girl.

Great, now I get to deal with the host and my inner demon.

When the host tries to seat us out in the main room, Alaric asks for something a little more private. My stomach does a flip-flop.

Relax! It's probably just so we can talk about the case without being overheard.

Or maybe it's so we can get naked and not talk.

I rub my temples, trying to get out of my head and back to what's happening in front of me. Which at the moment is a filthy look being thrown at me by the host behind Alaric's back. A sigh slips out before I can stop myself. Sometimes pettiness is just exhausting. I try to draw on my angelic nature and my psychology experience to garner some patience, but my inner demon is more interested in slicing her up. I settle for taking a seat.

When she finally leaves, I'm left sitting across from Alaric, and I take a minute to just look at him. His chiseled jawline, straight nose, and those deep blue eyes. His shoulders and traps are defined even beneath the blue T-shirt he has on, and his arm muscles are obvious, despite him being relaxed. He looks good enough to eat.

I force myself to drag my gaze back up to those hypnotizing eyes and feel myself blush when I realize he's staring right back at me. He doesn't call me out for checking him out though, just sits ever so patiently, watching, waiting, looking like he might be ready to devour me too.

Someone clears their throat to get our attention, but it takes us a full two seconds to turn and look at the server.

"Yes?" Alaric growls at the man.

I pull my lips between my teeth, trying to rein in both the angel and demon in me at his anger over the interruption ruining our moment.

The waiter turns a cherry red. "Uh, excuse me, sir, ma'am. What would you like to order?"

Alaric orders his steak rare, then turns to me expectantly.

"I'll have mine medium, thank you."

Once we agree on drinks, sides, and sauces, the poor man scurries away, likely glad to avoid returning for the rest of the evening if he can help it.

We quickly turn back to each other and our heated silence, and I wonder what we might talk about. My musings somehow manage to sour the moment, and it begins to feel awkward.

"So, uh, how long ago did you move over to Sydney?" I ask.

He shuffles in his seat. "I came over with the Council after their last move, so just a year or so ago now. What about you?"

"Maybe a year before that, I think? I came over with Clara. She wanted something completely different from our last place in eastern Europe. Mostly I just go where she wants to."

He tilts his head to the side, an assessing look on his face. "Why don't you go where *you* want to go?"

I feel a smile build to rest on my face. "You know, I think you're the first to really ask." I raise my shoulders in a shrug. "I love my sister. After my mother was killed, we lived with our father. Then after his downfall, well... I didn't have anyone else. I wanted to stay with her."

"And in that many years, she hasn't let you pick?"

I twist my lips to the side, trying to recall some of our conversations about moving over the years. "You know, I don't think so, now that I think about it. She's just always kept her ear to the ground for rumors of our father's killer, and we move to the next place so she can hunt the demons down who might have been involved."

Alaric appears to mull the information over as our drinks are delivered—a whiskey for him, and a glass of red wine for me. The waiter thankfully comes and goes quickly this time, obviously warned by our server.

"If I may," he says quietly, "you don't seem the type to be consumed by vengeance. Does it not bother you, to follow your sister around?"

I reach out and pick up my glass, swirling and sniffing the woodsy and fruity scent before taking a sip. I roll it around in my mouth, tasting the varying hints of flavor before swallowing it down. After breathing out, I open my eyes again and catch Alaric staring at me. His tongue darts out, wetting his lips. Instinctively, I do the same, lost in the moment.

His brows rise slowly as he watches my lips. "Does it bother you?"

I shake my head a little, trying to clear it. "It's Clara's way of grieving. I used to... participate... in the hunts, in the early days, but I haven't for a long time. I don't judge my sister, but I do worry for her." I snort indelicately. "Though, in some ways, she seems more adept at moving forward than me. At least she has a boyfriend. Even if he is a demon." I shake my head, still disbelieving of her choice.

He chuckles, the sound deep and sultry, and I can't help but stare.

He sounds and looks good enough to eat. Maybe we shouldn't wait for dinner.

"Well, I might argue about your assumption of her moving forward better than you. Especially now. Blake is a questionable choice at best, and it seems like you've made a couple of supernatural friends as well."

I grin openly, energy filling me in a way I'm not used to. "Yes, I didn't think I'd ever have any supernatural friends, really. Most of my early days around the community, people seemed to just hate me on sight. And I mean... you know what happened in Paris. Supes have always targeted me and anyone remotely close to me. It was always easier to stay away."

He frowns when I mention the time we met but then smiles, his features softening. "Well, I think Tess and Raine are equally happy to have you as their friend."

"They are wonderful. Life is so different with them in it. More than I realized it might be. But... what about us? Would you consider us to be friends?" A heated flush fills my cheeks.

"Friends...." He seems to try the word out, thoughts flitting across his face in the form of micro changes to his expression.

He makes sure he has my attention before he answers, "Yes, I'd like to be your... *friend.*"

My stomach does another flip-flop at his slight hesitation, my body clearly wondering about the potential of more with an unexpected keenness.

Another female waitress chooses that time to arrive with our dinners. Her eyes hook straight onto Alaric's fine form. I look over to him to see if he notices, but he's just gazing at me, and butterflies seem to take root in my stomach.

Friend indeed.

Raine and I sit in the guest bedroom with Clara waiting for Delilah to arrive. We've both taken the day off work to be here in case she needs us while setting wards, and as my friend reminded me, so that I have support no matter how things turn out.

"So tell me all about this dinner date, you little minx." Raine waggles her eyebrows at me. "I'm sure Clara would love to hear about it as well. She's always telling you to live a little."

I laugh at her enthusiasm and wild expression. "There isn't that much to tell. We just went to a steak restaurant near the harbor."

She blows a raspberry at me. "Oh, please give me details. What did you guys talk about? Better yet, did any clothes come off? I would seriously undress that delicious hunk of a beast if he wasn't already spoken for."

I choke on my tea for a second, coughing and spluttering through my laugh. "The clothes all stayed on, Raine. We were in a restaurant. Though—" I pause and give her a salacious wink. "—I may have undressed him in my mind at one point or another. And I'm damn sure the waitresses would have ripped his clothes off if they'd gotten half a second of opportunity." I roll my eyes, recalling their needy stares.

Raine leans forward and perches her elbows on her thighs, resting her chin in her hands. "Do tell, was he tempted by this waitress?"

I flush. "He didn't even look. Alaric kept his eyes on me the whole time."

My friend leans back and fans herself. "Girl, you have got to make a move."

I laugh as I try not to let the thoughts start running away and catching my inner-demon's attention again. "Hey, I'm calling last night's dinner progress. It's the first time we've really just sat and talked about anything other than a case, and him not trying to protect me from everything. And he agreed that we're actually friends. Not *just* partners. I'll take that for now."

She waves me off. "Sure, sure, *just* friends. For now. Time will tell."

The loud knock from the front door draws our attention, and I'm pulled from my little fantasy land of Alaric, back to the hard reality in the room. I stand, squeeze Clara's leg gently, then head upstairs with Raine to greet Delilah.

Raine opens the door, and our guest's standing in the hallway, arms full. I rush forward to help her with the load, which looks like it might weigh more than she does right now.

"Hi, Delilah. Thank you for coming. Let me get that for you."

She passes over the woven basket full of crystals and other ingredients with a smile. "Everleigh, Raine, good morning to you both."

I move inside with her items and place them on the wooden dining table we rarely use. Delilah follows me. Raine locks the door and then follows Delilah.

After removing all the items except the white crystals from the large basket, Delilah looks at us both. "All right, the first thing we need to do is place these crystals in the corners of each room in the house."

Raine laughs lightly. "Well, no wonder you have so many crystals in there. I'll do the bedrooms." She sets enough crystals out for me to do the living areas where we are currently sitting and then bounds away with the rest in the basket.

"She has such a beautiful, positive energy about her, especially for a vampire," Delilah says to me with a warm smile.

"That she does. She's a beautiful soul indeed, and I'm more grateful than you can imagine she was put into my path."

The witch nods, a knowing look on her face.

I'm tempted to ask, but she picks up some of the crystals left behind and walks to the corners of the room to place them, so I do the same. Within a few minutes, we're done, and Raine is already back in the kitchen brewing us a pot of tea.

When it's ready, she places the pot on the table for us while she nurses her thermal mug of blood, this time decorated in Tigger from *Winnie the Pooh*. A nice match for her bouncy personality.

Rather than talking, Delilah sits with her eyes closed, her face completely relaxed as she enjoys the tea. She hums between sips.

The gentle flow of her barely visible aura, the soft colors of serenity interweaving, lull me into a more relaxed state than I've managed in some time.

"Uh, Ev, are you okay?" Raine says, a tinge of concern in her voice.

I startle and blink, turning away from Delilah to look at my friend. "Sorry, I'm okay. Did you say something?"

Her brows draw down. "No, you just looked like you were in a trance or falling asleep or... something. I don't know. I was getting worried."

"Oh, thanks. I didn't realize. I was just watching Delilah's aura, or what I could see of it anyway."

At this, the witch opens her eyes and looks at me, curiosity plain to see. "Oh, I'm sorry, deary. I was just preparing myself to do the wards. I didn't realize you could see my aura, or I would have warned you to look away."

I offer a smile. "That's all right. It was nice to feel relaxed for a few moments."

"Ev, it's been nearly five minutes."

"Oh, well, I guess I should be more careful. I can't say I've had that happen before. I've certainly seen witches perform magic before, but I don't recall that being a side effect."

Delilah appears a little chagrined. "Ah, well. It probably wasn't so much doing the magic as the nature of what I was doing and the fact that your barriers are likely more relaxed than usual since I am here to help you."

"That's interesting. What makes you think that?" Raine asks.

"Most of the time, those who can see auras tend to keep very tight mental shields in place, usually because innately, they know they might be vulnerable. They can 'see' out but nothing gets in. Or at least that has been my experience in the past. *Sometimes* though, if those beings are feeling safe and not actively blocking, certain things can slip through. Now, if I was doing something inherently dangerous, I imagine your shields would have recognized it immediately, to keep you safe."

I lean forward on the table towards the witch. "Ahh, but because I know you're here to help and I could see the colors were calm and relaxed, I was able to just be drawn in."

She nods. "Precisely. Also, I wasn't doing a spell so much as preparing for one, which usually involves some meditation. My favorite of which involves enjoying a nice fresh pot of tea."

"Witches are *fascinating*! Between teaching at the school and being around you and Henry, Ev, I am learning so much about all the supernatural species. It's just amazing."

My lips pull up into a smile as I look at my friend. "You are exactly the right kind of being for this life, Raine. I think you're going to be such an amazing teacher and mentor to a lot of the supernatural species the longer you do this."

"Oh, I concur," Delilah adds. "I foresee you helping many supernaturals in your time."

Raine whips her head around to look at the witch. "You see the future?"

Delilah simply smiles but doesn't say anything else.

I grasp Raine's hand across the table and give it a squeeze. "Our world is lucky to have you."

She grins at me and a pinkish tear drips from her left eye. She returns my gesture, then rises to clear the now empty mugs from the table.

The witch stands. "Now, the only things I will ask while I do the wards is that you pick a place in the house and stay there so that there is limited disturbance while I lay the foundations. That you do not speak to me or interrupt in any way, and that you do not open any doors or windows. Any questions?"

We both shake our heads and go and take a seat on the couch to wait. I watch idly and with some curiosity as Delilah begins chanting words in a language I don't understand. She then picks up her large black candle, with symbols etched around the base, and lights it. She takes it to the first crystal, speaks some words of magic, and the flame from the wick spits off and flies into the crystal, lighting it up until it appears to glow from the inside.

The witch continues her task, moving from one crystal to the next, from one room to the next. I look at my friend, who is watching in complete awe, her eyes wide, her mouth slightly open. I feel the same. I've seen wards done in the past, but never like this.

Somehow we manage to sit silently, listening to the rise and fall of the witch's powerful words as she moves from space to space. Eventually, she re-enters the living areas, looking drained, but still chanting.

She makes her way back to the crystal she started with and says some new words. Powerful words. And when the flame flies into the first candle once more, several things happen simultaneously: The flame goes out, Delilah sits on the floor, and a light so bright it burns shoots out from each crystal and covers every inch of the walls, floors, and ceiling. They all connect for a fraction of a second, and it's as though the foundations shake. Then, the light is simply gone. The crystals are back to normal. And Delilah has fainted on the floor.

"Holy cow!" Raine whispers to me. "That was, like, the most amazing thing I've ever seen in my life."

I look at her, eyes wide. "You know, me too. I suddenly understand why the wards around the club are so good. This was only in a *house*. Can you imagine the power it must have taken her to do the entire street where the club is?"

We both turn and look at the witch sleeping peacefully on the floor.

How in all the hellish realms did anyone capture you?

VISITORS

Hours later, I hear Delilah begin to stir on the couch where Raine and I laid her down. Raine heads out to pick up some food from the local healthy takeaway store so that our guest can regain some energy.

I wander into the kitchen and put on the kettle, preparing some more English breakfast tea. Once it's ready, I pull out one of my ornate trays and load it with the tea pot, two saucers, milk and sugar. I pull out some blood for Raine and fill her thermal mug. Fully prepared, I wander over to the lounge chair opposite our guest and wait patiently.

After another few minutes, Delilah stretches out, then sits up, rubbing her eyes, a soft smile on her sleepy face.

"Are you well?" I ask.

"I'll be better after some tea, and maybe something to eat if you have anything? I should have thought to bring food with me."

"It's not a problem at all. Raine will be back any minute now. She popped out to get some food so you could replenish some of your energy. Placing the wards was obviously very exhausting."

"Ahh, yes, well I am a little out of practice after all this time. I wouldn't have crashed so hard when I was younger and working consistently. I'd built up some endurance, but," she looks at me, sorrow filling her eyes and making them glassy, "after I was taken... well let's just say, I haven't done spell work in almost sixteen years."

I let her sit with her emotions for a moment while I make her tea.

Once I pass it over, she brings the cup to her nose and inhales the scent absentmindedly, her gaze miles away from here. "I was pregnant when they captured me, rather more defenseless than usual of course. The coven who captured me had been after me for many years at that point, but they'd obviously been biding their time. They took me in broad daylight, just hit me over the back of the head. When I woke up, I was in that cave you found me in."

Shock courses through me. Nobody mentioned she had been pregnant. Unable to help it, I feel her pain, the sharpness piercing my chest and making my eyes fill before I blink them away. The deep blue of despair almost drowns the other colors from her aura. I move and sit next to her, hesitantly wrapping an arm around her, trying to provide comfort as she shares the horrors she experienced.

She barely seems to notice as she continues talking. "I had my baby girl in that disgusting, depraved cavern. I couldn't stop the labor once it started. I... I didn't even get to hold her. They took her and gave her to a witchling to kill as part of their initiation, to try and make her powers emerge."

Delilah sobs, her breath heaving in and out, and when our front door opens, she jumps.

"Shhh, it's okay, Delilah, you're safe. It's just Raine with lunch. You'll be okay."

Raine looks at me in alarm, but I shake my head, trying to signal there is no danger.

How could they do this to you and your baby, you poor, poor woman.

My friend brings the food to the coffee table, then takes her mug and wanders into the kitchen, trying to give our guest some privacy.

When Delilah has calmed a little, she continues her story, obviously needing to release it. "I tried to take my own life so many times after they killed my baby. But they wouldn't let me. Someone always watched me in those days. No amount of begging or pleading to any of them granted me freedom. They didn't seem to want anything from me other than simply to watch me suffer. They stuffed the magic binding potion down my throat every month so I couldn't even use my magic to help me. They never placed the witchling who took my baby on guard duty in my room, so I could never try and get revenge, or even ask what she did, if she buried her somewhere. The hole in my heart has never healed, but I did eventually stop trying to end my life."

"I'm so sorry, Delilah, for you and your baby girl. I'm sure she is resting in heaven with the angels, waiting for the day she will see you again." I know, deep down, that it is not true, that we have no afterlife, but sometimes it's better to suspend reality and offer a bit of comfort.

She nods forlornly and pats my hand. "Yes, I'm sure she is with the Mother. I will see my beautiful girl again one day. She got her wings far too early, but I will try to live on. Try to help others again. Do things to honor her ever-glowing soul."

"I'm sure she is watching over, waiting patiently. Time feels much different there. My mother told me when I was younger."

After the room has been silent for a while, Raine speaks from the kitchen, "Would you both like some lunch now?"

By early afternoon, Delilah is ready to try and work out which poison is affecting Clara. We move the items she'll need down to the guest bedroom. A buzz in my pocket alerts me to a text. When I see it's from my partner, my stomach does its new little flip-flop it seems to do whenever I start to think about him.

Alaric: I think I tried to visit earlier to see how things were progressing, but I somehow ended up back at the office. Assuming the wards have worked.

Me: Hey, sorry about that. I'll check with Delilah about how to make exceptions to the wards when she's done with Clara. Let you know soon how it goes.

"Let me guess," Raine says teasingly, "The handsome beast?"

"*My* handsome beast, yes." I poke her in the ribs and laugh, unable to help myself playing along with her teasing and the fantasy.

"Ohhh, yes, girl! He's yours for sure."

Delilah wanders into the room as both of us are laughing. "Are you two talking about that rather ruggedly handsome werewolf you were with when you saved me, Everleigh?"

I'm fairly sure I turn the color of a ripe tomato. "Uh, yes, but really we're just partners, and friends. I'd very much appreciate you not mentioning this to him."

She smiles knowingly. "Of course, dear. I wouldn't dream of it."

"Thanks!" I poke Raine in the ribs, trying to get her to stop snickering about it. "Speaking of, I was wondering if there is a way to allow particular beings to bypass the wards to come and visit. Said werewolf mentioned he tried to come and visit earlier to check in but somehow ended up back at work, not sure what he was doing."

Delilah's face lights up. "Perfect! I was going to talk to you about testing the wards later, but it seems your werewolf has done that for us. The trick to these wards is that you need to invite someone to visit before they try to come here. As a safety precaution, it is more tied to your internal intentions, not just *saying* they are welcome. That way, you can't be coerced into it. I set all of that up during my preparation. I much prefer wards for residences. They can be much more refined than those in public places."

"Wow," I say quietly. "That's incredible. Thank you, Delilah, seriously. I feel so much better about us leaving the house for work while Clara is still here and unwell. Are you sure I can't offer you any kind of payment, or anything in return?"

"No, deary, you've done enough. I'd likely be in that cave for the rest of my life if it wasn't for you. Now, if you're ready, I'm going to try and identify that poison."

Hope and dread find their way to the front of my mind as soon as she mentions being ready, but I nod in agreement anyway. I need to know.

She walks over to stand by Clara's side and pulls the sheet down to her waist to take a look. "How was she poisoned?"

"I didn't see how it happened. I experienced some of the poisoning during a vision and the pain started in the throat and went down, so I assumed she ingested it."

"Hmm. Okay, well from the black veins, there's already a lot I can cross off. Just give me some time to work, all right?"

Raine rushes out and brings back two couch cushions, planting them on the ground near the door and beckoning me over.

I walk to my friend and sit down next to her, allowing myself to be pulled into her embrace. Her arm around me eases my distress a little as we sit silently and wait.

Delilah places a few ingredients and materials onto Clara's chest and then begins more chanting, though it sounds vastly different from the words she used while doing the wards. Colors light the air at different times, and she swaps materials around more than once. After a while, she begins looking more frustrated, her brows drawn down and her eyes squinting.

My stomach churns and I shift about on the floor, unable to sit still like I usually do. The longer I wait, the more I notice signs of stress in my body, like my heart racing a little faster, my breaths getting a touch shorter.

Raine gives me a squeeze and rests her head against mine, reminding me she's with me. I lean into her, trying to wrap the comfort around myself like my mother used to with her wings—accepting a new kind of support that I've never had.

When Delilah turns to look at me with sorrow in her eyes, I know her answer. "I'm sorry, Everleigh, but I can't identify the poison. It's not one made by any ingredients from the human world."

"Oh hells. This is worse than I thought. How do I figure it out if the ingredients aren't even of this world?" Despair overwhelms my senses, and for a moment, I can't hear anything. All I can do is try to breathe.

After a time, I feel Raine humming something in my ear and stroking my hair. When I can, I take a deep breath in through my nose and an extended breath out through my mouth, slowing myself down, offering my body a reset.

I look over to our guest. "I'm sorry, Delilah. I am so appreciative of everything you have done here today. I'm just having a bit of a moment. Clara is the only blood family I have left, and she's going to die once she is out of this stasis if I can't find an antidote of some description. Do you have any idea about where I might look for answers?"

She pauses collecting her items back into the woven basket. "It's okay, deary. I know this is terrifying for you. My best suggestion is to try and speak to supernaturals who are not part human—angels, demons, and the fae. The poison will likely be found among them, but I fear it may not be easily identifiable. Speaking with those who are very skilled in poisons or who have been around for a very long time may be your best hope."

Angels, demons, fae. The most closed-lipped and difficult to access of the supernaturals. God help me.

Me: You're safe to visit now if you still want to. I could use your opinion on some stuff.

Alaric: Be there soon.

"He's coming around, Raine," I call down the hall to my friend.

She appears at my bedroom door after about ten seconds, already dressed up to go out.

I raise my brows. "And where are you off to, young lady?"

She rolls her eyes back at me. "Puh-leaze, Mom. I'm not getting in the middle of you and your wolfman. I'm going out so I can catch Henry up and see if he's found anything interesting from his little information hunt in the media about these cases."

My brows draw down. "He's been pretty absent lately. Is that what he's been doing?"

"Yep. If I don't call him on repeat, he's lost in his own little world over there. I'm surprised he manages to get himself to work most of the time. He needs to pare back the obsession, I think."

I suck my lip into my mouth and chew on it while I think. "Maybe I should cancel Alaric coming and go speak to Henry about this. It sounds like he's in over his head."

Raine walks into my room and grabs both my hands, looking right into my eyes, making sure she's got my full attention. "Listen, you have enough on your plate to deal with right now; plus, Alaric might have some helpful ideas to work out a next step for Clara. *I* will go and see Henry and help him to refocus. I promise if he doesn't listen, I'll tell you, and then you can intervene."

"I mean, I feel bad because I've barely had time for him since starting this enforcer job."

"Look, to be honest, I don't think it would have mattered. He's down this little rabbit hole for better or worse learning about supernaturals. Any free time he has, he spends doing that. Or hanging out with me if I pester him enough." She winks. "Just let me do this one, Ev."

I sigh, exhaling a huge breath. "All right, fine. But if you need me, just tell me. And make sure you tell him I want to catch up again soon."

She grins like the Cheshire cat. I can't help but feel a little suspicious, wondering if her motive goes beyond what she just said.

She does seem to talk to him *a lot*.

"Now, before I head out, what are you going to wear?"

I look down at my gym pants and tank top, then back at my friend. "Uh, well, I was just going to wear this?"

Raine's already shaking her head. "No, no, no. That won't do. He's coming to see you, and you like him. Put in a little effort. Hold on." She shoots off out of my room and returns twenty seconds later, holding some clothes out to me.

I groan as I take her choice. "We're just friends. I'm sure he's just in normal clothes, anyway. I can't look like I'm going out. He's coming to talk about how to help Clara."

"*Blah, blah, blah*. Listen, even if he's only coming to talk about that, there's something there between you guys. Put on the pretty outfit, which will make him look. Just think how disappointed your sister would be if you didn't 'live a little,' or however she likes to say it."

Feeling a little flustered, I pull the clothes up to look at them again. "Ugh, fine. I'll wear it. Give me a minute." I strip off my pants and singlet, glad for the fact I always wear nice underwear, and pull on the mid-thigh-length black skirt and teal three-quarter sleeve V-neck shirt.

Raine does a little spin and squeals in delight. "You. Are. Perfection."

I laugh at my friend's enthusiasm and try to let her mood soak into me a little. When my inner demon peeks her head out, I'm only slightly surprised given the topic.

We deserve a little admiration from our wolfman. Hells, maybe he'll even take it off for us.

No way. He's coming to help plan to save Clara, not to get naked.

No reason we can't do both...

A hand being waved across the front of my face pulls me back to the room.

"You having a vision or something?" Raine asks.

"Or something," I mutter.

She snorts. "Don't tell me you're having a little sex fantasy with me in the room."

I just about choke on air. "What, no! Of course not. Just... talking to myself."

Raine rolls her eyes, then winks. "Sure, sure. Okay I'm going. Text me when you're done for the night, yeah?"

"You are incorrigible! Yes, I'll text."

I hear my friend laugh all the way to the door, but when she opens it, there's a brief pause and she calls out very loudly, "Ev, your date is here!"

My cheeks suddenly feel about a thousand degrees, and I smack my hand on my forehead.

I'm going to kill her.

Alaric chuckles, clearly amused by my insane best friend.

"I'm coming," I call out as I head out of my room and up the stairs. When I get to the top, I can see the door has been closed, and Alaric is standing near the dining table. His hair looks freshly washed and he's wearing a newer, non-faded pair of jeans with a dark gray shirt that clings to his abs.

He looks good enough to eat.

No, we're not going there.

C'mon, how about just a taste then?

"Raine said she was in a rush, so she left right after she... called out to say I was here." He rubs the back of his neck with his right hand, causing his bicep to flex a little.

My eyes can't help but follow the movement. It's a huge effort to look back at his face. "Uh, yeah. Sorry about her... greeting. Did you want anything to drink?"

Alaric seems to be having a little trouble of his own. I watch as his gaze runs over me from head to toe and then back up.

The movement causes a pulse in my core, making me want to press my hand to myself to soothe it.

He can press a hand somewhere else that might soothe it.

"Yeah, a drink would be nice. Do you have any whiskey or a beer or something?"

"No one here drinks beer, but I can pour you a whiskey. Do you want to grab a seat on the couch?"

He moves over to the couch that faces the kitchen, and I smile tightly at him, knowing he's going to be watching every move I make.

I walk over to the kitchen and pull out a bottle of aged Irish whiskey, bending from the hips instead of at the knees, unable to stop the demon in me from teasing him a little. I pour us two fingers each, then carry the glasses over to him.

He watches me like a starving wolf who's just found a nice juicy steak.

I bet he wants me raw too.

I move to the side of the coffee table, bending down in a way that gives him a perfect view of my breasts and the lacy edges of my black bra. I hold out his drink, and without looking away from my breasts, he reaches out to take it. His fingertips close over mine as he grasps the cup, and a zap of energy jumps between us.

A purr-like sound rumbles in Alaric's chest, and it reverberates down to my wet core. Our eyes lock together, and I'm sure he can scent my interest. I pull my bottom lip into my mouth, biting down, trying to decide what I should do.

His gaze moves to my lips and suddenly he looks ravenous.

VULNERABILITY

Alaric leans forward and my heart races. He's so close to me now that I can feel his wolfish heat penetrating my own. My inner demon groans along with me.

An insanely loud buzz causes us both to jump back, sloshing the scotch in both of our cups.

"Fuck," he mutters. His phone skitters across the coffee table, and he looks at it with murder in his eyes. I see Tess's name on the screen and know she'd kick herself if she knew what she'd just interrupted.

He groans as he picks it up and looks at me apologetically, the heat fading from his eyes, and our chance slipping away. "I'm sorry. I have to take it."

I nod mutely, and head over to the kitchen to get a cloth for the whiskey that spilled on the table. I run some cool water over the fabric and rub it on my neck briefly, trying to leach out some of my own heat. I rinse it again and squeeze it out before heading back.

Alaric looks grumpy as all hell on the phone, giving Tess clipped single-word responses. I cringe a little, knowing how it feels to be on the other end of one of those calls from him. It's hard to be too sympathetic right now, though, after what my friend got in the way of.

Come on, girl, she had no idea. She's a friend. You wanted him here to help with Clara anyway. There'll be other chances.

After I clean the spill, I come back to sit down. I briefly consider sitting next to him and placing my hand on his lap. My inner demon jumps for joy at the idea, but ultimately, my angelic side wins. I sit on the couch opposite and take a swig of my whiskey, wrapping one heel behind the other as I wait patiently for him to finish on the phone.

When Alaric finishes with the call, he places the phone down and collects his drink, his other hand rubbing the back of his neck, a seemingly nervous gesture.

"Sorry, Everleigh. I had to take it in case a time sensitive lead came up in the case. I... I really wish she hadn't interrupted."

"It's all right," I murmur, "I know things are rough with this case right now, and we can't ignore calls about it. Was everything okay? You don't need to go?"

He shakes his head, regret lining his features. "No, it's okay. Nothing I need to act on right now. What is it you wanted to chat with me about? You sorted out the wards?"

I can feel my own regret mirroring his, wishing for a way to get the moment back. "Yeah, the wards worked perfectly. She is *really powerful*, Alaric. We need to invite anyone we want to come to the apartment before they can; otherwise, like you, they'll just get turned around."

"That's great, Everleigh. I'm glad she was able to help you."

Maybe I can lower his guard again by offering a little vulnerability.

"You know, you said we were friends, you could call me Ev too. If you want to, of course."

He smiles at me, and I feel the wall come down just a little. "Ev it is."

A warmth fills me at his acceptance of my offer, at having more familiarity in our relationship.

It's hardly intimate. Just take his damn clothes off. He'll taste so good.

I shake my head slightly, trying to clear the intrusive thought and focus on how things are going right now instead. Even if my inner demonic side does have a valid point.

"So, while the wards working is good news, there's also some not so great news alongside it. Delilah wasn't able to identify the poison. The only thing she could tell me with certainty was that it wasn't of the human world. She suggested it is angelic, demonic, or fae in nature."

Alaric frowns at the news. "I'm sorry, Ev. I'm sure that isn't what you were hoping to hear. It's still good news in a way, though. It rules out quite a lot of options and gives us somewhere to go next."

I feel my eyes well up a little at his positive take on what was feeling rather hopeless, and that he's finally treating us like real partners. "This was why I asked you around. I was thinking you might have an idea about what a useful next step might be. I just don't know where to go from here."

When he sees a tear spill over, Alaric stands up and walks over to me. He sits down next to me on the lounge chair and places an arm around my shoulder, pulling me in towards him.

I close my eyes and lean into him, resting my head against his shoulder and neck. His warmth soaks into me as he squeezes me closer. I take a moment to just breathe in his intoxicating scent.

Once I take a calming breath and become still, he talks again. "Personally, I would go with the angelic and demonic directions first, since your sister is both. It's more likely they would at least know if it has been seen before in their kind and what could be done about it. You know how treacherous the fae are, and needing to ask a favor of one of them would be my last resort."

I snuggle into him a little, feeling reassured by his logical approach to the problem. "That sounds like a really good idea. And I definitely do not want to owe the fae a boon if I can help it. I know a lot about angels and demons from my parents' lessons, but I don't know who to go to about this kind of thing. Have you come across anyone in your time as an enforcer that you think could help?"

He stills for a moment, and I feel him hold his breath for a few seconds. Long enough for worry to seep back in despite his embrace. Fear for Clara. I'm grateful he doesn't make me wait too long, though.

"I think, given you are part angel and demon, and an enforcer, you have a direct connection to both Raphael and Nicon. Speaking with them might be your best option. Especially given the time-limited nature of this problem and the fact that you suspect there is a connection to the case."

"They're under no obligation to help me, though. Do you think they will?"

Alaric is quiet for a few moments, showing me he's taking my worries seriously and thinking about his response. "I think if we go together to see Nicon, he will share. He's too morbidly curious not to want to take a look, and he took too much joy in pairing us up for this job for whatever reason."

I chuckle, remembering his gleeful voice when he declared Alaric would be my partner, since he was in charge of the enforcement unit. It was so out of place in such a serious situation. Alaric's deep chuckle joins mine and reverberates through my body, causing us both to laugh a little louder.

"He definitely had some kind of agenda making that decision." I pull myself away just a little and turn so I can look into his deep blue eyes. In an instant, I'm lost. They have such a depth, and when his walls aren't up, it's like I can see into his soul. And I like what I see.

The way he's looking back at me gives me hope. When he lifts his hand and rests it on my cheek, stroking it with his thumb, I hold my breath so I can focus on the feeling. His skin is hot and soft, and he touches me with a reverence that makes my heart skip a beat.

I lean into his touch for another moment, relishing the feeling of his affection, and then I take a chance. I tilt my head back, eyes locked to his, and move closer. Alaric's hand stills on my cheek and then he shifts to meet me.

My eyes flutter shut as I feel the warmth of his breath on my lips. I reach out and snake my own hand around his back, running my hand gently across him. His body shivers as our lips meet. Slowly. Gently. We kiss, moving our lips together in a gentle dance. Sweet. Perfect.

For a time, there is nothing but us in the world. I relish in the feel of being in each other's arms, connected by lips and tongues. Alaric runs his hand down my back, causing me to shiver with need. I want to push myself closer, but I feel him loosen his hold and begin to move back. With a new kind of reluctance, my body complies, and I move back and meet his eyes again.

He reaches up and tucks a loose strand of hair behind my ear before gently running his thumb over my lips. I'm lost and found at the same time, and the sweet perfection of the moment welds itself into my very soul. Unable and unwilling to stop myself, I mirror his movements, enjoying the feeling of his soft skin and lips beneath my own fingertips.

He reaches up and takes my hand in his and pulls it to his lips, kissing my fingers gently—like a prince might do with a princess upon meeting for the first time. His eyes never leave mine though, so I remain in the safety of his gaze while my body experiences a sweet kind of bliss under his gentle attention.

It's as though the world has stopped spinning just for us, to have this moment with each other, and I can't feel anything but grateful for it. This was meant to be.

Alaric turns me gently and pulls me back to rest against him on the lounge. We sit peacefully in each other's company, simply breathing, and being.

After a time, Alaric rests his head on mine and finishes his thought from earlier in a soft voice, not disturbing our bubble of contentment. "Given Raphael's helpful nature and demeanor, and the potential connection you both have, I think he will also agree to help if he can. I see no harm in asking."

Once we agree on a plan, I stay curled up with Alaric on the lounge. I send an email request off to both the Archangel and the Ruler of Demons on my mobile phone, then put a show on the television. Despite the general chaos of Clara and the case, pausing in Alaric's arms feels so right.

The next morning I'm unable to stand still as I wait in the foyer for Alaric. My stomach is full of butterflies, unsure what to expect.

When he left last night, we shared another soul-shattering kiss that I couldn't stop thinking about. But now, I have no idea how I should greet him. I've never needed to worry about how to approach someone I work with but have also been kissing.

Maybe I should act like nothing happened. We are at work.

Or maybe jumping into his arms and locking legs around him and making out is a better option.

Well, it'd be the more fun option, but "better" might be pushing it in the foyer of our office building.

"Hey Ev," Alaric says warmly from behind me.

I jump a little, completely startled out of my own little world. I feel the heat rush up to my face. "Hi, Alaric. Sorry! I was in my head for a second there. I didn't hear you walk in."

He smiles, but keeps his distance, giving me a fairly clear signal of how I should behave with him at work. I understand it but still can't help the sliver of disappointment that echoes in my chest.

"It's no worries. You ready to head up?"

I take a deep breath, then nod. "Yep, let's do this. We're seeing Raphael first. Want to lead the way?"

"Let's do it. You'll be fine. He's an angel, after all. Come on."

I follow him to the elevators and then ride up to Raphael's floor. Instead of focusing on the room and the hallway, I distract myself with the view in front of me. Of Alaric's broad shoulders, slim waist, firm arse, and muscley legs.

I'll bet it feels good to have that beast on top, running nails down his back, squeezing that perfect arse.

I move my head from side to side, trying to drag myself back to the hall and away from the fantasy my demonic side is crafting for me to enjoy.

Alaric opens the door and steps to the side for me to enter. I smile at him, hoping I don't look like I want to devour him as much as my body is keen to right now. He seems to be working hard to hold his stern look in place as I move closer to him to go past, and it only makes me grin more widely, wanting him to lose control a little like I have.

When I step past him and into the room, I immediately jerk to a halt, feeling like I've just witnessed the Rapture.

Both Raphael and Nicon are in the room waiting for us.

PERSPECTIVE

MY BRAIN SEEMS TO just short out for a moment. I don't move anywhere or say anything. I can only stare. Raphael is sitting behind his desk, looking straight at me, his expression slightly strained. Nicon is lounging in a chair in the corner with his ankle over one knee and his fingertips together like some villain in a television show. He looks half-pissed about something, but in a flash, his expression morphs into relaxed amusement. I can tell just by looking at him that his favorite show is about to start. It helps calm the need to stretch out my wings.

The heat of Alaric's body behind me seems to restart me again, and I step further into the room, hearing Alaric pull the door closed behind him. When he's standing next to me, I look over to him, unsure what to say about this, wondering if he knew this was going to happen.

Of course he didn't. He'd have said something in the elevator or downstairs.

Just say hello for hell's sake.

"Good morning, Raphael." I bow deeply, then turn to the Ruler of Demons and lower my head in respect. "Nicon."

Alaric does the same, though only dips his head to both since neither has his fealty.

"Hello, Everleigh," Raphael says in his usual calm tone. "I do apologize for our unexpected guest. I was meeting with Nicon for another matter, and when I mentioned the need to wrap up for our meeting, he indicated he was also to see you today. If this is the same matter, would you like to speak with us together?"

Since I'd been fearing the worst, I try not to collapse in relief at this unlikely coincidence.

I take a peek at Alaric, curious if he might object, but when he says nothing, I shrug. "It *is* about the same thing. I just didn't think to try and arrange a meeting with you together. I thought that it would be rather difficult to make happen and the reason I am here is time limited."

"Oh, do tell then," Nicon drawls with interest.

Raphael simply inclines his head to indicate I should speak.

I feel somewhat awkward just standing, but since we haven't been invited to sit, I just suck it up. "I've come to talk with you about Clara, my sister."

Nicon takes his leg down and leans forwards, continuing to hold his fingers together as he looks at me, brows raised and a twinkle in his eye I don't love.

"She's been poisoned."

Both the Archangel and Ruler of Demons frown at me, disbelieving.

"Surely that just went straight through her system and disappeared?" Nicon interjects.

I shake my head, reminding myself to breathe through the panic welling up inside me at their response, my hope slipping further away. "I found her just in time and was able to put her into a magical stasis using my own aura."

Raphael pales behind the desk. "Everleigh, you know you cannot keep that in place. It will kill you. Our auras are not meant for such a thing. I'm surprised you would even know how to do it."

I force myself to stay still, to not show weakness to these supernatural leaders, but I feel Alaric turn to stare at me as well. I shift uncomfortably, since I certainly hadn't mentioned that tidbit of information to him.

"I know. That's why I am trying to find a way to reverse the effects of whatever poisoned her quickly. I knew it was unlikely to be a poison of this world, but I had a skilled witch check to be sure, in case her magical resistance was lowered somehow allowing a poison to affect her. But the witch confirmed it was not of this world, and suggested I would need to consider alternatives."

Nicon leans back in his seat, amusement replaced with perplexity. Raphael seems to withdraw into his mind, his eyes moving as though he's reading, except there is no text in front of him.

After what feels like an eternity, Raphael returns to the present. "There is no angel-made poison that I can think of that might affect an angel. I do have books of healing, which may be of some help for rare ailments over time. However, without identifying the poison, this may be futile." He looks to Nicon.

"Well, I can think of some potential options that might make an angel sick, but not necessarily that could kill. None of which should be in the human realm." His eyes flash a vibrant red for a moment, his anger bubbling to the surface. "I think the best option at present is for me to come and see your sister. I have seen most poisons at work and know how their symptoms might appear in an infected being." He turns to look at Raphael. "I think it pertinent that you also attend. If these are any of the things I fear, and they have been brought to the human realm, they may pose a danger to others of your kind, should whoever is in possession choose to use them."

Raphael nods. "So be it. Ordinarily, we do not concern ourselves with the lives of individual supernatural beings. However, it seems the risk here may be far greater. Where is your sister residing at present?"

Shock rattles me down to my bones that not one but both of these powerful beings are offering to help. Even if it's not for me or my sister, but for the greater good. I'll happily take any help I might get to save her.

"Of course, thank you both. She's at my apartment presently, so you would need to come there to see her. When is a good time?"

The leaders look at each other and nod slightly before looking back at me.

"Now will be the most appropriate time," Raphael says.

"We can take my limousine," Nicon adds.

I freeze for a moment, not sure how to get out of such an offer. Despite the thoughtfulness, the idea of being trapped in such a confined space with them both makes my heart stutter in fear. Nicon especially can be incredibly temperamental.

"Thank you, Nicon. While we appreciate the offer, it might be best if we meet you there. We need to take my motorbike, as we have business that's related to the case to attend to after we are done."

Yes, wolfman. Swooped in for the save. A delicious thank-you coming your way later.

Nicon pouts, looking extremely put out at not getting his way.

What in the hells were you hoping to see, Demon Lord?

"Very well. We shall see you both there presently."

Seemingly dismissed, we both offer bows and head out of Raphael's room and down to the basement level of the building. When we reach Alaric's bike, he grabs my arm and pulls me behind a pillar. He shoves me into it and slams his mouth onto mine. It's all tongues and teeth and heat. I push myself into him, determined to be closer, but far too quickly, he pulls his mouth away from mine and flashes me a grin as I melt in pure ecstasy.

"I've been wanting to do that since I arrived this morning."

I put my fingers to my lips for a moment, feeling the swollen heat of us merging together so abruptly. "I'm glad you did," I say breathlessly. "I wish there was time for more, but I'm assuming we need to get moving to beat them there."

He leans forward, placing a hand on each side of me against the pillar. When he's close enough, he kisses me softly on the cheek, driving me wild with the need for more. Then he whispers in my ear, "Time for more is *exactly* what I want." He steps away, leaving me wanting.

Fuck yes!

I almost feel a little lightheaded from the excitement, but I follow him and take the helmet he offers.

He holds out the keys. "Would you like to steer again this time?"

My lips pull up into a grin. I contemplate for a moment, but decide I'd much rather wrap my arms around him. "Not this time. I'll be the pillion."

"As you wish, Ev." He winks at me, then pops his helmet on and mounts the bike.

Ohhh, you can mount me like that. Vroom vroom, baby.

We zip through the city traffic in a way a car never could and get back to my apartment in record time. I let Alaric lead the way up the stairs so I can check him out. He occasionally pauses and looks back with heat in his eyes. He knows I'm watching.

My demonic side has me biting my lip at him and giving him "fuck me" eyes before I even get a chance to reject the thought.

His responding growl is possessive, and it turns my insides molten, wishing he would take me right now, here in the stairwell.

"Getting along well, I hear," Nicon says from right around the bottom corner. I squeak in surprise and Alaric's growl cuts off immediately.

Holy never-loving hells, when did he arrive?

"Now, now, no need to fear. I knew the pair of you would get on splendidly." Nicon comes into view a second later, an outright grin of triumph lighting his features. "Although, I am surprised it took you both that long to realize."

"Nicon," Raphael interjects from the next flight of stairs. "This matter is not our concern. Let us focus on the task at hand."

The Ruler of Demons snorts, looking somewhat disgruntled by the Archangel's comment. "Speak for yourself."

I shake my head, completely at a loss for words once more. Instead, I hurry up the stairs past Alaric and to my door, which I unlock to let everyone inside.

Raine flits up from her room. When she sees who files in behind me, her eyes bulge out of her head for a split second before she manages to pull herself together.

"Uh, welcome. Would anyone like a drink?"

Nicon's face lights up immediately. "Scotch. Neat. Don't be shy when you pour."

Raphael merely shakes his head.

"Right," she says. "And you pair?"

"I'm good. Thanks, Raine." I turn to Alaric, waiting to see what he will say.

"No. Thank you."

Hmm, we're going to have to work on his bedside manner with my friends. Although, maybe it's because of our visitors.

I smile at Raine, and she disappears for ten seconds before returning with a rather large glass of scotch.

"Ahh, excellent," Nicon says when she presents it to him. He downs the contents of the whole glass in a few gulps and makes a refreshed noise. "Lovely. All right. Carry on, little hybrid. Where is your sister?"

The demon seems far more accepting of my half-blood status than most.

I walk down the stairs, and Alaric falls into step immediately behind me, protective, despite our guests doing us a favor.

Clara is lying in the bed, looking rather like Snow White with her overlapped hands resting on her stomach. I rearrange her hair for my own comfort and to greet her. Then I pull down the sheet so that the blackness on her neck and chest are visible. I move back a step and gesture to the others to come forward.

Raphael and Nicon move up to Clara on the other side of the bed. Raphael makes eye contact with me briefly, his irises illuminating to a gold to match my own, a showing of empathy for the pain I work so hard to keep shoved down. Nicon simply bends down to inspect my twin.

Nicon mutters a few incomprehensible things, and then after a moment, he holds his hand out over the blackness and closes his eyes. He begins to speak in demon tongues that sound vaguely familiar from my father many years ago.

A burning sensation rips through my chest, and I clutch it, hissing in pain. Alaric steps forward with a growl, eyeing Nicon suspiciously.

Thankfully the pain leaves just as quickly as it appeared, and I manage to relax. I reach out and touch Alaric's arm and try to give him a reassuring smile, despite the echoes of fear now floating in me after the poison responded to Nicon.

After another moment, the Ruler of Demons opens his eyes. His face is carefully neutral.

"You know what it is," Alaric accuses.

Nicon nods, looks at Raphael, then over at me. "I do know, but I'm afraid it is not good news. Your sister has been poisoned by liquified obsidian from the deepest realm of the hells."

My heart is racing, as though it is trying to jump right out of my chest. "And what can I do? How can I save her?"

Nicon doesn't answer, and I turn to look at Raphael, the pain in his eyes telling me the truth.

Tears well up and spill over like the sorrow inside me. It's so big it feels as though it can't be contained. "Please, there has to be something," I beg, the worry spiraling into despair.

Raphael tries to give me a thread of hope, of something to hold on to. "You can look through my library, to see if anything might be done, but I can recall no instances of reading such a thing."

When Nicon meets my desperate eyes, all I see is pity and a determination to be truthful. "I'm sorry, Everleigh. Demons are immune, but no angel has ever survived this kind of poisoning. It seems she has enough angel blood for it to be deadly."

ASTONISHED

MY KNEES HIT THE floor with a dull thud. I lean forward and rest my head on the side of the bed, pulling my vision into blackness. The sound in my ears is like white noise that pulses, drowning out anything that might be going on around me.

Clara.

The burning pain in my chest is nothing compared to the grief that's drowning me now. I can't lift my head above it. Breathing is too hard.

My sister.

You can't leave me.

I can't be without you.

This can't be the end.

I don't know how long I sit in this hollow grave, my emotions feeding on my life force, as if they'll consume me and I'll be left here, an empty shell.

A minute or an eternity passes, and I feel Alaric's heat behind me. He must be saying something, but I can't hear it over the static in my head. I let him pull me back towards him, my eyes scrunched shut, trying to keep the world out and the pain in.

We're on the floor together, with my back against his chest and his arms are holding me together, and I'm suddenly sure that if he lets me go, I'll unravel.

I wake up in the dark in my bed, my covers pulled up around me. A soft snore makes me turn my head. Alaric right next to me, sleeping peacefully on top of the blanket.

He didn't leave.

Raine appears at my door a moment later, concern clear on her face. She moves closer, quietly, and at a human speed so I can watch her, then bends down next to my bed.

"I heard you moving, so I came to check on you," she whispers, trying not to wake Alaric.

I try to smile, but I can't make myself do it. The sorrow in my soul is too heavy. My vision blurs; tears have welled up in my eyes again.

Raine reaches out and strokes my hair. After a minute or so, she whispers to me in a fierce, resolute voice, "I don't care what they say, Ev. We are going to find a way to save Clara. I know we will. You aren't alone in this. You have me, and Alaric, and Henry, and Tess. Hells, even Delilah has offered her help. We *will* find a way."

"She's right, you know," Alaric murmurs from behind me. "There are lots of us here to help you, and we won't rest until we find a solution and whoever the hells did this. None of us want you to lose your sister."

I turn to look at him, pleading in my eyes. I don't know what it is I'm pleading for, but I know the feeling.

"The most important thing right now, Ev, is not to give up hope. No matter what Nicon says. Even if what he said was true about no angels having survived before. Clara is half demon too. She also has a twin who is keeping her safe in stasis. We have time that no angel had in the past to find a solution. We'll find one."

The resolute look in Alaric's deep blue eyes tells me he believes his words. He has hope that we can do this.

Raine leans down and gives me a hug. "We're with you, Ev. We'll figure this out and save Clara. We won't give up, but you can't, either, okay?"

Much like the pleading in my eyes, I can hear it in her voice. The need for me to not collapse in on myself and surrender. But to fight.

Come on ya, bad bitch. Get up and save Clara.

I take a deep breath and try to pull some of the sorrow in, wrapping it carefully in the warmth and love of my friends. I can feel it inside me, but I can breathe too.

Okay. I can work like this. Come on, Ev. You've got this.

I give Raine a squeeze and drag myself to a sitting position. Alaric quickly follows, a sense of awe in his gaze. He leans forward and kisses me chastely on the lips.

"That's it, Ev. We can do this."

It's Sunday morning and I'm sitting in the Technical Division office with Alaric, Tess, Oldin, Stella and Zeke. The rest of the team is working on the current case, especially since we know another body and video are due to show up today. The tension in the room is high, and I know everyone is worried about me from the quick glances they all keep shooting my way, especially Alaric and Tess. While they work on damage control and look for any new clues to try and find those responsible for the "catch, release, kill" case, I'm poring over ancient angelic texts that Raphael granted me access to.

I turn the pages of the ancient tomes carefully, most of which are made from papyrus, the ink handwritten. I try to keep my emotions under wraps, but with every passing chapter of the books I read being absolutely no help, it surges. And every time it does, Alaric is there with gentle reminders of patience.

By mid-morning, I'm feeling a little tired, which is completely unlike me. I slept yesterday and only recently before that. Normally, I only need to sleep once a week. Worry begins to stir in amongst my sadness. If the weight of the stasis is already affecting me, then time is starting to run thin. Admitting that to anyone here will only make them worry when we should be focusing on the case. I keep quiet.

"You okay there, Ev?" Tess asks.

"Yeah, just a little tired," I say. "Deciphering all of these old texts in different languages is pretty exhausting."

"Can I get you anything? A cup of tea maybe?"

It won't help, but it won't hurt either.

"Sure, thanks, Tess. I appreciate it." I do my best to pull up my lips into a smile through the weight of sorrow and fear holding me immobile. I know it looks strained, but it's the best I can do for now.

She squeezes my shoulder and walks off to make some tea.

Alaric appears in her stead, a deep frown furrowing his brow. "Can we chat?" At my nod, he signals that I should follow him. We walk until we reach my office where the wall-sized screen is still showing the garden I didn't change. Once I pass him to enter the room, he pulls the door shut behind us. "Why didn't you tell me, Ev?"

A sinking feeling pulls inside me, thinking I know where this might be going, "Tell you what?"

"That using a stasis on Clara would eventually kill you?"

Well shit. Just distract him with making out.

Not likely. He's about as distractible as a saber tooth tiger with a bleeding bison in front of it right now.

"There's no easy way to say that. I can't say I was thinking about the potential side effects at the time anyway. I was just trying to save my sister before it was too late. Then, well, I guess I just avoided it. I didn't want anyone to worry."

He stares at me, a slow burning fury rising in his eyes. "You can't sacrifice yourself. You dying here is not an option."

"I'm not letting her die, Alaric."

"So your plan is to what?"

I glare at him, frustration overtaking my sorrow. "My plan is to save her, like it's always been. You're the one who said we can do this, that we can find a way."

He huffs a sharp breath out. "Yes, we're going to keep working, but I refuse to lose you." His tone is stubborn, final.

"I hear you. Can we please just—"

The door bursts open and Tess is there, bordering on being out of breath. "Reception just called. There's a mage downstairs, who says he was captured but got free. He has information."

Both Alaric and I pause, shocked, before our brains catch up with our mouths.

"Where can we talk to him?" I ask.

"No, I'll talk to him. You go back to reading the books to save your sister," Alaric says, tone sharp. I know he's just worried I'll expend too much energy, but I've already worked hard to convince him to let me in. I'm not about to let him go back to pushing me out again.

"I'm still working these cases as well. I need to be there in case I can pick up any visions while we speak to him. And if I don't take a break from translating these bricks, I'm going to start throwing them anyway. Probably at you if you try to get in my way."

We stare each other down for what feels like an eternity.

"Ev is coming, Alaric. This is the first big break we've had. Hells, the only break we've really had. We need all hands on deck. Let's go."

Alaric looks like he wants to bite Tess's head off, but she doesn't wait around for him. She simply turns and leaves.

I dart forward and kiss him on the cheek, trying to thaw him out a little. "Come on, handsome. Let's go."

He sucks his cheeks in, trying hard to keep his glare, but it's failing quickly. When I grab his hand and pull him towards the door, he loses his fight with himself. Without warning, he yanks me back to him and kisses me thoroughly.

"Hurry up you two!" Tess yells from down the hall.

We pull back from each other, and now his look is one of satisfied possession. I smile back, shaking my head a little.

Possessive man.

He can possess me anytime. Bite him next time. He'll like that.

I walk out the door, sticking my nails into my palm in an attempt to get my ill-timed intrusive thoughts to shut up.

Tess leads us into a small office on the fifth floor. When we enter, a man stands up, fists closed, ready to attack. He looks terrible, his hair matted to his face, bruised and beaten. He looks like he went through hell to get here.

Tess stops and observes him. "My name is Tessa. I'm the head of the Technical Division. We're responsible for investigating the case you wanted to talk to us about. This is Alaric"—she points to him, then to me—"and this is Everleigh. They're both enforcers and working this case as well."

The mage collapses back into his seat, sagging over the edge.

Alaric opens the door and barks into the corridor for the receptionist to fetch food, medical supplies, and to alert Solomon Trite, the head mage. He then closes the door and gestures for us all to sit.

I take a seat close to the mage, while Tessa sits further away. Alaric comes and stands between the mage and me, and I stare at him. His expression is unrelenting. I roll my eyes and go and sit in a chair a little further away, and he takes my seat, giving me an affirming nod.

I shake my head and look back at the exhausted mage. "What's your name?"

He seems to startle, and I wonder if he was sleeping. "I am Ragnor Partik. I work directly with Solomon."

Another insanely powerful supernatural. It seems whoever is behind this isn't afraid of power.

So they're either powerful themselves, or too egotistical to recognize their limits. Either way, it sounds like a good kill.

I pinch my arm, trying to stop my inner demon from taking over the case. If that happens, the focus shifts from logic to instinct, and I'll be kicking in doors without a plan. Maybe holding Clara in stasis is rubbing off on me too.

"So, what happened?" Alaric asks, filling the silence I left.

"I was out yesterday to get my morning double shot espresso, taking my usual route through back alleys to avoid the humans. I was jumped by two supes. I was getting demonic vibes, but I wasn't completely sure because they knocked me out pretty quickly."

He sounds so disgusted in himself that I want to reach out and comfort him, but I doubt the mage would accept that. I'm yet to meet one who doesn't have an ego bigger than they are.

"When I came to, they'd taken me to some old stone building in an industrial area. It was a fucking demon. Only one if you'd believe it. The bloody fools. As if one demon could take me on its own."

And there's the ego.

"They had me tied down and he was trying to possess me. I don't know the moron's name. He was in a human form. He obviously didn't consider that I'd have magically infused tattoos in place to fight against possessions. He tried to beat the shit out of me to make it easier for himself. After a ridiculously long scuffle, I knocked the fucker out and escaped. I had to run back here through back alleys, though, hence the exhaustion. It was a good twenty kilometers. I could probably take someone back there, but it didn't look like a base of any kind, just a place of convenience."

Alaric frowns at him. "Did he give you any inclination of what he was trying to do? Why he was trying to possess you?"

The look the mage shoots at Alaric is witheringly sardonic. "No, nothing, he was too invested in the possession and trying to beat me into submission to give a victor's speech."

You know, I think he's gonna be just fine.

Alaric and Tess both look to me—

The door smashes open.

Solomon Trite stands in the doorway in his full mage garb, looking ready to commit murder.

CONFUSION

"ALL OF YOU GET out," the Arch mage demands. "I need to speak with Ragnor."

When Alaric looks like he might object, Tess stands up and gives him a look that clearly says to shut up. She then turns back to our mage. "If you could report up to the Technical Division once you are able, that would be helpful. I am sure there is more information that could assist with this case."

"Of course," he says. "I also expect to assist. I don't take too kindly to this type of behavior."

This time when Alaric opens his mouth, Tess not so subtly kicks him in the ankle and jerks her head towards the door. The demand is clear.

I suck my lips between my teeth, trying not to smile as my badass witchy friend puts Mr. Grumpy in his place.

When Alaric sees me trying not to smile, I see a flicker of an idea cross his features, one of wicked, wicked things. As he walks past me, he bares his teeth at me, looking like pure sin and mischief.

I don't know whether to smile, run, or be excited. A mischievous Alaric could be a truck load of fun.

I'll take a truck load of anything from that beasty. Yum, yum, yum.

Smiling now at the filthy fantasies my inner demon is contemplating, I keep my eyes averted from Solomon. Knowing the nature of his insanely large ego, he'd probably think I was having thoughts about him.

Ugh. No. That pompous arse can fuck himself.

I try really hard not to snort at the thought of telling Solomon Trite he could go screw himself. And in that moment, I can't help but think my demonic side has some kind of death wish.

I feel his eyes on me as I walk out of the door, but I resolutely keep mine away.

Once we make it into the elevator, Alaric turns to glare at Tessa. "What in the hells was that? Why did you leave our one lead in a room with that power-hungry prat?"

Tess rolls her eyes at him. "Have you ever stepped on the wrong side of Solomon? If I had tried to stand my ground, his next step would have been throwing every possible blockage in our way, and it would take so long for us to get in a room with Ragnor again that we'd be far too late for him to be of any help."

Alaric grunts, clearly annoyed, despite the sound reasoning.

A smile comes over me at his intense stubbornness. I look at him with curiosity. "What strategy do you think you might use to get Solomon to allow Ragnor to come with us?"

He's quiet for a longer-than-usual moment. "Honestly, I'd probably just have demanded that's what needed to happen for us to solve the case really—"

"Hence why I did the talking," Tess interjects.

Back in the Technical Division, Tess calls the rest of our weekend team over.

"What's the news?" Oldin demands, his voice strained.

"The biggest break we've had," Tess answers. "The supe behind the attack is actually a demon, or rather two or more of them. They've been abducting supes and possessing them to attack the humans they capture."

"What pieces of shit," Stella says blandly.

"Well, that is handy news," Oldin adds, then looks at me. "It especially makes your visions make sense, Everleigh, where you were saying something about how the attacks felt wrong."

"Yeah, you're right, Oldin. It definitely makes more sense, especially when I couldn't see the eyes of the attacker."

I wonder if one of the demons involved is also responsible for poisoning Clara?

They'll be a dead demon soon.

Tess sighs and flops herself down into a chair, less concerned about being professional with only the team around. "This is a huge leap in the case in some senses, but in others, it still means nothing. We have no specific ideas on which demons might be involved. And, ugh, the boss is going to lose his shit."

Nicon's day is definitely about to get that much worse.

I walk over and take a seat next to her, then reach out and rub her arm, trying to offer a small measure of comfort. "It's definitely a big break in the case, and not only can I try and work with Ragnor to get visions, but we can also look at the location he was held. And he can likely do a sketch with Zeke. I'm sure Nicon can identify them, or we can find a demon who can. And unless I'm mistaken"—I look around the room at each member of the team—"I don't think we've had a victim show up on any channels today, have we?"

Zeke's face lights up a little when I say this, more than happy to agree. "Nope, no new victim as yet. This has definitely put a spanner into their plan."

"And the body dump?" Tess asks quietly.

"Yes," Stella says. "But, in saying that, we knew that was inevitable. As Everleigh mentioned before, that's one more opportunity for clues in this case we didn't have. We're getting somewhere."

Tess nods, but doesn't say anything, instead sitting quietly while she processes the information.

"What I want to know," Alaric adds, "is why the demons are trying to possess every other supernatural species to expose them but leaving themselves out. What's the end game?"

"Well, maybe they're planning to place themselves in the best light, you know, to swoop in and save the day. It's a perfect opportunity to paint themselves as the misunderstood strangers, the saviors of the humans against the other supernatural—"

The beach spreads for miles in front of me.
Nothing but waves and sand.
I pull out my mirror glass.
Copper hair and a single pale brown eye reflects back to me.
"Come on, magic! Emerge already!"

The office comes back into view and the whole team is looking at me with hopeful expressions. "Sorry, guys, I think... I think this one might actually have to do with my sister. I just... I have no idea how."

Tess leans over and pulls me in for a hug. "That's great, Ev. I'm sure it'll become clearer for you soon."

"Yeah, hopefully. It's something at least."

Alaric shifts his weight, pulling my attention. "It's a big improvement to what we were told yesterday. Stay hopeful, okay? This means there's a stronger possibility."

I smile gratefully at my friends, my heart thawing a little. "You're both right. Thank you. Shall I go down to the morgue now and see how I go with the latest victim?"

Tess looks at her mobile, then at me. "Yeah, you may as well. I have no idea how long it'll be until Ragnor comes back."

Zeke coughs nervously from the corner. "Uh, guys. Who's going to tell the boss man that it's some of his demons that are responsible for this? I imagine we need to do it soon, so he doesn't find out from Solomon." He shivers involuntarily and looks at the other team members around me. "Do you all remember that other time he was the last to know something? It went terribly."

Alaric stands up when he sees Tess cringe and my heart melts a little. "I'll do it this time. It'll be fine."

Tess looks up at him weakly. "You sure?"

"Of course. I'll go see him now."

My angelic intuition tingles in my brain, determined to get my attention. "I think I should come with you before I head down to the morgue, okay?"

WILD

Nicon is sitting on a thronelike leather chair by his fireplace, waiting for Alaric and me to enter. The room looks like a mockery of the hellish realms my father talked about. My brows slide up towards my hairline.

This looks rather trashy for the Ruler of Demons. He dresses far too stylishly for this to be to his tastes.

The demon's sensual laugh draws my attention. "Tell me what you really think, love."

Heat builds in my cheeks at being caught out, and I bow my head in apology. I feel the color deepen when Alaric looks at me as well.

When I glance up, his expression is one of amusement, and I exhale, relieved I haven't pissed him off right before we're about to do exactly that.

"So, what is it that you both needed to see me for? Need a relationship disclosure form?"

Just give him some bloody popcorn.

"Nothing quite so delightful," Alaric grinds out before closing the door.

I whip my head around to look at my partner, who is staring at the demon, his hands clasped tightly behind his back.

I smile to myself at the words that likely slipped from Alaric without much thought and turn back to where he is looking.

Nicon stands, and pours himself a drink, a whisky of some kind. He sculls it before pouring another and then moves in front of his fireplace, staring into the flames.

"Out with it then," he deadpans, no trace of amusement left flickering in his tone.

Alaric opens his mouth to tell our boss the answer, but my angelic intuition rings so loudly in my head I push a hand to my forehead to try and ease the pain. When he sees me, he closes his mouth and looks at me questioningly. I point to myself and then to Nicon. Apparently, I should be the one to bear the bad news.

He looks at me consideringly, then shrugs, and waves a hand in the demon's direction. A clear "be my guest."

Nicon turns to look at us, impatience shining through in the set of his jaw. I hurry to talk before we make this any worse than it's about to be. "We've had a break in the case."

He frowns at me, clearly unsure how this could be a bad thing.

"A mage who was captured, Ragnor Partik, escaped and made it back to the Accords building this morning. We haven't had much time with him, but before we needed to leave him, he gave us some information." I realize I'm dragging this out and try and draw up some courage to spit out what he needs to hear. "He was captured by a demon. The demon was trying to possess him when he broke free."

I hold my breath as I watch the Ruler of Demons shift through emotions so fast, I can barely follow them. Within a few seconds, his eyes turn a darker red, then blue, and finally black. Involuntarily, I take a small step back. His eyes lock on me, then he turns and launches his lowball glass straight into the flames, causing them to burn brighter.

He turns back to us, and his face blurs between his human form and the melted rubbery red of his demonic self.

I'm careful not to move an inch while he tries to get his burning rage together, but I feel my inner demon react—my eyes begin to glow a heated red, matching his anger. It's as though his demon self calls to mine. He's tossing fuel onto the fire with every second he remains enraged, threatening to burn us all. A part of me knows the only thing stopping him from ripping me apart for the bad news is my own demonic blood.

By the time he speaks, his features no longer blur, but his eyes remain the same obsidian as my sister's poison. The moment I notice this, I feel the red heat abandon my eyes, and tears well up as I'm dragged back to his words.

"No angel has ever survived this kind of poisoning."

My tears seem to drag the demon out of his fury, his eyes quickly dulling back to their usual red hue. When he steps forward, I flinch.

An inscrutable expression crosses his face before he resets it back to a trained neutrality.

I quickly rub the tears that slid onto my cheeks and look at Alaric. My intuition telling me the pain that was forced on show for the Ruler of Demons changed my partner's fate should he have delivered the news on his own.

It's always one pain for another.

Knowing I've served my purpose here, but still smarting from the freshly torn reminder, I jut my chin towards Nicon.

Your turn, wolfman.

His body shifts towards me half an inch, enough to let me know he wants to come to me, to comfort me. Ultimately, he stays in place, though, and accepts my message that it's his turn.

When he locks eyes with Nicon, the demon addresses him. His tone is as carefully bland as his face, and it makes me wonder if he truly regrets upsetting me. "What other information do we have?"

Alaric straightens, his voice moving into one of professional boredom, which he reserves for unstable, powerful supes. "We have not yet been able to identify the demon that attempted the possession—he was in his human form—but once we have Ragnor, we will arrange for a sketch to be brought up to you. Perhaps you will be able to give us an identification."

He nods stiffly. "Anything else?"

"Yes. There are at least two or more involved, according to Ragnor. It's possible there are more, though."

He leans forward, pressing his fingertips together in contemplation. "And do we know if this is definitely what has happened with the rest of those taken?"

Alaric answers for me without skipping a beat, keeping the attention on him. "Everleigh's visions have indicated something being *wrong* about all of the other attacks. If we place that together with the fact most victims would not have willingly hurt humans and exposed us in such a way, then I am comfortable drawing that conclusion."

Nicon bobs his head in acknowledgment. "So some of my demons have been taking other supernaturals, possessing them, and forcing them to attack and kill humans to expose us. In the worst possible ways."

"Yes. That is what makes the most sense given the evidence."

He lifts his head and looks from Alaric to me, then back to my partner. "And who else knows this information?"

"I imagine Solomon knows since he interrupted our talk with Ragnor so he could have his own. Assuming he is now aware, you know it will not be long before word spreads." The Council would never miss an opportunity to paint each other in a bad light, especially since this releases the rest of them from suspicion.

The red in his eyes begins to deepen, and he closes them. "Very well. Leave. Continue with the case. Report back as needed."

I don't need to be told twice.

Let's get the never-loving hells outta here.

Alaric pushes the door open, and walks inside, waiting for me to follow. The room is lit only by the hallway lights, giving it a private feeling.

"Everleigh, I wasn't going to leave you to come down to the morgue by yourself. You nearly scratched your eyes out with one of the recent victims."

I tilt my chin slightly to the left. "You didn't say anything when we were with the team."

He shrugs. "I didn't want to argue with you or Tess about it."

"Why would I argue?"

Alaric smiles wryly at me. "You seem to have a problem accepting my help."

Has he looked in a damned mirror?

"*I* have trouble with that?" I fold my arms. "I don't recall *you* being willing to accept any help, Wolfman."

He relaxes his stance and steps closer. "You could be right. But you're the one I'm worried about. You're a little more vulnerable than me when you've been pulled into a vision.

Especially when it's so unpredictable how far in you get—if you start acting out the dreams."

When he says the last, the double entendre makes my heart skip a beat.

Alaric, you're driving me wild.

"I suppose that's true. I have noticed as well that I seem to be more affected by the visions in this case for whatever reason." I step into his personal space, my chin tilted up slightly so I can keep eye contact. "In this case, I wouldn't have objected to some company, though, just so you know."

A rumble sounds in my partner's chest, and it gives me the impression of a satisfied cat, purring.

I bet that would feel good with our bodies pressed together. Move closer.

Unable to resist such a reasonable suggestion, I move forward into Alaric's arms. I rest my face against his chest and hold him closer. With my body flush against his, the rumble increases, and the vibration radiates through my body.

Holy hells, it does feel delightful.

I feel Alaric's cock harden against me, and a small moan escapes. I bite my lip to try and stop myself.

I want you so bad right now.

Claim him.

He picks me up by my arse, squeezing and massaging it with his fingers. When I lock my legs around him, I feel his hard length push into me through my own clothes. He walks us towards the door, and closes it, shutting us into the darkness. My back shoves into the door right when his mouth locks onto mine. I arch my back, pushing my breasts into him, feeling that vibration down in my wet core.

Alaric moves a hand up to my face, slides it into my hair, and I moan into his mouth. He grabs my hair and pulls it back, giving him access to my throat, and my breath catches. His hand blocks my head from hitting the door. He pulls away from my mouth and nuzzles into the base of my neck before licking his way up to my earlobe, which he sucks and nibbles on.

A shiver of need radiates through my body, and I try to move my arms up and out of the way to give him more space. I need him to be closer. He shifts his hand from my hair and locks his fingers with my own. He begins to slide them down, and we bump the light switch. The entire room illuminates in a split second, causing us both to squint and block our eyes at the sudden onslaught.

"Shit," he murmurs. "Sorry, Ev. I should've... I mean, we shouldn't be doing this here. Christ. We're in the morgue, for fuck's sake." He lowers me with more care than I've seen him take with anyone who hasn't been traumatized.

My inner demon and I grumble together. "I don't mind. I was quite enjoying that myself. Although," I say reluctantly, "you might be right this isn't the best place for it."

Hmph. It's not like the bodies in the compartments care.

I cringe at my inner demon's callousness.

Yeah, definitely not the place.

Alaric looks at me, and his gaze softens. "You'd mind later, Ev. We both would."

I bite my bottom lip, hard, then take a deep breath in through my nose. After holding it for a few seconds, I let it out. The calming response cools some of the intense heat that was building inside me.

"You're right. Let's go and see this body."

"Oh, uh." He rubs his hand on the back of his neck, a nervous gesture I've noticed. "There are two bodies. Remember, his wife was killed as well."

I sigh deeply, resigned once more to the shitshow that is this case. "Okay, fine. Let's just look and hope we can get some kind of clue."

Alaric pulls both compartments out, aligning the morgue tables next to each other, together in death as they were in life. When he pulls back the sheets, my heart breaks a little.

The woman's neck is sliced open, a look of terror marring her petite features. The husband looks and feels as though he is made of sorrow, his throat cut wide as well. Pentagrams have been roughly sliced into them both, and it appears whoever did this put salt into the wounds. I shake my head at the horror and waste of it all.

I look at Alaric whose face is stoic, holding any emotions at arm's length to deal with this.

Maybe that's what I'll be like after years of this job. I hope not.

He nods to give me the go-ahead, and I raise my hands above the woman, feeling for the psychic pull of a vision. After a few minutes of trying, I shake my head and turn to her husband.

I follow the same process, and when my hand is over his chest, I'm pulled in.

"Lady, please, stop! Leave my wife alone!"

"Honey! Honey, I'm here! I love you."

Tears stream down her perfect face.

I reach out, desperate, thrashing in my restraints.

The witch's eyes are dead, like voids.

"Please, stop! Leave her."

She kneels next to my bleeding wife.

Looks at me with those hollow orbs.

And smiles. A feral, empty grin.

She raises the knife to my wife's throat as she thrashes on the floor.

"Stop!" My voice is hoarse. "I'll do anything! Stop!"

UNEXPECTED

ALARIC'S WARM, GENTLE VOICE in my ear brings me back to the present. I focus on the rhythm and tenor of his words to center myself, to slow down my terrified heart. When my breathing returns to its usual pace where I no longer have to think about it, I open my eyes.

I look at Alaric's worried expression, and a yawn escapes me. "Sorry, I'm a bit tired."

His worry turns to alarm. "From the vision? Does that usually happen?"

I yawn again, shaking my head. "No, not usually. It must be because of the psychic energy I'm already using to keep Clara in stasis." I rub my eyes, trying to focus back on the room and the case.

"So there wasn't much overly useful about the vision that we didn't already know. I assume the witch was Dorothea like we thought, and if I see a picture of her, I could confirm for sure. I could see her eyes this time. It's as though knowing about the possession opened up the vision. She had the void-like eyes of the possessed."

He lifts his chin in understanding. "I don't think it gives us any more clues, but at least we essentially have confirmation of what is going on now. We can start targeting our searches and strategy more towards the demons. Although I am sure Nicon is out there causing hell on Earth right now trying to work out who has betrayed him."

I cringe, thinking about seeing his complete loss of control in his office.

Yep. Fuck being on the receiving end of that.

Back in the office, I explain my vision and ask Tess to show me a photo of Dorothea. She scrolls through her phone for a few moments and holds it up for me to see.

"That's definitely her, Tess, but as I said, she was clearly possessed when it happened. She isn't responsible for anything she did."

My friend nods, looking dejected. "I don't suppose you got any indication if she's still alive? There doesn't seem to be any trace of the supes who were taken and possessed."

"I'm sorry. It wasn't clear either way. I only saw what happened during the attack. I promise I'll tell you if I figure anything else out."

"Thanks, Ev. I appreciate it."

Alaric comes closer and squeezes Tess in a one-armed hug. "We'll find her. I told you we would. For now, though, has there been any word on Ragnor coming back?"

Tess waves towards the private rooms at the end of the Technical Division. "He's doing the sketch with Zeke as we speak. He seemed to be in a pretty feral mood after he returned from talking to Solomon, though. I'm not sure how much help he's going to be."

"Who's going to check out the location he came from?" my partner asks.

"That'd be us," Stella calls from across the room. "We've been tied to these desks since this God-awful case started. We'll take a couple of the crime scene techs with us as well, in case we can find anything helpful."

I try to stifle my yawn, but it only makes the next yawn louder. "Sorry, guys. Just a little tired."

The team all turn to me with confused and concerned looks.

"Okay," Alaric says, drawing everyone's attention before the team's concern for me worsens. "Ev and I are going to work on Clara's case for a bit since you all have this under control. Call if you need either of us."

The twins nod and return to their work and Tess comes closer, her brows drawn down. "Anything you need, Ev?"

I shake my head. "This is news to me. What are we going to do, Alaric?"

"Raphael has put together a collection of old books for us to look through. We'll take them back to your place and go through them there."

"And maybe grab a nap," Tess adds.

"Thanks, guys. Okay, let's do this. Tess, you'll call us with any updates or if you need us, yeah?"

"Of course. Off you go."

Home is quiet when we arrive since Raine is still at work. We pile the books on the coffee table, and I text her while I walk downstairs to check on Clara.

Me: Alaric and I are here looking through some books for answers about Clara.

Raine: Suuure that's all you're doing with Alaric.

Me: You're a terror ;) See you after work!

My twin looks completely peaceful in stasis—vastly different from how she is when she's conscious. I'm relieved to see the black hasn't spread much at all, even if holding the stasis is exhausting me more easily. I wasn't expecting my visions to make me feel more tired since they don't usually do that.

My aura and visions must be linked in some way.

What the hell will that mean for visions every time the aura darkens from using Dad's demon power?

I sigh deeply. *It won't matter if I can't save Clara anyway. I won't be here to find out.*

My inner demon is surprisingly quiet. I almost expected the demonic part of me to say I don't care what happens to Clara. To let her die.

"Ev, are you okay?" Alaric asks from the door.

I spin, my hand clutched to my chest. "Gee, you startled me. Sorry, I didn't hear you come down."

He frowns when he sees my face and walks closer. He reaches out with his right hand and wipes a tear from my left cheek. "You're crying?"

"Oh." I reach up and wipe my eyes and cheeks, feeling only a tiny bit of moisture. "I hadn't noticed. I was just thinking about Clara."

His expression becomes carefully neutral, and I have no idea what he's thinking now. The change makes me feel vulnerable and confused, but I hesitate to bring it up in case he asks difficult questions.

"Should we go and get started?" I offer.

Alaric, thankfully, catches my hint. "Lead the way," he says, then steps to the side.

I walk up the stairs in front of him, and feel as though his eyes are boring into me. I peek back about halfway up, and his eyes scream of hunger, but they aren't looking at my face. Heat rises into my cheeks and a delicious shiver vibrates through me.

What in the hells is this wolf doing to me? What kind of angel am I, with my sister sitting in the room downstairs, fighting for her life, and my body just wants my wolf?

Needs the wolf, more like.

I can't need him. We've not even spent that much time together. And almost all of the times have been fraught with danger.

My inner demon seems to have nothing to add, leaving me to ponder the times Alaric and I spent together in Paris and here in Sydney. A lot were dangerous, and he did spend time protecting me.

I'm half angel, half demon. I shouldn't need a protector.

And Clara?

I walk the rest of the way up in silence, cursing myself for following such a useless train of thought right now.

In the lounge room, I see that Alaric has spread the ten or so books across the coffee table. Although, from looking at them properly, tomes might be a more accurate description. They are all very old—some with fading covers and most handwritten on papyrus.

I avoid Alaric's gaze completely this time, collect a smaller tome called *Angelic Ailments*, and curl up on the couch to start reading. The heaviness of my partner's gaze rests on me for a solid minute, and it takes most of my energy to just continue flicking through the pages.

Finally, he picks up one himself and settles on the opposite lounge chair. His decision leaves me warring with relief and disappointment.

Just focus.

The door opening startles me awake. I blink my eyes and rub them, realizing I must have fallen asleep. Raine is standing over with us by the time I manage to sit up.

"Raine, you're home," I mumble, then look at Alaric. "Why didn't you wake me up? It's been hours."

"Aww, sweetie, you look like you needed the sleep. Of course he wasn't going to wake you."

"Yeah, what she said," Alaric adds, looking up over the top of *Angelic Prophecies: An Extensive History*. He closes the cover and stands, stretching his arms into the air.

My mouth drops open slightly when his shirt lifts up and leaves his abs bare. The V shape running down into his jeans makes me want to crawl over the tables to get to him.

Raine does a giant fake cough, pulling my attention from Alaric's abs. My eyes dart up and connect with his and he's watching me with a big grin. When I look over to my best friend, she's smiling and laughing quietly. I don't know what to do with myself.

"So... have you guys had dinner?" Raine asks, letting me off the hook.

"I could eat," Alaric rumbles.

Raine snorts. "Oh, I bet. What about actual food, though?"

I smack my palm over my mouth and try to muffle a laugh. Even Alaric manages to smile, and relief runs through me at my best friend and my love interest getting along.

"I'll go pick up some dinner," Alaric says, as if he knows he's outmatched here. "I'll be back soon."

Raine curls up on the other end of my lounge chair, and after Alaric shuts the door, I peg a pillow at her. "Girl, you are a bundle of trouble!"

She chortles back at me, her delicate features crinkling in amusement. "Oh, please, he started it being all 'I could eat,' and clearly talking about you."

Warmth spreads through me at the thought of Alaric wanting me in the same way I want him. I shake my head to free the thoughts and focus on my friend. "How was work? Is everything going okay there?"

Raine's energy expands immediately—her smile growing, her posture straightening. "Oh my goodness, it is the *best*, Ev. I'm so glad I got this job. The kids are fantastic. They all know so much, so we learn from each other. They make my heart happy!"

Her joy is like the color of a beautiful sunrise or watching a flower blossom. She draws the same emotion from within me, just as she always does, and I'm struck again by the happiness that Raine will be with me for a very long time.

"No one you've had to show who is boss?" I laugh, thinking back to Tess's advice.

Raine cringes good-naturedly. "No, not exactly." She seems to pause for a moment, caught in thought before she continues. "There are a couple of teens, though, now you mention it. They don't need to know who's in charge—it's definitely them, just ask them—but some who are on the brink of changing or emerging are a bit tough to manage."

Curiosity pulls me in, and I lean closer. "What do you mean?"

"Well, the shifters and witches mostly. The ones waiting to shift for the first time, and those yet to have their powers emerge. They're really... I'm not sure how to describe it. Kind of unstable?"

"Hmm... have you asked the other teachers?"

"Yeah. They just say it's normal. I can't help but be a little worried. I've been keeping a closer eye on two in particular, more so than the others. A witchling named Kiah, and a shifter called Rowan."

I reach forward and squeeze my friend's hand. "They're lucky to have you, Raine. Even if they don't realize it right now. Just remember that."

She nods, her expression now pensive. "They're both orphans. So they actually live at the school along with some other kids without parents and some whose parents have sent them to stay for the school year. They just... I don't know."

"Hey, you'll figure it out. And if you need help with those kids, I'm sure Alaric and Tess would be willing to give you some advice."

My friend smiles back. "You're right. Okay, enough of that. Let's work on these books."

Hours later, our stomachs full from Chinese takeout—or blood in Raine's case—we're most of the way through the collection with nothing useful to show for Clara. A loud knock on the door startles us all from our piles. Alaric is immediately on his feet, and I can sense his wolf close to the surface.

"Who is it?" he growls at us. "Did either of you invite someone over?"

I shake my head as another sharp set of raps sound. "Raine?"

Her brows pull down in the center and her forehead crinkles. "I mean, I can only think of Henry. I was chatting with him earlier, but I don't think he said he was coming."

The knocks grow more agitated, and then a muted man's voice sounds from outside.

Alaric stalks towards the door, so close to the change I can feel it in the air. He yanks it open, and Henry almost stumbles into him.

"What the heck took so long? I've been knocking for ages."

My partner simply stares at him while Raine and I jump up to say hello.

"Sorry, Henry. I didn't know you were coming! How are you?" I ask as relief floods me that the wards haven't failed since my human best friend is always welcome here.

Henry glances quickly at Raine, and a look of resolution covers his features. "We need to talk, Ev."

Alaric's metaphysical hackles stand on end, and I edge a little closer as I address Henry. "What's going on? Do you want to sit?"

"Yeah, okay. Fine."

The corners of my lips pull down, hurt and confusion echoing through my mind. "Raine, would you mind popping the books out of the way?"

She looks somewhat alarmed and miffed by the turn of events, but hurries to do what I've asked.

I lead Alaric back to the lounge chair. He sits next to me, while Raine and Henry take the opposite one. I mentally inspect the tightness in my chest, and the color of my friend's aura. It's a strong mix of reds and deep oranges.

"Damn it. Just show yourselves, stupid bloody powers!"
I shove my copper hair out of the view of my arm.
Inserting the razor into my skin, I drag it across.
It hurts and feels good all at once.
But it doesn't do what I need.
"Come on!" I scream. "I need my damn magic."
"I'm nothing without it."

"Hey! Everleigh! Are you even listening?" Henry says, voice raised.

"Henry, relax!" Raine says.

Alaric's growl rumbles into the space, the vibration reaching me through the lounge chair. "You better settle the fuck down, mortal. Or I'll remove you from the house."

I open my eyes to Henry's deeper red aura, the colors troubling me. "Sorry, Henry. I was just having a vision. I couldn't hear anything anyone was saying for a moment. I can see you're really upset. What's going on?"

"What's going on is that you're being incredibly reckless, Everleigh."

I sit back, my head pushing back further as my eyebrows shoot up into arches. Alaric's growl gets deeper, more intimidating.

Henry doesn't seem to hear it. "You're being reckless. This stasis is killing you, for God's sake. Trying to keep Clara alive when she doesn't even care about you.... What do you think is going to happen if you die, huh? What about Raine? You don't think she's scared about this?" He stands up and looks down at me. I glance over to Raine, who has her eyes locked onto her hands. "You need to fix this. Clara is selfish. Just let her go. Take care of yourself and Raine. You're the one responsible for her." By the time he stops talking, he's pointing at me, and breathing deeply.

CHAOS

My words feel trapped in my throat, unable to pass the bubble of hurt from Henry's words. He's so angry and worried. My mind is overlaying his face with all of the victims who died because of me, or around me. And of the families of those who were lost—the pain and betrayal.

I hadn't even thought of Raine, and not only am I thinking of the losses in Paris and in Sydney, but now of the potential future loss. I've only ever had my sister since my parents were both taken away. It's never mattered what happened to me before, as long as I could care for her.

I look around the room, and I realize the beings in here will be hurt if I'm gone—if I let myself die in an attempt to save my sister. Raine. Alaric. Henry. Even though he's furious, I know it would break him as well.

What in the never-loving hells am I meant to do here? What's wrong with me?

"I—"

Henry holds out a hand, defensive. "Save it, Everleigh. Words don't matter here. Actions do. Stop this nonsense and think about everyone—not just you and your sister. I might seem like a shitty friend right now, but you matter to us as well. We should count for something too." His voice is a yell by the end of his rant.

The betrayal and anger in his voice pierce my heart and my pain wells up and pours from me in tears. I don't try to speak again. I can't. My throat feels so full of emotion, I can barely breathe, let alone talk. I look to Alaric, needing his help this time. If I try to speak on my own, I'm almost certain I'm going to cry.

Alaric is on his feet as soon as he locks eyes with me, and he moves swiftly in front of me, teeth bared. A growl so low and feral comes from him, it's as though his gray wolf is in front of me, not his human form. He turns his head to Raine, who looks somehow paler and more frozen in place. "Remove him now, or I'll rip him to shreds," he grinds out.

I reach out a hand to try and calm Alaric, to stop him—this kind of violence isn't the answer and definitely not something my angelic side would ever consider to be help. The movement seems to shake Raine free of her stupor, and she moves in a blur to Henry, who looks both angry and terrified of Alaric.

"Come on, Henry. You need to go now," Raine says quietly. "You're not helping. Look at Ev. Really look at her. This isn't easy, and this definitely isn't the time or way to talk about your worries."

Henry gets a stubborn set to his shoulders and jaw that sets another growl off from Alaric, who takes a step forward. I reach out and grab his shirt in an effort to distract him since I still don't have the words.

Raine huffs, her shock wearing down and frustration and concern picking up. She picks Henry up and shoots over to the door, opens it, and takes him through, pulling the door shut behind them.

I stare through my tears at the blurry door my two best friends disappeared through, wishing I could do something to make this better. But I know deep within myself that losing my twin isn't an option—and the pain echoes through me, seeming to expand with each ragged breath.

I feel Alaric sit down beside me and pull me back into his lap. He tucks my hair behind my ears, then holds me closer, his chin resting on my shoulder. "It'll be okay, Ev. I promise. Raine is learning to understand the concept of our incredibly long lives. Henry is... human," he says with a civility I wasn't expecting of him. "He can't comprehend the consequence of letting your sister go, especially when your parents are gone."

For the next sliver of eternity, Alaric simply holds me. His arms around me feel like the only things holding my shattering heart together. His heartbeat against my back keeps my guilt from crushing me under its weight. His heat keeps me tethered to the here and now, instead of being stolen away to the harrowing thoughts of "what if".

All I can do is breathe.

One in.

One out.

By the time Raine returns, my tears have dried, and I feel empty.

She walks over to me, and I feel a low rumble in Alaric's chest. A warning. Completely unsubtle.

She glares at him for a moment but doesn't bother to engage with him. Instead, she meets my eyes, and I immediately see them well with pinkish tears. She comes over to where I'm sitting and kneels on the floor in front of me, taking my hand.

"I'm so sorry Henry said all of those things, Ev. He's just scared to lose you and clearly didn't know how to say it in a helpful way."

I nod, my chest aching from the weight of the pain. "Thanks, Raine. I mean, I get it. And I really don't want to hurt you. I'm sorry I haven't been thinking more about you in this situation. I'm-I'm not used to having anyone care about me except Clara."

"Hey." She squeezes my hand. "I don't want you to worry about me. Between this case you're managing and trying to find a way to save Clara, that's like... enough to sink a ship or something. Let's just focus on those. Finding a way to save your pain-in-the-arse sister is what we need to work on. And you guys need to work on solving that case so everyone is stressing less generally. I know that's amping up tensions too. Especially Henry's, okay?"

I suck in a deep breath, feeling as though it's the first I've really taken since Henry arrived. "You're right, Raine. We should focus on the things we can control for now, which is our behavior." I turn around in Alaric's arms and kiss him on the cheek before resting my forehead against his. "Thank you," I whisper, "for holding me together."

"Always," he rumbles back at me. "No matter what, I'll always protect you, Ev."

His words are a salve to the cracks in my heart, a soft layer that seems to reconnect the pieces tenuously left sitting after Henry's explosion.

"You should get some rest, all right. It's late and you look exhausted." When I open my mouth to interject, he shakes his head. "I need some sleep as well, okay?"

I feel my lips curl up at the corners after he says the only thing that would make me agree with him—that he needs sleep too.

"We can meet at work in the morning and see where we are up to with the case. It's hard to know what's going to happen to the timeline now that Ragnor escaped, and we'll need some extra energy to hit the streets for demon hunting."

My brows draw up at his last statement. "You're taking me demon hunting?"

He pauses for a split second, reconsidering, before nodding at me resolutely. "Yes, I think that's just what you need right now."

I drive into work with my car radio off on Monday morning, needing to leave my more-fragile-than-usual brain some time to settle. It's one of those days where too many sounds would be overwhelming, and I wish I could return to our family home deep in the Carpathian Mountains.

At least I'm not as tired this morning. Just exhausted.

When I pull into my parking space and get out, I see Alaric waiting for me by his motorbike. He's in his usual faded denim jeans and wearing a gray shirt, which brings out the same color in his eyes. Once I get out, he comes and joins me, his gaze never leaving my face.

"Ev, how are you?"

The concern in his tone touches my heart and forces me to recognize again the connections I'm making and the specialness of this one in particular.

"I'm all right, thank you." I look deeper into his eyes, finding the blues swirling through the grays. "Did you manage to get some sleep?"

He nods and we start heading inside. "It was a little hard getting to sleep, but once I was there, it was good."

As soon as we walk through the door, Tess is on us, a desperate look on her face. "Ugh, thank the Mother you're both here! Nicon has been down here three times since he identified the demon from Ragnor's sketch. I can only distract him with so much gossip before he starts to get antsy."

I pull my bottom lip down, exposing my lower teeth as my brows draw down. "That sounds unpleasant. Why didn't you call?"

Her gaze cuts sideways at Alaric, then rests back on me. "Let's just say I was under strict orders not to unless it was an emergency. If you guys hadn't shown up in the next ten minutes, I would have buckled and called. Not because of the case, but Nicon is fraying my nerves."

I smile at my friend, grateful for her patience. "What can we do?"

"The team has a few locations for you guys to go and check out that we've pegged as the most likely places to find him." She turns around and calls across the room, "Hey, Zeke, can you send Ev and Alaric the photo of the demon, please?"

My phone buzzes in my pocket a moment later, and I see Alaric pull his mobile out to have a look as well. The man is tall with non-descript short brown hair. The only thing really identifiable about him is the mean glint to his eyes. So half of the adult population, then.

"Yeesh. An average-looking guy with mean eyes. I hope the places to look aren't overly populated."

"Yeah, right," Alaric says, amusement coloring his tone. "I'm willing to bet at least one of those places is that filthy demon club in Kings Cross."

I swallow a groan. A club, with its blasting music is the last thing my brain needs right now.

Tess cringes. "Yeah, sorry, Ev. The first couple you can check today, but we aren't holding much hope. We think he might work at the club, so that's probably your best bet." She forces a smile. "If Alaric is right, and it's the club I'm thinking of, you should both dress to impress. Don't want to stick out and give anyone a reason to run."

It's one in the morning, and Alaric and I are standing in the line at Wicked Sensations, the demon club in Kings Cross. The trance music is so loud and unending, it makes me want to cover my ears. It isn't helping the tired and agitated vibe I have going after a day of searching for this damned demon with Nicon breathing down our necks. He's like a clingy partner. He wants updates on our locations, on what we're thinking, on what we're planning.

When Alaric pulls his phone out again, I lean against him to check the message. His lips curl up to one side as his eyes cut to me as I clearly enjoy acting the part of his girlfriend.

Nicon: If you don't have him soon, I'm going to get him myself.

Alaric: We'll be in touch soon.

I laugh and say, "You know that is going to make him pissed, right?"

His grin is half-feral, half-mischievous. "I've had enough of him for today. Serves him right."

I smile in tired amusement at his dangerous antics.

He'd better not show up here or Alaric might fight him just out of pure agitation.

That would be a delicious sight to see. My turn for the popcorn.

"Next," the bouncer yells.

I link my arm with Alaric's and move to the front. He checks our Accord issued driver's licenses and signals we can go through. The female host is dressed in tight black leather, accentuating all of her curves. She grins salaciously at Alaric, and I pull him towards me possessively.

She winks at me and takes the money Alaric hands her for entry. She stamps both of our wrists. "Enjoy the sensations!"

I laugh at her attempt to sound sexy while needing to yell over the deafening music in the club, and wander into the main room. The lighting inside is a deep red, making it hard to see everything. The occasional strobe shows men and women in outfits so scant, they make the host look overdressed. I look down at myself.

"I don't think I dressed right for this," I call in Alaric's ear.

He leans away and looks me over from feet to face, pausing to appreciate the split all the way to my lacy underwear, and the mounds of my breasts through my fishnet overshirt. "I think you look good enough to eat."

I think finding a dark corner to give him a taste is a great idea.

I bite my bottom lip, incredibly turned on by Alaric's insinuation and my inner demon's intrusive thought. Having him devour me right now sounds perfect.

I move into his personal space, pressing my body flush against him. With my stilettos, I'm tall enough to lean close to his ear. "Don't tempt me."

Bite him!

Too interested to deny the idea, I take his earlobe into my mouth and suck it hard once and bite down.

His cock immediately hardens against me and the rumble in his chest vibrates down to my now pulsing core. Alaric pulls me back by the hair and slams his mouth into mine, kissing me furiously. We're all tongues and teeth and heat, and I can't get enough.

When he steps back, his gaze is feral, and his eyes have the slight glow of his wolf. "You're the temptress here. We need to find this damned guy before I lose control completely."

I like the sound of that.

I'm sure I look just as unhinged and wanton as he does, but I'm not convinced I'd have stopped us.

"You've got more self-control than me," I call back.

His hungry eyes stay locked on mine, his lips swollen from kissing. Now we definitely fit in with the club's vibes.

If I can't have him, then I can at least tease him a little.

I walk past him, running my hand across his lower stomach, just above the waistband of his black jeans. His shiver and the gentle, seductive touch echoes through my own body, and it takes every piece of willpower I have to keep moving.

I feel Alaric at my back as I walk amongst the human and demon crowd, devouring each other with lust, their bodies pressed together, impossible to tell mortal from supernatural. We look as we walk, but after a solid thirty minutes, I turn back to my partner and shake my head, libido dead and replaced by more frustration. I raise my brows askance, but he echoes my sentiment—no sign of the demon we need.

A scream makes me turn immediately towards the back door of the club. A woman—or demon—rushes back through, panic painting her face, which is lit up every few seconds by the strobe lights. Most don't seem to notice, but a few do, and they look outside, only to run back in moments later, looking equally as terrified.

"I think that's for us," I yell, moving as quickly as I can through the throng of tightly packed clubbers. Alaric follows me closely, his familiar heat a source of comfort in the chaos as more people and demons join into the panic.

The area around the back door is now deserted and I rush outside with Alaric and immediately come to a halt. The alley is painted in the blackish-red ichor of demons. Right across from the door, on the opposite side of the space, a male is standing over the demon we're searching for. He's covered in the same blood, his eyes lit up—half madness, half enjoyment—as he stares at us.

Immediately, I pull my deadly sharp hair pins and ready myself to attack. Alaric crouches down and pulls a knife from an ankle sheath.

"Step away from that demon," I call.

The psychotically unhinged laugh sounds familiar enough that I pause, and my partner does so as well, trusting my instincts.

In that hesitation, the demon blasts the one we came for with a ball of fire straight to the chest. He immediately turns to ash as he's pulled back to the hellish realms.

MESSY

My heart stops for a moment. Another clue is gone.

What is with this fucking case?

The demon stands up and wipes some ichor from his face, smearing it rather than removing it because of how much he is coated with. "Everleigh. Alaric. Fancy meeting you here."

Alaric growls low and deep while my jaw simply drops open.

"Blake, what the fuck do you think you're doing?" Alaric grinds out. "We needed that demon. Why didn't you stop?"

Blake mocks Alaric, exaggerating his words in an annoying whiney tone. He does it for long enough to make me wonder if Alaric might just bite his head off. "Why did I need to find out from a contact that Clara was poisoned by a fucking demon?" His tone is pure venom, and this time directed right at me. "Why didn't you keep me in the loop like you said you would? And why the fuck are you following down that stupid supernatural case instead of saving Clara?"

I cringe away from the hatred and judgment in his voice. "I am working on saving my sister. And I didn't tell you because I didn't have anything specific." I wave my hands at

the gore-soaked alley. "Look what you've done with half the information. How many demons did you torture and banish tonight?"

He sneers back at me. "Not enough!" he yells. "Because I still haven't killed the one responsible."

I shake my head. I don't even know what to say.

Fucking chaotic demons.

It might be half my heritage, but the carnage is always beyond excess, and my angelic self doesn't comprehend it. I look at my partner and lift my hands, palms up.

Alaric turns his gaze back to Blake. "The demon you just killed. Did he say anything useful about our case? Do you know who he works with?"

Blake looks disgusted, assumedly because we are not focused on Clara again like him. "He didn't say anything useful. Just begged for his useless existence on Earth. And he doesn't work with anyone who isn't already dead. And before you ask, they didn't have anything useful to say either."

He better not have banished anyone who could give us a fucking clue about the connection between Clara and the case.

"You'll need to come with us and present to Nicon, Blake. Unsanctioned killings on a human street is an offence," Alaric says, clearly done with this situation.

Blake doesn't bother to answer with words; instead, he brings flames to each of his hands. I dive to the ground a split second before he starts launching them at us, jamming my pins back into my hair. Alaric is forced to take cover as well. Blake takes a step closer to us, and I drag a fuming Alaric back into the club, knowing Blake likely won't bother pursuing us—he's too motivated to hunt for revenge. A fight with us only risks getting himself caught and dragged in.

I'm right. The blasts stop after a few more hits against the reinforced door. I open it slowly, peeking through the gap. I see Blake close to the exit of the alley, almost at the road. I rush after him, trying to stay quiet. Just when I think I might have a chance at catching him, another male speeds to a halt in a black mustang, flinging the door wide open. He flashes his demon face at me—a malformed red and black face with large tusks—for a few seconds before reverting to a bald human-looking man with tattoos up his neck. My hesitation is enough for Alaric to catch me and for Blake to escape.

The car speeds off, leaving me and my partner alone in the alley smeared in ichor.

"Fucking demons," Alaric grinds out.

The office is a flurry of action when I arrive, finally free of the demon ichor after several showers and a small nap. Alaric is with the twins looking over our geographic profile for whoever is behind the case. Oldin is pointing at a few key places, and I move closer to see.

Tess cuts me off. "Morning, Ev. How are you?"

I smile at my friend, who looks as though she's been living on coffee and adrenaline instead of sleep. "I'm all right. Are you? You look pretty wrecked."

"Oh, yeah, I'm okay. I haven't been home, so I've been taking rejuvenation potions. They're starting to not work, as you can tell. I'll have to crash soon."

"How come you guys didn't head home once we called in the bust with the demon?"

"Because we got another break in the case, if you can believe it. Sort of."

I take in her irritated look. "What do you mean?"

"Someone attempted to take an angel but evidently botched it. They escaped and reported back to Raphael."

"Well, that sounds good. What's the problem?"

Tess rolls her eyes and pinches the skin together in the middle of her forehead. "The issue is that even though Raphael sent her down here to help, she won't talk to Zeke to give us a description. She's really old and won't even answer me. Nicon is still in a foul mood, so I don't really want to call him yet. I know you're not friendly with any of them, but do you think you could give it a go?"

My heart sinks for my friend. She's been through so much with this case, and trying to deal with a stubborn angel on no sleep has got to be rough. "Of course, Tess. No guarantees of course, since, you know"—I point to myself—"much disliked hybrid and all, but I'll try."

She draws me in and gives me a quick hug. "You're a godsend, thank you!"

I laugh, shock coursing through me. "I don't think I've ever been considered that before."

She shrugs, clearly not changing her mind. "The very lovely angel is in your office, waiting."

I snort softly. "Sure I was going to see her, were you?"

Tess winks at me, then walks off towards Alaric and the twins.

As I make my way down the hall to my office, I take a deep breath, trying to ground myself and pull on some psychological armor to deal with the potential hatred waiting inside.

The angel sits in the chair at the end of my meeting table in a floor-length dress with one ankle tucked behind the other. She's playing with my screens, changing the backgrounds to different cities around the world.

"Places you've lived?" I ask her.

She turns hazel eyes to me, looking at me from head to toe and back up. She looks unimpressed.

"So, you're one of the hybrid twins."

It doesn't sound like a question, but I nod anyway, hopeful she might just move on.

No dice.

"What's it like to grow up hated by all supernaturals?"

Bitch.

"About as pleasant as it sounds," I deadpan.

"Mmm, I see."

Bored of her attitude, I press on. "Are you ready to do the sketch of the demon now?"

She considers my request for a moment before shaking her head.

I try my best to be patient, but considering how tired I am now, I don't manage it as well as usual. "And why is that?"

"Because I find myself curious about you. I knew Estelle, your mother."

My brain shorts out for a moment, and I have no idea what to say. It's been a long time since I found someone who knew my parents. The angel says nothing, just watches me, her head tilted to the left slightly, as though she's looking at an experiment. But unless she plans to trap me in a test tube, I'm not interested in playing this game with her.

A sliver of anger bubbles at the thought, and I feel the tell-tale heat of my red eyes flashing.

The right side of the angel's lips pull up into a smirk. "Ahh, and there is Arinthall. You look so much like your mother, I wondered how your father might come through."

My brows pull down. "I'm not a puzzle or a game you know."

"Indeed. Although after so many millennia, one does not come across originals very often. I find myself curious about you and your twin. Where is she?"

I cringe, the reminder of my sister on top of my parents making me feel raw. "She's indisposed at present, and unless you know anything about poisoning by liquid obsidian, I'm afraid there isn't much to talk about."

"Nothing positive, I'm afraid."

I draw in a deep breath, hold it for a few seconds and then release it, determined to put my limited energy into something helpful. "Very well. Are you ready to do the sketch now so we can help the humans and hopefully prevent more abductions of supernaturals?"

She shrugs. "Very well. Bring in the clumsy baby vampire."

I shake my head as I turn around and pick up my work phone and dial Zeke's extension. "She's ready when you are for the sketch, Zeke."

"Coming!"

By the time I place the phone down, Zeke appears at the door with his tablet. He pouts a little when he sees the angel and slows to a human speed to walk inside my office, very careful not to bump into anything. He reaches for his bracelet, only to drop his hand away, looking ashamed.

Clearly the angel bitch said something to him. Should kill her.

Killing someone for a nasty comment is not a reasonable decision.

My inner demon continues to try and get in my head, but I do my best to shake her out of it, pulling strange looks from both of my companions. "Okay, are we ready then?"

"Oh, yes, of course," Zeke says quickly, an apology in his tone. He doesn't look at the angel, but addresses her as he opens his tablet instead, his speech rushed. "If you just describe the features, I'll draw the demon. Then you can tell me what adjustments need to be made."

"Very well," she says with a bored tone.

The angel spends the next several minutes describing the demon using details so intense, it's as though she had stared at him for an excessively long time.

When Zeke shows her the sketch, there is only one minor adjustment needed to the thickness of the lips.

She stands. "My work here is done. I'll be leaving now." She looks at me, doubt clouding her perfect features. "Well met, daughter of Estelle. May God guide you."

"And you," I murmur in reply, although given she is a full-blooded angel, the sentiment is largely wasted.

When we walk back into the office, Tess calls out, "The boss man is on his way down to look at the sketch. He refuses to waste any more time. The other Councilors are riding his arse."

"It's not surprising really, considering the number of deaths and the exposure in the human media."

"Speaking of," Oldin calls out, his tone dry, "the religious sects have started joining into that. I was down in my local community last night and the priest was handing out flyers on how to protect yourself from the monsters, and how not to be tempted by them." He lifts a wad of said flyers, warnings printed across them in bright, bold lettering. At least half the information is wrong, from what I can tell.

Alaric frowns at him. "That is problematic. Religious zealots are harder to dissuade than the media and general public once they sink their teeth into something."

"At the very best," Stella says, "we'll be looking at another rise in supernatural novels and art, as well as a rise in conspiracy theories and fear mongering."

"Well, the art I don't mind," Zeke chirps.

I smile at the young vampire, his interest and talent in art are palpable, and I'm sure being able to share his world at times would be freeing.

"I'm all for the books," Tess adds, "especially those smutty ones."

I laugh. "Well, I won't say no to those either. It's always interesting to see how humans perceive us all, what traits they think we have."

Whether someone like me could ever feature in one.

Zeke smiles sadly. "Unfortunately, I think this round we'll be seeing some of the macabre versions."

Stella shrugs. "I'm all for the doom and gloom. Blood and a side of sex sounds great to me."

"Well," Nicon says as he walks into the office, thankfully looking amused, "I'm glad there is some positivity that might come out of this mess."

"I think finding a moment of lightness amongst this shitshow was just what the doctor ordered," I say, enjoying the brief reprieve.

Nicon is in a better mood today.

Tess nods. "Precisely. Zeke, do you have that sketch for the boss man?"

He darts forward, holding the image up on his tablet for Nicon to see. When Nicon reaches for the tablet, Zeke looks like he might run away with it, but ultimately, he lets it go.

"Don't fear, young lad. I won't smash your tablet today."

Zeke melts in relief, telling me this might have happened before. Tess gives his arm a reassuring squeeze and a sympathetic smile.

Nicon sighs then looks at me and Alaric. "This is one of the demons Blake destroyed in his revenge plot for Clara."

"Of course he did," Alaric grumbles. "He's turning into a gigantic pain in the arse. I assume you haven't located him yet, Nicon?"

"No, he's a surprisingly elusive fucker. He hasn't been Earthside for that long. I can't say I actually know that much about him. He's fairly young and was only created after I left the hellish realms."

"Do you need us to take over the search?" Alaric asks.

Nicon shakes his head. "No. I'll deal with him. The team's focus needs to remain on this case."

Oldin waves to get Nicon's attention. "Have the Council decided if we'll be starting countermeasures for the exposure, or if we'll be starting to move towards revealing ourselves?"

I spin around to look at the vampire twin, shocked. "I didn't even know we were considering the latter."

"Yes, we've had no choice but to consider it," Nicon says, "but ultimately, the majority has still voted that this is not the right time, and certainly not the right circumstances, when the demons responsible have shown the worst possible side of our supernatural brethren."

"So countermeasures then?" Oldin asks.

"Yes, it will be starting sometime today. Key social influencers, who are supernaturals, will start to push doubt back on the supposed hoax situations, and ruin the credibility of the videos that were released. It should work for the vast majority of the humans, who are ultimately followers. Those remaining will be too few to get any traction. It's not the first time such a situation has occurred. Simply the most difficult since the rise of technology."

The team collectively nods, understanding the plan.

Zeke flitters around anxiously until Nicon passes back his tablet, at which point the young vampire visibly relaxes. "I'm wondering, since Blake appears to have taken out the entire set of demons connected to those we managed to identify, could this be over?"

Everyone pauses for a moment, considering the possibility, a small air of hope entering the space. Only for it to be dashed in less than a minute.

"I think not," Stella says, pointing to a headline by a major news company on the television.

"Three people have been found dumped in a public park in Sydney's CBD, all of which appear to be covered in supposed vampire bites. More details tonight at 6:00 p.m."

Nicon rubs his temples, his eyes beginning to pulse, drawing the heat to my own. When he sees the reaction he is causing, he simply turns and walks out of the room, leaving us to do our jobs and clean up the mess.

HISTORY

I WALK INTO THE apartment, tired after a long day of damage control, watching my rose tattoo bloom as I get closer to Raine.

"Honey, I'm home," I call, trying to draw on our usual friendly banter as I rush downstairs to check on Clara. I breathe a sigh of relief when I see nothing has really changed.

"Why hello, beautiful," Raine says, appearing beside me with a smile and almost her usual cheerful tone. "How was work?"

I kiss my twin on the forehead and straighten her sheet.

"Ugh, it was long. Did you see the news about three supposed vampire attacks? We've been trying to manage the spread, and I tried to get visions from the bodies, but no dice."

"No, I haven't seen it yet. It seems like that really specific timeline has gone out the window," Raine says, frowning.

"Yeah. Completely gone. It's a huge escalation and change of behavior."

"Do you think it could be someone different responsible for these deaths? Three is so far different."

My angelic intuition gives a metaphysical tingle at Raine's suggestion, and I sigh. "Seems like you might be right. Maybe the original demon was banished by Blake in his ragey spree." I pick up my mobile phone and send a group message to the team with the latest development. "It seems like supes are starting to use this as an excuse to break the Accords. I hope Nicon is going to call in some reinforcements. We're seriously going to be outmatched if more cases pop up as a result of the main one still ongoing."

"This is such a nightmare, Ev. I'm sorry there isn't anything I can do to help. I'm feeling so useless lately."

I reach out and hug my friend. "You're doing everything you can, Raine. I couldn't ask for anything more. Just having you in my life and supporting me is more than I've ever really had in this world."

Her eyes fill with pinkish tears, and she pulls me closer again for another squeeze, causing our rose tattoos to blossom completely. They close a touch as she steps back from me.

I look at the time and realize it's almost 6:00 p.m. "Oh, the report is about to come on. Let's go upstairs and take a look at what they've come up with." Once we reach the lounge room, I grab the remote and switch it on to the news channel advertising the body dumps earlier in the day. We take a seat on the lounge side-by-side.

A different reporter is standing in the middle of the park where they found the bodies and I'm immediately frustrated again that the demons keep alerting different news teams about each new victim.

Why is catching a break in this case so damn hard.

A section that is the crime scene has been taped off behind the reporter. Beyond them a group of teens are hanging out on some tables. I lean forward, seeing familiar copper hair.

Raine shifts to get a closer look as well. "Is that—"

"Damn it. Just show yourselves stupid bloody powers!"

I shove my copper hair out of the view of my arm.

Inserting the razor into my skin, I drag it across.

It hurts and feels good all at once.

But it doesn't do what I need.

"Come on!" I scream. "I need my damn magic."

"I'm nothing without it."

"Ev, are you okay?" Raine asks when the vision fades and I start coming back to myself.

I shake my head to clear it. "Yeah, sorry. I got another vision of that girl. I think I just saw her on the news report in the background. The one with the copper hair."

Raine looks confused. "That was Kiah, from the school where I teach. The one I was talking to you about."

My eyes widen, wondering if this might be the first real link to how we can help Clara. "Do you think I could come and meet her? She's the one I've been getting visions about. Maybe she might be able to help with Clara?"

Raine looks uncomfortable. "Uh, I don't think I can just let you come into the school. I'll need to check with Octavia first and get permission and stuff. Just for safety and everything, you know?"

My heart drops a little. "I understand, of course. Do you know much about her? You said she was an orphan, right?"

"Yeah, I mean I can't say much, because of confidentiality, but also because we really don't know a lot about her. She was dropped at the school as a baby and has been there ever since. I don't even know who brought her. Maybe Octavia will let you look at the files if you speak with her."

"Okay, that sounds like a plan. I'm sorry, Raine. This is just the first hint of real hope for saving Clara I've had. I don't know how Kiah is meant to help, but the visions and my intuition are telling me she will. Actually." I pause, guilt filling me. "Sorry, I should have led with this. I feel horrible. In my vision, Kiah was cutting herself with a razor, trying to get her powers to emerge."

A look of understanding crosses Raine's face. "Ahh, well that explains her wearing jumpers on the hot days we've been having. I tried to ask her about the jumper, but she just shut down. I think it's probably safe to assume that vision has already happened. I'll speak to her again about it, though." She sighs. "I know she's desperate for her magic to come and all witches get it differently. Unfortunately, self-harming happens more than it should at the school I work at. She's probably been doing plenty of risky things trying to make it happen sooner."

"That sounds pretty intense. I wonder what Tess needed to do to get hers." I'm drawn back to Delilah and the initiate who took her baby and killed it to have her powers emerge.

Surely that kind of behavior is reserved for blood witches. Surely most wouldn't do anything that drastic.

"Octavia will be at the school in the morning, Ev. How about you come in with me and we'll see about you talking to Kiah?"

I lean in and give my best friend a hug. "Thanks, Raine. I really appreciate it."

I walk into the old stone building with Raine, looking around curiously at the offices. "Do you have an office?" I ask.

"No, those are for the administrative and executive staff. The rest of the teachers just share a staffroom, and then we have our own classrooms. I usually just work in mine and then come and join the other staff for break times." We walk a little further and then Raine stops and knocks on a door.

"Come in," Octavia calls from inside.

We go inside together, and Octavia looks at us with her brows raised. "Raine, Everleigh, what a surprise. How can I help you both?"

"Hello, Octavia. I'm sorry to show up unannounced. I need to make a request involving one of your students. A little roundabout, but are you aware of what ails my sister?"

She nods, her expression grave. "Yes, I heard she has been poisoned by liquified obsidian."

"Yes, that's right. I've been having visions of one of your students, Kiah. I learned her identity last night. And my angelic intuition tells me she may be able to help my sister in some way, although it's not yet clear how."

The High Witch raises and lowers her head slowly, processing what I have said. "And I take it you are seeking permission to speak with her?"

"Yes, that's my hope. Perhaps to explain and ask if she might be willing to help, if she is able to."

Octavia sighs deeply. "That is a predicament, Everleigh. I am reluctant to say either yes or no, given the stakes for you while also considering Kiah's protection."

She's quiet for a moment, and I say nothing, waiting.

A smile lights her face as she comes up with a solution she is happy with. "Okay, well knowing Kiah, I think a nice compromise to this idea would be that you join Raine's supernatural history class this morning, which Kiah attends. You share a bit about yourself and your history, and then you can ask Kiah if she'll talk with you. How does that sound?"

Like torture?

But also like the best chance I have.

"Okay," I agree. "Thank you, Octavia."

"Yay!" Raine says. "What a brilliant opportunity for the students!"

Octavia grins at Raine and nods to me, seeming satisfied with her solution. "Very well. In that case, I will leave you both to go and prepare. Should you need anything, feel free to reach out."

I can't help but feel a sense of lightness as we walk into my best friend's classroom. She has several single lounges and beanbags set out across the room and the walls are decorated with posters of modern-day bands and sports teams, a mix of humans and supes.

"This is great, Raine. I bet your students love it in here."

She looks really proud. "Yeah, sometimes they pretend they don't love it, but I know they do. None of the other teachers have setups like this."

"It's amazing." I move further into the room to look closer at everything. "Where would you like me to sit?"

She laughs. "Maybe just wait until they sit down first before you do. That way no one will start off being extra grumpy. The whole teen hormone thing is next level at this school, or rather with the supes in general."

"Good plan."

I move over to Raine's desk and lean against it, waiting. It's not long before fifteen teens come into the classroom, including Kiah. I try to stay calm but even seeing her has my hope doubling in size. The first tangible sense of hope since Nicon's surety there was nothing that could be done.

"Good morning, class. How are we today?"

"Who's the newbie?" one of the boys calls out, jutting his chin in my direction.

"Rowan, I assume you're well then." She drops her chin and raises her brows at him, a subtle reminder to be polite. "This is Everleigh Cole. She's here today so you can ask her some questions about the history of angels and demons."

A girl leans forward in her chair. "Usually our visitors only answer questions about one of the races. Why is this lady doing both?"

Raine gestures to me. "Everleigh, would you like to answer?"

You've got this, girl. It's a class of teenagers.

I force myself to relax and smile. "Because I'm half angel and half demon."

The students start whispering among themselves, and then openly staring at me.

Eventually one of the boys says, "But that isn't allowed."

I nod at him. "You're right—it's not. But here I am."

Kiah is sitting at the back of the room, her face full of distrust. "Which of your parents is an angel and which one is a demon? How did they get away with it?"

Okay, time to prove myself.

"My mother was Estelle, an angel. My father was Arinthall, a demon. I wouldn't say they got away with it, per se. When they refused to separate, they were cast out of both heaven and hell respectively and trapped on Earth."

Kiah bobs her head, looking more curious than disbelieving now.

"That's pretty sweet," a girl with dark blonde hair says. "Choosing exile so they could stay together, even if everyone else like hated them for it."

Rowan gets a mean glint in his eyes that makes my stomach knot up a little. "Well, when they broke the Accords to have a kid, I'm willing to bet that sent them on their path towards death."

I fight back the flash of red I can feel building up in my eyes, reminding myself he's a teenager.

"Rowan," Raine says sharply. "If you can't be respectful, you'll miss out on these opportunities and make up for the classes with additional essays."

I just breathe in and out, letting the surge of emotion pass. My parents have been gone for a long time, but I still miss them dearly, and with Clara in danger, hearing this makes me feel even more raw.

Thankfully, the boy just crosses his arms and sits back in his seat.

A fae girl, who has been sitting quietly at the back of the room, decides to send the room into further chaos. "How long after your parents had you and your twin were they killed?"

Raine flinches next to me, clearly not aware any of her students might know who I am. I'm less surprised, though, certain Clara and I have been a warning tale for many supernatural children since we were born, and our parents perished.

The students are all a flurry of excited whispers, sideways looks, and curiosity.

Once they settle down, I answer, "My mother was killed by a demon when we were about thirty years old, and our father lost his life in a battle to avenge our mother when we were seventy years old."

"And how old are you now?" a boy asks.

"About one hundred and thirty years old."

The students mutter back and forth amongst themselves for a time. I leave them be, trying to keep myself focused on staying in the present rather than becoming fused with those losses and the potential for Clara to meet the same end.

We spend the rest of the hour with the students asking more general questions about angels and demons, which are much easier to answer and far less stressful.

"Okay, guys," Raine calls, "that's enough for today. We'll pick up again next time." She looks over to the young copper-haired girl. "Kiah, could you stay back for just a few minutes please?"

She shrugs and stays in her seat, her face a mixture of curiosity and mistrust. She adjusts the sleeves on her sweater almost automatically.

All the other students file out, waving to both myself and Raine as they go, some offering a quiet thank-you as well. The whole session went rather well, and I'm hopeful the upcoming generation might see Clara and me as just individuals instead of a broken rule.

Maybe there will be more supes like Raine, Alaric, Tess, and the team in the future. Ones who are less judgey.

The rest are killable.

I almost hear the shrug through those words, and I shake my head, trying to get out of such a thought before talking to the girl.

"So," Kiah says, "what is it you guys want with me?"

"Kiah, as I mentioned in the class, sometimes I get angelic visions and intuitive feelings about things. Recently, I've been seeing visions of you."

Her face shuts down completely, and I hurry to try and explain.

"This is actually about my sister, Clara. She's been poisoned by something we have no cure for, and I keep getting the sense that you can somehow help her."

Kiah folds her arms across her chest defensively. "And how am I supposed to do that? I don't have powers or anything yet."

I nod. "I know, it's okay. And honestly I'm not really sure how you can help yet. I just wanted to see if you might be willing—"

"I'm sorry, but I don't want anything to do with this. I'm no one, certainly not anyone's savior." She stands and grabs her bag, and I reach out, touching her arm lightly to ask her to stay and hear me out. Two things happen simultaneously; first, I feel her slip from my grasp, second, I'm dragged into another vision.

MISSING

"Who are you? What do you want from me?"

I can't see anything.

I try to smell what's around me.

I inhale a large amount of dust and cough.

"Hello? Who's there?"

Mother, help me. I am not dying like this.

I've worked too damn hard.

A sharp pain flares in my stomach.

"Shit!"

It builds until I can't breathe.

My whole body is on fire.

"Ahhhhhhhhhhh!"

Raine has hold of my arms and is shaking me enough to make my brain rattle. I realize I'm screaming as though I've been lit on fire, and I force myself to stop, dragging in deep breaths. When I can see again properly, I look at Raine and her eyes are orbs of pure panic.

"Sorry," I puff, completely out of breath.

"What's going on?" she asks, voice tightly controlled with strain.

"Kiah. She's in some kind of danger. I don't know when or what's happening, just that it's like she's on fire. Where did she go?"

Raine pales beyond her usual vampiric whiteness. "She ran out of here right when you got sucked into that vision. We need to go and tell Octavia. Come on."

We rush across the school yard, the students looking at us in alarm. Raine tries to reassure them we are fine, but I don't think her stressed tone or rushed words help much.

We burst into Octavia's office, but it isn't her sitting behind the desk.

Raine takes over. "Jean, do you know where Octavia is? We need her."

The witch looks alarmed by Raine's panic. "I'm sorry, she's left for the day. She had something urgent she needed to attend to."

I'm starting to feel rather desperate myself since I have no idea if this vision is happening now or not. "Do you have a PA system or something? Or does Kiah have a mobile phone? Can we call her?"

"Is Kiah in some kind of danger?" Jean asks quickly, her wide eyes indicating she is being affected by our panic.

"Yes, we think so. Can we try to find out if she's still on campus please?"

"Now?" Raine adds.

Jean goes to a small cupboard-like compartment at the rear of the room and opens the door. She leans down to a small microphone, takes a steadying breath and says, "Kiah H, please attend the front office immediately."

Raine and I peer out the window, looking for Kiah's telltale copper hair. Jean tries to call Kiah's mobile phone, and then Octavia's.

"They've both gone to voicemail. I'll have all the on-duty faculty check their areas for her. They'll message back as soon as they've had a look."

I turn to Raine. "Could you go and ask any of her friends if they might know where she went?"

She nods and disappears from the office.

After around ten minutes, Jean looks up at me, her round eyes pleading. "None of the teachers have been able to locate her. Is there anything else you can do?"

"Thanks, Jean. I'll go and call my team to see if there is anything we can do. Please let Raine know if either Kiah or Octavia turn up."

"Of course," she says, voice tight.

I walk outside the office and pull the door closed behind me, my intuition telling me she's already gone, that we're too late to stop whatever this is from happening. I feel sick. For Kiah. For Clara. For all my friends when this goes badly.

I pull my mobile from my pocket and dial Alaric's number.

"Ev," he answers, "how's it going at the school?"

"I've had a vision, Alaric. Are you with the team? I need help."

"What's wrong?" he growls, immediately in protective mode. "Where are you?"

"I'm fine," I say. "It's not me. One of the students, Kiah, she's in trouble. She's been taken."

His growling cuts off abruptly when he realizes I'm unharmed. "Okay. Yes, I'm with the team. What do you need?"

"Is there a way we can try and track her last known location or something? And does Tess happen to know another way to get in touch with Octavia? We can't find her anywhere."

"Text me her mobile number, and we can do a trace. I'll ask Tess and call you back."

I rush back inside to Jean, get Kiah's number, and send it to Alaric right as Raine blurs into the room.

"None of the kids who usually hang with Kiah have seen her," Raine says quietly. "Have you heard anything?"

"No. She hasn't shown up or returned any calls. I've got the enforcement team looking for her and trying to find another way to get in touch with Octavia."

My phone starts ringing. "Alaric, anything?"

"There's nothing on the girl, Ev. The phone went dead just outside of the school. Tess said she can attempt to scry for Octavia, but she isn't holding her breath. The High Witch likely has methods in place to stop even the most powerful witch finding her. She could try and find Kiah if you have something that belongs to her. But if she's being blocked by someone, it will be the same problem." He pauses for a moment. "You could ask Delilah? If anyone has enough oomph to their magic, it's her."

"Yes! Perfect. Thank you! I'll call her."

Within half an hour, Delilah is standing at the front of the school with a basket of materials.

"Delilah, hi. Thanks so much for coming. We're really desperate to find Kiah. She's in some kind of danger, and we can't get hold of Octavia either."

"Of course," she murmurs. "Caring for Witchlings is everyone's job in our community. Do we have anything that belongs to Kiah? She'll be much easier to find than Octavia will."

I look at Raine, who hands over two items—a hairbrush and a locket.

Delilah runs a hand over each item, but takes the hairbrush, a curious look on her face. "I'd have expected the locket to have more energy. Interesting. Okay, we need a space."

Raine leads us to her classroom, and we both rush around to pull down the blinds to give Delilah some privacy.

She lays a map of the local area down, and places a map of New South Wales to the side. She pulls a crystal on a leather core from her basket and four candles. As she lights each candle, she places them in the positions of north, south, east, and west on the map, holding it in place. Delilah chants some words of power, which make the candles flare white. She picks up the brush and crystal, wrapping the cord around the handle.

When the witch holds the brush and hanging crystal above the map, she begins a renewed, more intense chant. After a few moments, the crystal begins to spin, the circles getting bigger each time they make a loop. Once the circles reach their maximum circumference, they start to shrink. Delilah simply holds the brush steady and continues to chant with her eyes closed. The crystal spins in smaller, faster loops, then drops.

Delilah opens her eyes, and we all look down at the map where the crystal is standing on its point. "It's a theater in Surry Hills. It should take about fifteen to twenty minutes by car." My heart races, and I know there's every chance we're going to be too late. "Come on, Raine. We need to hurry. Delilah, are you okay to get back home?"

"Actually," the witch says, her face serious, "I think I need to come with you. Something tells me it's important."

I nod, no time to argue. "Okay, let's take my car."

We rush out, and I let Raine drive, in case another vision takes over. Delilah keeps the crystal and map in the back seat in case anything changes. I send Alaric a quick update text.

As we get closer, I see dark gray smoke in the air. My stomach is in knots.

We can't be too late, please, God, no.

I hear a creak from next to me and I turn to see Raine squeezing the never-loving hells out of my steering wheel. "Raine! Hey!"

She immediately releases the wheel, which has a crack along where her hand was sitting. "Sorry, Ev."

"It's okay—don't stress. I just didn't want to end up in an accident and not get there. The car is fixable, all right."

"Look at all the smoke," she whispers, gesturing ahead of us.

"It might not be her. It could all be fine."

"Mmm," she murmurs quietly, as she tries to get us there as quickly as possible through the traffic.

Realizing Delilah has been very quiet, I turn to look at her. She looks completely confused but simply shakes her head at me when she notices me looking.

When we arrive on the correct street, Raine shrieks in alarm. Four bodies lay on the ground out the front of the incinerated theater. She jams the brakes on just before we reach the building, and I'm completely confused why there aren't emergency service vehicles everywhere, and people out looking.

We all jump out of the car and move towards whoever is on the ground. "Why isn't anyone here?" I ask the others.

Delilah grabs us both by the arms, pulling us to a halt. "Stop," she adds.

We both look at her, confused.

"There is a giant ward around the building and the street around it. If we charge right into it, it will pull it down. It has Octavia's magical signature, but it's been thrown up with a lot of haste."

"But, Kiah," Raine says, clearly considering trying to break free.

"I think the girl is okay, Raine." Delilah points behind us.

We turn, and see the four supes begin to move, amongst them Kiah and Octavia.

Octavia sits up, her usually poised appearance ruined. She is covered in dark ashy smudges, with holes burnt into her cloak. When she sees us, she waves towards us, mouthing something I can't understand.

Delilah seems to understand, though, because she steps past us both and says, "Follow directly behind me."

Once we're inside the wards, Octavia waves her hand in a downward motion to close the wards and then leans back where she's sitting.

The group of four all appear to be witches. I can't see Octavia's aura, much like I can't see Tess's, but the others are the typically muted colors of shock—an interweaving show of varying shades of orange.

"What happened?" I ask as we reach them. Raine moves to help a confused-looking Kiah stand up. "Is everyone okay?"

Kiah turns to Octavia, her aura morphing to a solid red.

"Grab her, Raine," I call out quickly, sensing she's about to attack the High Witch. My friend pulls Kiah back and holds onto her, but squeaks in pain as her skin starts to sizzle, resulting in Raine quickly letting go.

"What in the *hells* did you all do that for!" Kiah yells.

To her credit, Octavia manages to look regretful. "Well, if a witchling has not managed to emerge on their own by their sixteenth birthday, the coven tries to help them in a controlled way."

"A controlled way!" Kiah screams. "You kidnapped me and kept me blindfolded. I was terrified!"

One of the other witches coughs. "Well, it worked, didn't it. And honestly, I think we copped the worst end of the deal."

"Margot," Octavia scolds the woman.

My brain completely flat lines for a moment, complete and utter shock taking over as I realize what happened. My eyes feel like they are about to pop out of my head as I look at Octavia. "Are you *kidding* me? We've been running around completely panicked thinking Kiah was in peril. The entire enforcement team has stopped their case to track her down. We thought she was one of the missing victims."

Octavia stiffens, and I'm suddenly reminded who I am talking to. "This does not involve non-witches, Miss Cole. The practices we use to support our own are not your concern."

I turn away, trying to calm my raging heart. I tuck my hair behind my ears and catch sight of Delilah, who looks as pale as a ghost. Forgetting my own worries, I rush to her. "Are you all right? What's wrong?"

Octavia is at my side after a moment. "Lilah, are you well?"

Delilah simply stares past us, looking as though she's seen a ghost. We both turn to see where her attention is. Kiah.

The girl is looking between Raine and Delilah, confused. She clearly has no idea what is going on.

I turn back, and when Octavia and I reach out a hand and touch Delilah's arms at the same time, she crumples forward.

We catch her together and lower her to the ground. Her eyes are so full of tears, she surely can't see anything but a blur.

Octavia lowers to her knees beside her old friend. "Lilah, what is it?"

Delilah points to Kiah, and with a raspy voice, whispers, "My baby girl."

ROGUES

The world holds its breath for a moment. I look between Kiah and Delilah, as confused as everyone else in the clearing. The two witches look nothing alike.

Kiah looks terrified, and is trying to back away, but ends up walking right into Raine, who holds her gently.

"Lilah, are you certain?"

Delilah looks past us. "I'm sure. She's the spitting image of her father."

Everyone seems frozen, with no idea what to say to anyone. Kiah is crying and shaking, and starting to get pink in the face.

"Everleigh," Octavia says, voice quiet and strained, "she needs to breathe or we're all going to get roasted." She looks meaningfully at the house that's nothing but a burned pile of rubble.

I nod, get up, and move quickly to Kiah and Raine.

"Kiah," I say softly. "I need you to look at me, okay? Your newly awakened magic is building. I need you to breathe with me, all right?"

She looks at me, panic bleeding from her eyes.

I reach out and offer her my hands, careful not to force her into anything.

Kiah takes my hands, and I begin to guide her. "Just breathe with me. In for four seconds." I pause and exaggerate taking a deep breath. "Hold for four seconds. Now breathe out for four seconds." I model breathing loudly out through my mouth. "Hold for four seconds." I can see she's clinging to my words and breathing with me. "Good, Kiah, that's it. Keep going with me."

After a minute of breathing, Kiah is more relaxed—the pink flush has left her face and the panic is gone from her eyes.

"Well done, Kiah. You're okay. Good breathing."

"Thanks," she murmurs quietly.

"Are you ready for me to move now?" I ask gently.

She takes another deep breath, looks back to Raine behind her, who smiles reassuringly, then meets my eyes and nods. I let go of her hands and move to the side to let her see Delilah and Octavia. The other two witches have moved away towards the building and are working to douse the remains in magical water.

Delilah walks closer to us now that Kiah is calm. Octavia is holding her friend, supporting some of her weight. When she's a meter away, she dashes the tears away from her. "My name is Delilah Shelldrake. I'm—" She sucks in a breath and tries to control the sobs trying to escape her. "I'm your mother."

The young girl looks at Delilah, her eyes round and teary. "I'm Kiah H—" She looks at Octavia. "Is that my last name too? My real one?"

When Delilah nods, Octavia answers Kiah. "It is."

Kiah looks back at her mother, a storm of emotions riding her. "Could I— Can I give you a hug?"

They move closer to each other, gazes locked, exploring the face of the one they've missed for sixteen years. When they embrace, it's as though the world is right again. Just in this moment, it's all okay. They cling to each other, refusing to let go.

At that moment, my phone buzzes, distracting me from the precious embrace. I open it to look.

Alaric: Have you found them? We have a lead for the vamp body dumps. Will you make it back or should I head there without you?

Me: We've got them. You can let the team know to call off the search. Everything is okay, minus a building that's now burned to a crisp. I'll be in soon.

I look over to Octavia and Raine. "I need to go, guys. Raine, do you want me to drop you back?"

She shakes her head, pinkish tears filling her eyes at the scene in front of her. "We can find another way back. Be careful, okay."

I nod, then leave Kiah and Delilah to their reunion, trying to ignore the ache in my heart at her refusal to help my sister.

Alaric meets me in the garage, waiting by a black Mustang GT. I raise my brows at him. "New car?"

He shrugs, a grin on his face. "I needed a new toy with some oomph."

I smile back, his joy infectious. "Well, it is rather sexy." I walk closer to him and lean in. "Just like its owner."

He pulls me close and kisses me slowly and deeply. By the time he lets me lean back, I can feel my lips are swollen, a feeling I'm starting to enjoy.

"Are you ready to go? I've loaded the weapons kit into the trunk already."

"Let's do it. Where are we heading?"

Alaric opens the passenger door for me, and I kiss him on the cheek before I slide in. He closes it once I'm inside and then hops into the driver's seat. "We're heading over to Potts Point. There's a restaurant these guys seem to frequent. You were right about them being unrelated to the case. There's nothing to indicate a connection, and the fact they aren't missing is a pretty clear sign they've just taken it upon themselves to enjoy a feast."

"Ugh, these are the monsters humans need to be kept safe from." I frown. "How did you find them?"

Alaric comes to a small stretch of free road and pushes his foot to the floor, forcing us both back into the comfortable leather seats.

"Once you gave us the heads-up, we had Oldin and Stella look through local footage from all directions leading to the dump site, which Orpheus is going to murder them for."

I snort. "What idiots. Surely they knew they'd get caught. I imagine the Vampire King will make an example of them, as a warning to anyone else silly enough to think they should try the same."

"He was already pissed when I left, so I imagine he'll be pretty worked up by the time we collect the pair of them. Oh, speaking of...." Alaric unlocks his phone, opens to a photo of the two vampires, and hands it to me.

The names underneath the images say Stefan and Elonzo Ruiz. Once I feel I can recall their faces well enough, I pass the phone back to Alaric. We drive in companionable silence, until my mind shifts back to Kiah and Delilah, and then onto Clara.

"So what happened with the girl?"

Alaric's question makes me jump slightly as my mind and reality clash, startling me. "Actually, the whole thing is sort of unbelievable. I don't even know where to start." I pause, trying to assemble my thoughts so the details make sense to someone who wasn't there. "Well, you know she was missing and that I called Delilah to help. She scryed for Kiah and found her at a theater in Surry Hills. But when we got there, the whole building had been incinerated, which I think was Kiah's emerging power."

"Wow, that is some powerful magic for a witchling."

"Yeah, it is," I murmur, "but are you less surprised if I tell you she's Delilah's daughter?"

He turns to look at me, eyes wide. "I didn't know she had one, but yeah, I'd definitely say less surprised."

"Mmm, Delilah thought she'd been killed years ago. It was a huge shock."

"I'm sure it was. But wait, how was she okay if you guys didn't make it and the theater burned down? Was anyone hurt or killed?"

I harrumph grumpily. "Everyone was fine, because apparently, it was just some crazy witch initiation to try and get Kiah's power to emerge. Octavia and a couple of other witches literally kidnapped her to scare her powers out of her."

"Wow, that's pretty rough," he mutters. "Did you say anything to Octavia?"

I cross my arms, feeling rather petulant. "I did, but not as much as I would have liked. She reminded me it wasn't exactly my business since I wasn't a witch, with a subtle side of 'I'm the High Witch.'"

Alaric snickers, and I suck my lips in to try and stop a smile while I glare at him, feeling myself relax a little from the stress.

When he talks again, his voice is gentle and hesitant. "Did she agree to try and help with Clara?"

There's the weight back.

The lightness is gone, and I feel weighed down, forced to bring my sister's decline back to the front of my mind. I shake my head, then realize he probably can't see me while he's driving. "No, she wasn't interested in helping. I.... Maybe she'll change her mind. I don't know. It wasn't the time to ask again once we found her, though, not when she and Delilah just reunited."

He reaches a hand out across the center console and I place mine in his. He squeezes softly, reassuringly. "We'll save her, okay?"

I look at him and nod, but the hopelessness has already begun to snake its way back into my heart. My angelic gifts haven't given any other indication there is another way.

Not that I know how Kiah could help either.

We drive past the Italian restaurant and pull to a stop around the corner. Alaric pops the trunk and we pull our weapons out. I strap my twin blades to my belt, and pop another into my thigh sheath.

Alaric leads the way back to the restaurant. When we walk inside, it appears just like any other city dining venue—the humans are socializing loudly, some on dates and others with family. I'm suddenly glad I pulled on my long overcoat, especially since I hadn't considered there would be children.

Thanks for the heads-up wolfman.

He walks straight through the dining area, past the kitchen, despite the staff hollering at us, and towards a room out the back. We approach a tall man, who I'm fairly sure is a vampire from his lack of movement.

"We're here to see Stefan and Elonzo Ruiz," Alaric states, tone neutral.

The vamp at the door just stares at my partner but says nothing.

After waiting twenty seconds, Alaric speaks again. "My name is Alaric Bane. I am an Accord Enforcer. This is Everleigh Cole. She is also an enforcer. I suggest you move aside and let us through."

The guard continues to ignore Alaric, and I can feel the violence in him building at an alarming rate. My partner doesn't bother asking again. In a swift move, he slides a blade of silver from his belt and drives it straight into the guard's abdomen, causing him to fall to the floor in pain. Alaric leaves the blade in, and the sound and smell of sizzling flesh become potent.

That's my wolf.

I feel my eyes heat and flash red as I'm drawn to the ruthless violence. I step up next to my wolf, and when his gaze meets my crimson one, he smiles knowingly.

Before we need to move, the door swings open from the inside, and Stefan is standing there with a cigar hanging from his mouth. When he sees us, it drops to the floor. He takes an automatic step back, showing us his palms.

"Who is it, Stef?" a man calls from inside. "Are the drinks here?"

He keeps moving back, hands raised. We follow him, and I close the door. Once it clicks shut, I turn and lean my back against it and cross my ankles at the heels. Watching Alaric take the lead fuels my desire, and when my eyes heat and the redness shows, I know it's my inner demon keen to watch the chaos.

Alaric identifies us both by our names and titles and the three vamps who aren't Stefan and Elonzo stand up and back away against a wall. The level of fear in the room is palpable, from all except Elonzo, who looks pissed.

"What in the flying fuck do you cretins want?" he demands as Stefan moves back to his side.

"You've been identified as the vampires responsible for the murder and dumping of three humans in a park in the Sydney CBD."

The angry vamp pauses for a split second then stands up, throwing the table right towards us. Alaric puts a booted foot up immediately, causing the table to crack down the middle, then Elonzo is on him. He throws a punch at Alaric, who ducks and weaves to the left before throwing his own punch—*with* a stake in his hand, I realize when the vamp hisses in pain.

"You're going to regret that, you mongrel."

Elonzo launches at him, diving from both feet. He grabs Alaric around the middle and knocks them both down to the floor. The vampire's fangs go straight for Alaric's throat, which he blocks by throwing a right hook into the side of the vampire's face.

I look over to Stefan from my post against the door and see panic in his eyes. "He's going to get killed, you know," I warn.

His gaze darts to me, and his eyes bulge when he notices mine are red. Immediately, he darts closer to his brother and tries to pull him away from Alaric.

"Lonz, let go of the damned wolf!" he yells with a grunt, but his brother refuses to give up. "You're going to get us all killed. Just. Let. Go." He punctuates each word with a yank, finally dislodging him from my partner.

When Elonzo takes another step, Stefan grabs him around the middle and starts whispering furiously in his ear. I can't hear what they're saying when they speak so fast, but it seems to be calming Elonzo down to an angry simmer instead of being outright violent.

Alaric gets up from the floor, his lip bleeding from the scuffle. The urge to wipe it off and kiss him senseless is enough to make me uncross my ankles and stand up. Thankfully, I recall our job and remember to stay by the door, lest our soon-to-be prisoners decide to make a break for it.

After a little more back and forth between the brothers, Elonzo holds up his hand to Stefan, silencing him. Then he sneers at us. "We'll come along willingly."

The shock from the three vampires who have studiously stayed out of the way is clear. Evidently, Elonzo is not one to give himself up.

Points to Stefan. He must have said something persuasive.

I reach behind my long coat and into my back pockets, pulling out two sets of lined, silver cuffs. I lob one to Alaric, and gesture for the brothers to turn around where they are. Stefan does so first, and shoves his brother hard in the ribs, reminding him to comply.

I put the cuffs on Stefan, careful not to let the silver touch his skin since he didn't cause us any trouble. Alaric, on the other hand, is none too gentle or careful putting on Elonzo's cuffs.

I look over to the three statues against the wall and am tempted to draw my red eyes to the surface and shout, "Boo." Instead, I ask, "Do you three have anything to do with this?"

They all shake their heads, and I look to Alaric for his orders. He shrugs. "You can all leave. Remember, though, anyone caught breaking the Accords will be punished. Swiftly."

They nod and disappear out the door.

"Fucking pussies," Elonzo grumbles after them.

EXCEPTIONS

I sit in a chair at the back of the room with the entire Council of the Accords in front of me. Alaric is so close in the double-seater lounge that he is pressed against my side. He could have left some space between us when he sat, but I'm glad he didn't. Being in this room is always stressful. Thankfully though, it isn't us in the firing line today.

Elonzo and Stefan are standing side by side in their cuffs, facing the Council. Elonzo's posture looks belligerent while his brother's appears tense but respectful.

There are no introductions today. Orpheus simply stands and stalks towards his underlings. "So, pray tell why the pair of you thought brutally killing three humans and dumping them in a public park was acceptable?" His tone is quiet, tightly coiled, deadly.

Elonzo says nothing, simply ignoring the Vampire King.

Squash him like the filthy bug he is.

The urge to cheer Orpheus on is strong enough that I cross my arms over each other and pinch one in an effort to release myself from it.

Orpheus's eyes seem to flatten into a black deep enough to draw someone in and suffocate them. I look away at the other councilors. They all appear more strained than usual, the tension in their muscles ever-so-slightly more noticeable than in other meetings. Nicon looks downright sulky, and about a million miles away from what is happening in the room.

I peek at Alaric to see if he's noticed the way our boss is behaving, but his eyes are on the spectacle in front of us.

I realize that while I've been looking around, Orpheus has donned gloves and pulled out a giant silver net. Stefan takes a step back and looks at his brother, hissing something too quiet for me to hear, but the Vampire King does.

"Yes, Elonzo, why not just answer? Make this experience less painful. If not for you, then for poor Stefan at least."

"We did it," Elonzo growls, "because we thought we would get away with it. And because we've missed the hunt. These fucked-up rules stop us from following our true natures. We're meant to rule over humans. They *should* be scared of us. We're fucking predators."

"I see," Orpheus says, a maniacal smile now on his face. "And why is it you thought you'd get away with it?"

Elonzo raises one brow. "There have been supernatural murders all over the news. They haven't been caught and more keep coming. We just assumed our victims would get lumped in with the rest of the unsolved cases. Plus, maybe we wanted to help to prove a point," he adds, "that we should come out to the humans, and be in charge."

Stefan cringes at his brother's disrespectful tone.

Silence fills the room while the entire Council stares.

What a fucking moron. He's dead.

Orpheus turns back from the brothers to face the Council. "Has everyone heard enough?" His tone is like razor blades, just daring anyone to say something.

Each member of the Council simply nods. Orpheus walks over to his thronelike chair, drops the silver net and pulls out a giant pure-silver scimitar. He walks over to the brothers with it. "Kneel."

Stefan simply drops to his knees. "In the next life, brother," he says, resigned.

Elonzo looks as though he is going to argue, but Orpheus removes his brother's head in one harsh movement. The squelch and thud echo throughout the room.

Elonzo is silent, watching his brother's head roll across the floor until it comes to a stop. While he's watching, Orpheus blurs to his chair and back, exchanging the sword for the net. By the time Elonzo tears his eyes away from his brother, Orpheus throws the net over him, causing his skin to sizzle immediately.

The Vampire King whistles, and two guards walk in, and take Elonzo away. Another vampire shoots into the room and collects Stefan's head and body before darting after the others.

Ugh, I hope they aren't taking his brother to the same room.

Orpheus returns to his seat and places the scimitar back where he pulled it from before sitting.

"This is a problem," Conall, the Werewolf and Shifter King, states. "We have implemented countermeasures in the human media in an attempt to remain hidden. But if more supernaturals elect to try and capitalize on this situation before we can stop it, then we are going to be facing an even larger problem."

Raphael nods. "Yes, I concur, Conall. Not only will we not have the forces here to put a stop to this issue, but it will be the worst entrance into the human world we could imagine. Which I foresee would end in war and death for many from both sides."

"I'm of the same opinion," Octavia adds. "Polls where we monitor human impressions of supernaturals online, are showing a significant increase in fear and anger towards our possible existence. This case has destroyed the 'fairy tale' element humans usually possess when they think of us. We must do something to stop this and turn back to our previous course."

Nicon continues to stare into space, something clearly on his mind, although no one on the Council bothers him.

Iridessa crosses her ankles, and leans forward, somehow managing to look regal in the leather chair. "I suggest we put forth an edict decreeing death for those who expose us in any way to the humans until such time as this case is resolved. Perhaps longer if needed."

The room is silent as the leaders of our world contemplate the repercussions of such a decree, the potential death toll if they don't.

This surely needs some caveats—what about all the emerging supes. Has no one heard of an amendment? Surely it doesn't need to be that or nothing. Maybe if I just...

"Uh, excuse me," I say, standing up to address the Council.

Surprised glances turn my way, and I hear Alaric groan behind me. Nicon finally snaps out of his haze and looks at me with curious amusement.

"Yes, Enforcer?" Iridessa trills, her voice more dangerous than usual, the threat clear.

Fuck it. Just speak up.

"I just wanted to ask whether there would be any exceptions to that exposure rule?"

The Fae Queen looks irritated. "Enforcement is always an exception that is cleaned up when needed. I would think you know that."

Fae bitch.

I smile ever so politely back at her. "Indeed, I am aware of that rule. Although, since this edict will overtake all others, you may need some clauses that note the exceptions. The one I was referring to is for emerging supernaturals, though. They rarely have any control over their early magic or initial changes, which will of course result in accidents. I wouldn't think this should result in a death sentence either, right?"

Nicon has a wicked smile as he looks at the Fae Queen, clearly enjoying her being pulled up by an inferior. "Oh yes, I think my enforcer is quite right," he pipes up with a smile.

"Yes," Octavia adds, relief coloring her tone, having clearly not thought of this.

She must be pretty darn stressed if she's forgetting her witchlings in this conversation. I hope Delilah and Kiah are all right.

"Very well," Iridessa hisses petulantly. "The edict as it was, with the usual exceptions including those covering emerging supernaturals. Do we agree?"

Once everyone provides their affirmation for the edict, the Fae Queen stands and stalks to her personal exit at the rear of the room. I'm careful to keep my face neutral. I hadn't wanted to piss the dangerous fae off, but not saying something was too much of a risk in my mind.

Plus, it will make Raine breathe a little easier.

I walk back into the Technical Division leaning against Alaric, feeling a little drowsy from the constant stretch to my aura to keep Clara going. I try to ignore it for now, knowing I need to give Kiah at least a little time with her mother before I approach her again.

"Hey, you two, afraid I've got more bad news," Tess calls from across the room.

I pull myself away from Alaric and head over to see the latest video. Another woman. Another witch attack. I sigh, tired of all this terribleness towards the humans, and how horrible these demons are making the supernatural races look.

"How long ago was this released?" I ask her.

"A few hours ago, while you were out collecting the scummy vamps."

I nod. "Of course. One problem down at least. Oh, and guys." I raise my voice slightly to get the team's attention. Once they're all looking, I continue, "An edict is coming out, noting death as the penalty for exposure to humans. We still have an exception to the edict while working, and those emerging as well. But honestly, I'd suggest we stay careful."

"I agree," Alaric grumbles. "Make sure anyone going out *always* has their partner. Every time. It's not worth the risk of any accusations being made. You all know we aren't the most favored team in the supernatural world and anyone with a vendetta might think this is a good opportunity to throw us into the line of fire."

The team nods in agreement.

An idea pops into my head about Tess's mentor. "Hey, Tess, have the covens already done the call around to track anyone missing?"

She frowns, not understanding where I'm going with this. "Yeah. No one has been flagged as missing yet. Why's that?"

"I'm starting to think that the supernaturals from each species that were abducted are being held in case they're still needed for more attacks. So your mentor, she's probably still alive."

"Oh, yeah." She smiles back at me, tears in her eyes. "I was really starting to give up hope, but you're probably right." Her expression drops. "In saying this, if we find her, she's going to feel absolutely dreadful. This is everything she stands against."

"*When* we find her, Tess," Alaric says.

I smile up at him, impressed at his supportiveness and resolve.

"Ugh, stop being so cutesy, you pair," Tess says, completely distracted.

I wink at her, causing her to laugh while Alaric jumps into leader mode.

He looks over at the twins. "Do we have any idea where the woman might be? Have you flagged the location on our map with the others?

Oldin nods and walks over to the map, the team following. "We just got a ping on some possible locations. I've tagged them in orange since they aren't confirmed yet."

"We've already sent a couple of teams out to check the locations," Stella says.

"Both are still in the same zone, though. There has to be a base in here that we're missing. Has anyone checked for demonic portals or anything?"

"There aren't any seismic markers in that area for a portal to be ripped open," Zeke says, drawing my attention for the first time since we entered.

I smile at him and dip my head in acknowledgment. "How is the grid search going?"

"Still nothing," Tess says, "but we really don't have that much manpower doing the search. We just have to let it go slowly to make sure we're not missing anything. All of the supernaturals in the zone appear to be accounted for, though, and not housing any unwilling guests."

"Hmm. We'll figure it out soon. I'm sure of it."

"Angelic intuition?" Zeke asks hopefully.

I shake my head. "Sadly not, Zeke. Just some good old-fashioned belief in things working out."

He bobs his head with a sad smile, which makes me want to give him a hug.

My phone buzzes in my pocket and I pull it out and see Delilah's name.

Does Kiah want to help?!

I quickly move away from the group towards my office before picking up the phone. "Hello, Delilah. How are you doing? Is everything well with you and Kiah?"

"Hi, Everleigh," her voice sounds concerned. "I'm well, and so is Kiah. We're spending some time together, which is wonderful. It's not the reason I called, though. I rang to let you know that I am getting some signals from the ward around your home, indicating that someone is trying to penetrate it. I should have set these up to come to you, and I'll fix that later. But for now, I wanted you to know."

My stomach tightens in fear. "Is it serious? Can you tell if they're breaking through?"

"They aren't near the wards proper, just near the ones further out on the street, which should keep them from attending if you didn't invite them. It seems they've identified a work around to be able to stay near the wards but, no, they aren't moving any closer."

I breathe a sigh of relief that Clara is still safe right now. "Okay, thank you, Delilah. I'll go and check it out."

"Okay, that's a good idea. And Everleigh?"

"Yes?"

"The presence is demonic."

INTRUDER

I RUSH NEXT DOOR into Alaric's office, grab his bike keys, and then move quickly to the main room. "Alaric, I need you," I call out, pulling everyone's attention. "A demon is attempting to breach the wards at my house."

Tess shoves Alaric towards me. "Go! And take care of her."

When he's almost with me, I wave his bike keys and then toss them to him. We high tail it to the elevator together, and I start jamming the button.

"Hey!" calls the petite blonde fae, now standing behind her desk. "That isn't going to make it show up any faster."

Alaric growls at her, and she sits back down, cowed. My eyes flash red, my inner demon amused by Alaric basically telling her to shut up—the mean streak keeping me distracted.

The doors open and we ride down to the car garage. Over at the bike, Alaric hands me a helmet and climbs straight onto the bike before placing his own on.

Too many minutes later, Alaric pulls the bike to a stop a block away from my apartment. We dismount and put the helmets and gloves down. We split up, Alaric going right, and me going left, to meet up out the front. I run towards the end of the block since no one is in sight. I slow down before I reach it and peer carefully around the corner. A woman is sitting with her baby on a bench.

I step around and rush towards the next corner, sure that whoever the culprit is, will be on the next side if they are still trying to penetrate the wards. I try not to be loud or conspicuous, not wanting to draw the demon's attention, or that of the lady, in case she becomes curious and decides to follow me into a dangerous situation.

I slow again at the next corner. Stick my head forward and peer around.

Fucking Blake.

He's standing there launching fireballs, trying to weaken the ward to get in, but the only results of this are him clearly getting angrier and the ward absorbing his demonic flames.

I storm down the street towards him and see Alaric coming from the other end. I decide to draw his attention to allow Alaric a chance to sneak up on him.

"Blake," I hiss loudly. "What in the hellish realms do you think you're doing? You're out in public!"

He turns to me, his eyes a fiery red. Thankfully, he absorbs the flames back into his hands. He looks half mad.

I slow down once I get closer. "What are you doing here, Blake?"

He laughs darkly. "What am I doing here? What the flaming fuck do you think I'm doing here? I want to see my girlfriend. You haven't invited me over to see her. I haven't had any updates. Nothing. I'm going out of my mind. Is she dead?"

My brows draw down. "Last I checked, Blake, you were on the run and I'm an enforcer. My job if I see you is to bring you in. I can hardly invite you to my house. Also, yes. Clara is still alive."

He looks me up and down, homing in on the slight bags appearing under my eyes. Something I've never had before in my life. "Not for much longer by the look of you. I want to see her. Now."

His half-crazed state unsettles me, and the way he talks about Clara being dead soon makes my stomach knot up. I shake my head. "I don't think that's a good idea right now. I think you should come with me down to the Accords building and answer for all of the illegal banishments. That way when Clara wakes up, you're not still on the run."

He shakes his head at me with those half-mad eyes. "Oh no, I'm not going in. I still need to banish some more demons. I'm not done yet."

I squint my eyes at his wording. "For Clara, you mean?"

"Of course," he roars. "I will purge the Earth."

Alaric is close behind him now, and I try not to look at him, to pretend he isn't there. But Blake sees the flicker of my eyes and immediately starts firing behind himself. Alaric rolls to the side, evading the line of fire.

"I will get her back, Everleigh. Make no mistake!"

I begin to move towards him, but it's not long before I need to dive out of the way as well. I curse as I bang my shins on a small flowerbed.

When I look up, covered in dirt from the flowerbed, Blake is gone.

Alaric walks over to me, keeping an eye on the direction Blake just fled. "I don't know whether to be mad or not. On the one hand, if it was you being kept away from me, I'd tear down the world to find you. On the other, it's our job to enforce the Accords, and I don't think he could break any more of the laws if he tried. Fireballs on a public street?"

We both glance around, grateful the street is somehow completely deserted.

"He looks like he's going insane. I don't really know what to do, though. He's acting suspicious as all hells, too. Just showing up places and banishing demons, trying to break in. Do you think Tess would agree to moving the watch guys over to here, or maybe put up some extra security cameras?"

He nods. "Yeah, I'm sure she'd do that for you. We all look out for each other on this team."

At the end of the day, I walk inside my home and head straight downstairs to see Clara. I'm physically and mentally exhausted, the strain of the stasis and worry over my sister and the case are starting to feel too much.

I don't know how much longer I can keep holding out.

Tears well in my eyes at the thought I've been desperately pushing down and avoiding for days now. With no sign of Kiah changing her mind and no more visions to even show me what to do if she does, I'm lost. I have no plan. Nothing in the books could help, just as Raphael predicted.

I know deep down that Kiah is our only hope. But she's a child. This isn't her responsibility. I can't ask her to do something she's not comfortable with for a couple of supernaturals she doesn't know or trust.

I sit next to Clara, lean forward, and stroke her forehead with my thumb.

"This case is going terribly, Clara. I'm sure you'd know how to track down a demon way better than any of the team does. You're practically an expert." I smile sadly, letting my tears flow freely for a while. "The demons responsible are still eluding us, and we have no idea who they are. Every time we get a clue, your pain-in-the-arse boyfriend kills it." I shake my head. "He's bringing hell to Earth trying to get back to you, girl. I'm sorry I haven't let him in to see you. He's on the run now, though. Hells, you might kill him if you wake up."

A stabbing sensation punctures my heart when I realize I said *if*. "*When*. I mean when." I lean forward and rest my head on hers gently. "I won't stop trying until the end. I promise."

My tears drip onto my sister, and I pull myself away, drying them with the sleeve of my shirt. I laugh, congested with snot from crying. "You would totally hate me for sitting here crying over you." I take in a deep breath and push it out slowly through my mouth.

"Anyway. The case. The woman who was found on video has already been killed and dumped. On the same damned day this time. The nice, organized timeline has gone to shit. None of us know what to expect, or when. It's hard. And it's so damn scary, not knowing."

I sigh and sit back in the seat.

I just need to close my eyes for a while.

"Ev... Ev...." I feel someone gently shaking my shoulders.

"Mmm...?" I push through the layers of sleep until I can open my eyes. I blink several times, seeing a blurry version of Raine in front of me.

"Where am I?"

"You're in Clara's room, Ev. Are you okay?"

"Mmm, yeah. I'm just tired." I yawn and stretch out my arms and wings. My wing hits something and I startle, waking more.

"It's okay, I've got it," Raine says.

When my vision clears and I can see the room, I notice that the sun has already risen. I yawn widely and shake my head again. "Did I sleep all night?"

Raine looks incredibly worried. "Ev, I think you slept two nights and a day."

"What?!" I grab my phone from Raine—the thing I knocked down to the floor—and check the date and time. "Hells, I've got about twenty missed calls here that came in yesterday."

"Alaric called me, and I told him you were sleeping. That you must have been tired. But I had to go to work, and they needed me to stay back at the dorms, so I just got home and when I saw your bed hadn't been slept in, I came down here."

"Shit," I mutter. I unlock my phone and open it to send a text.

Me: Alaric, sorry, was sleeping. Raine just woke me. I'll be in soon.

Alaric: Don't stress. See you when you're ready.

I pull my wings back into the ether with more effort than it usually takes, not even recalling releasing them. Though, as I roll my shoulders back, I realize my back feels less tight after having them out.

"Thanks for waking me," I say. "How was work? Did everything go okay?"

"Yeah, work was all fine, Ev. Kiah's come back to school."

My eyes widen. "Has she said anything?"

Raine's eyes fill with pinkish tears, and she shakes her head. "Sorry, Ev. She hasn't brought it up, and you told me not to. Do you think... should I just ask? It seems like things are getting more serious."

My eyes fill as my heart sinks, hopelessness riding me. It feels so much worse when I'm tired.

Not that I should be tired after sleeping for so long.

"It's okay. She's just a child. I wouldn't force anything on her." I push myself up to stand, feeling a little wobbly for a second. "I'm okay," I say, seeing Raine's face. "I just need to eat something."

She nods. "Okay, you shower. I'll make you breakfast."

Heat rises to my cheeks.

She laughs softly and reaches out to give my hand a squeeze. "You're fine. Not stinky or anything. I just assumed you might like a shower after sitting on that couch for so long. And maybe a trip to the bathroom?"

As soon as she mentions it, it's as though my bladder wakes up, screaming at me with a vengeance. "Yep. You're right. Okay, toilet and shower. I'll meet you in the kitchen."

Raine takes a last lingering look, then shoots off up the stairs.

Once I've used the bathroom, I wander into the bedroom and look for something to wear. I pull out a matching teal lingerie set—one of the fancier ones to perk myself up—and then pull on my black skinny jeans and a short-sleeved teal shirt. It's more color than usual for me, but I decide I really need it today. I even add some matching earrings.

Once I pull on my knee-high boots, I walk upstairs to find that Raine has made me a full breakfast smorgasbord. I smile. "Raine, this is way too much delicious food. What's going on?"

She gives me a watery smile. "I just wanted you to have a nice breakfast, that's all, beautiful."

I walk over and hug my best friend. I can't lie and tell her it's all fine; instead, I say, "I'm sorry things are so hard right now, honey."

She hugs me back, squeezing my bones a little until I make a little "Oomph" sound. Then she chuckles and lets me go. "Okay. Eat up. You need your energy. I need to go to work. I'll see you when I get home, okay?"

"Of course. Have a good day."

Once Raine leaves, I slouch down in my chair and lean against the table. I look at all the food and know I need to eat, but there's no part of me that wants to. I reluctantly reach out and grab a waffle and some bacon, pour on some maple syrup, and eat it.

Each mouthful is an effort. Everything feels like an effort right now. I sigh, trying to convince myself to get up and keep trying. All I want to do is sleep.

HOPELESS

When I finally drag myself into the office, I bring all the extra breakfast Raine made with me and set it on a table. "Hey, guys, Raine overcooked if anyone wants anything."

"Ev, you're back!" Tess comes up and gives me a big hug.

I laugh lightly. "I've only been off a day, Tess. How's the case going?"

Her quick smile falls. "Unfortunately, not so great. We had a new victim turn up last night."

"Last night?" I ask, confused.

"Yeah, they've really gone off the pattern. I don't think there's any point in calling it that anymore. This one is different in other ways too. She was attacked by a demon. And it seems like she'd been kept captive a lot longer than the others."

I frown. "And she was dumped publicly like the others, but at night?"

She shakes her head. "She actually stumbled her way into a mental health facility where one of ours found her."

"How do you know it's the same demons?"

"It's the same traumatized, sliced-up pattern as the rest. This time she just happened to be dumped in the wrong spot. Well, right for us, wrong for them."

"Also, a news van showed up shortly after she was found. The werewolf healer that found her took down the details of the number plates, so we've sent someone to pick them up. Though of course, we won't bring them here. We'll have some police officers on our payroll speak with them about where the tip came from."

"Wow. Well, I mean this sounds all sorts of good and bad. What's next?" I look around the room. "And where's Alaric?"

She smiles gently at me. "Next, the Council is going to decide what approach we take with the woman, since we actually have her in our custody this time. She's sedated and being treated in the medical rooms at the moment."

I look down at my watch. "When's that happening? Is that where Alaric is?" For some reason, I feel like I need to know where he is.

"Yeah, in about five minutes. He went up to wait just before you got here. Told me to let you know where he was when you arrived."

"Thanks, Tess." I reach out and hug her, then turn and head upstairs.

When I enter the hallways, it's deserted, except for the mage guarding the door. Not thinking, I rush towards him, determined to get inside before they make any decisions. The guard puts his hand to his belt, and I force myself to stop in my tracks. I raise my hands in supplication.

He relaxes slightly, though doesn't take his hand away from his belt. "State your business," he says.

"I'm Everleigh Cole, one of the enforcers. I'm supposed to be inside with Alaric Bane to see the Council."

"Please wait a moment." He turns around and approaches the door. He raps his knuckles against it once, hard.

After a few moments and some whispered words, he opens the door wide for me to go inside. I nod my thanks as I go past, and he returns the gesture, a slight curiosity to his expression.

Odd for a mage. They're usually too wrapped up in themselves to be curious about others.

When I walk into the room, all eyes turn to me. I nod in the general direction of the Council but stop in front of Raphael to bow properly—a bow befitting his leadership over angels on Earth: the ones who have sworn fealty anyway.

When his gaze locks with mine, his eyes bore into me, as if they're seeing down to my soul—or maybe just to my aura. His eyes glow golden, pulling out the golden glow in my own. His brow creases for a split second, appearing to be concerned, but he smooths it away so quickly, I can't be sure.

I wait for another second to see if he'll say anything, but when he doesn't, I go and join Alaric. He nods to me in greeting, careful not to show too much familiarity in front of this audience.

"Just in time, Miss Cole," Nicon says, his usual amused smile somewhat more serious. "Alaric, please update the Council."

I wonder if he knows I've been away? Maybe the team told him. He is our boss after all.

"A woman was released by the demons. She is the first of all the victims in this case we have managed to have in our custody here at the Accords headquarters. It appears she was kept much longer than the usual three-day pattern. She is quite... psychologically damaged. It seems she was tortured often by the demon and has a body covered in scars to prove it. The woman is not in a fit state to talk about what happened, so we need for you to determine the most appropriate approach moving forward." He bows his head—a small dip—then waits.

The councilors begin arguing back and forth immediately.

"It seems the most humane action would be to let her be. She needs to recover," Raphael says.

"Humane, yes," Solomon says, "helpful, no. We need answers."

"Well," Iridessa sings, "perhaps she can join us in the fae realm, and we can pry it from her head."

Hells, that lady is sick.

"Please," Octavia says, "that is hardly necessary. If we need to get information, there are more peaceful ways of doing so."

"Yes," Conall says gravely. "She has been tortured enough by our kind. She does not deserve any more damage."

"I hear your point," Orpheus grinds out, "but we can hardly afford to take the soft and slow approach. This situation is getting rather dire, especially when we *still* have no idea who is responsible here, and the deaths are piling up. Supernaturals are starting to take more risks."

"Ohh, yes," Nicon adds, "that's very true. The edict won't keep them under control for long. Slimy vampires will do anything."

A laugh tries to escape, and I force myself into a coughing fit to try and cover it up, turning my face away from the Council. Alaric turns with me, appearing to check on me, but I see the same laughter on his face.

Nicon is one crazy son of a bitch.

Orpheus sighs exaggeratedly. "Could you try to be serious, Nicon?"

"You're right. My demons are in the shit right now as well. They're not even keeping it together anymore. *You're not alone, it's okay.*"

I keep my back turned, another bout of "coughing," keeping me occupied.

When I have it together enough to maintain a straight face, I turn back around to continue listening to them argue.

They're like a bunch of kids chucking tantrums to get what they want.

With Nicon in here messing with them for the popcorn.

I give my head a short, sharp shake to refocus on the room.

"This is going nowhere," Raphael states. "I think a vote may be a better use of our time at this point."

The rest of the councilors grumble in agreement, Iridessa flicking her hand in his direction to tell him to go ahead.

"Very well. All those in favor of allowing the woman to heal without interrogation."

Raphael, Conall, and Octavia raise their hands.

He sighs. "Very well. In that case, it seems our options are either witchcraft or the fae. Those in favor of the fae?"

I watch in disgust as Iridessa raises her hand with a maniacal smile that looks completely wrong on her lovely, childlike face.

Orpheus and Solomon raise their hands as well, humanity taking a back seat over progress on the case.

One life for the sake of many and all of that I suppose.

Screw that, they're just being impatient. The witchcraft way won't take that much longer. They should be put down.

More death is not the answer here. Besides, better the devil you know. Speaking of...

I look over at Nicon, knowing he is definitely the swing vote in this room. Raphael, Octavia, and Conall will all vote for the most humane option on the table.

Nicon puts his thumb and finger into a tick shape and rests his chin inside it, tapping his face with his index finger—a pantomime of thinking. Most of the Council look like they'd enjoy stabbing him. Raphael and Conall simply shake their heads and wait.

"Oh, just bloody choose, Nicon. We don't have all day," Orpheus demands.

Nicon pouts for a moment, then smiles. "Witchcraft it is."

I sag in relief at his decision. The poor tortured woman certainly doesn't need to be gifted to the fae to have her mind torn open.

"Very well," Raphael says. "In that case, we will leave it with you, Octavia, to make the arrangements for whatever is deemed necessary."

She nods briskly, then stands and leaves. The other councilors begin to follow, and I assume we should leave as well. I tap Alaric on the shoulder, and when he looks at me, I jerk my head towards the door, brows raised.

"Yeah, let's go. I imagine Octavia will be in touch soon once she makes the arrangements."

We walk towards the door, but Raphael calls out to me, "Everleigh, daughter of Estelle. A word if you will."

It's not a request, so I turn back to look at him. The rest of the Council has dispersed. Alaric has stopped as well, and is waiting, pushing on Raphael's grace.

The hopeless bubble sitting protected inside me by the distraction of the Council meeting begins to break down as I meet the Archangel's eyes. I feel the panic rise into my throat, and it must radiate from my eyes because Raphael asks Alaric to wait outside for a moment.

He squeezes my shoulder as I remain resolutely looking towards the seats. Then I hear my partner walk out and close the door behind him. I close my teary eyes and take a deep breath, feeling as though I know what's coming.

"Come, child. Sit for a moment." He waves at the seat next to him.

I look at it, unsure whether sitting in it would be a terrible idea given the level of power and heightened senses that belong in this room. Seeing my quandary, Raphael smiles softly and moves to the chair next to his, then directs me to his own.

At least I know that's safe.

I nod, and go and sit down, instantly sagging into the chair, knowing that the false bravado is wasted when Raphael sees me so clearly with his angelic vision.

He looks at me for a moment, and I have the intense urge to just pull out my wings, wrap them around myself and cry—a long, hard, ugly cry. He presses his lips together softly, care radiating from him. "Everleigh, you know you don't have long left if you continue holding this stasis with your own aura."

Tears turn the archangel into a blur of colors. I nod, feeling the tears spill down my cheeks, and then drip to my hands resting in my lap.

"I know your parents meant a lot to you, and losing your sister, the one last true connection you have, feels like too much to bear."

The lump in my throat is so thick that it's difficult to breathe. My voice breaks as I try to talk. "I can't let her go."

His head tips to the left slightly, no judgment, just empathy. "It does feel like that, I'm sure. But you know, there are many here now who think of you as family, and it would break their hearts, too, were you to leave."

I suck in a breath, which turns to a sob. Every time I try to breathe, it gets caught on the lump in my throat. And I think of them—Alaric, Raine, Henry, Tess, even the team I've gotten to know so well.

My first chance at love.

My best friends turned family.

Friends who could become more than that with time.

Time.

But my sister. My family.

I can't breathe. I feel too dizzy. This is just too much.

"I can't do this," I rasp. "I don't want to decide. I don't want to lose my heart. I don't want to fracture the souls of my friends. I—"

I feel my wings rip from the ether and automatically wrap around me. I suck in breaths. I try to remember the tune of the song my mother used to sing to me. But I can't. I can't remember it anymore.

I can't do this.

HELPING

I vaguely hear Raphael speaking outside my wings, but I have no idea what he says. I just continue to cry—soul-wrenching sobs that don't allow me to breathe. I can't make them stop. I hear more noises in the room, but they mean nothing to me.

Eventually, my chest is so painful, and I'm so exhausted from crying that my body forces me to stop. The tears run out. I feel like the walking dead. Still, I sit. Wrapped in my wings. Wondering if maybe death will just take me now. Take the choice out of my hands.

But it doesn't.

Of course it doesn't.

Instead, I hear a knock, then the sound of the door opening. Then a familiar heat soaks into my body, making me warmer by the second.

"Ev?" Alaric asks, his voice careful, as though he thinks I might break.

Maybe I will.

"Ev, I'm sorry to ask, but Octavia called me. She thinks it might help for you to come and support the woman, with your psychology skills and all. But... if you're not up to it, that's okay. I can ask her to find someone else."

I wipe my face, certain I look exactly like I have been bawling my eyes out. Then I release my wings to see Alaric.

He looks as though he wants to come to me, but I hold out my hands palms forward, trying to keep him at bay. If he embraces me, I'll truly break. I have so little left. I do my darndest to pull myself together enough so that I can help the woman. She's been through enough, and if I have to leave this Earth, then the least I can do is help someone else before I go. I turn around to look at Raphael, to see if he has an opinion, but he's left the room.

"Let's go," I say, turning back to my partner. "I want to help."

He opens his mouth, then closes it.

As I walk past Alaric and out the door, I work on stuffing my hopelessness back inside myself. Just for now, I build it into a container in my mind, knowing I can come back to it later. I imagine taking the feelings that will drag me into the abyss, curling them together into the shape of a ball. I conjure the image of a reinforced steel vault in the ground, with a circular lid made of even heavier steel—like I might find on a ship. I carefully place the ball of emotions through the open circle. I hold them there and then close the lid, spinning the round handle until I can't tighten it any more by hand.

As we reach the garage, I check on my vault. No hopelessness is leaking out. I know it's there. I know I can reopen that vault when I'm ready. But right now, helping the woman is more important.

We climb into Alaric's Mustang GT, but this time, he lets me open my own door. I try hard not to over analyze why. Instead, I start a simple mindfulness grounding practice. I push my feet into the floor of his car, focusing on the feelings and sensations it causes, and the subtle changes as I move them around.

I take a few deep breaths, then when I feel as centered as I can be, I open my eyes.

"So, where are we going?" I ask.

He inhales, then releases his breath slowly. I look at him and see a smattering of guilt in his expression. "We're going to Delilah's home."

I close my eyes, pushing my feet back into the floor. "And you didn't think to warn me about that before we left?"

"Honestly—" He pauses for a moment, waiting for me to look at him. When I do, he continues, "I know how much you value helping others. I thought being able to do that might help you to feel a little better when everything else has been so hopeless. If it's too much, though, tell me. I *will* turn around and take you back to work or to your house."

I allow his warmth and care to flow through me alongside his heat. It's a nice feeling. I allow myself to bask in that, choosing to focus my attention on it for just a little while. "No. It's okay. You're right. Let's go and help this woman."

After another ten minutes, Alaric enters a driveway and pulls up in front of the large gates. Once we've stopped, he presses the intercom. When someone answers, Alaric states his name, and the gates open slowly inwards, allowing us to drive up the laneway. It takes another few minutes for us to reach the grand manor at the end.

It's a gorgeous stone cottage set into a small forest. It looks large, but somehow still manages to look at home amongst the trees. The large windows are spaced evenly around the house, letting the natural light shine into the rooms.

A myriad of small ornaments line the front porch—different types of animal and goddess statues—a nod to Delilah's beliefs and interests.

After parking, we walk slowly together along the open porch, and I try to remain in the moment. I check quickly on my mental vault, glad to see it's still locked tightly away. Once we reach the door, I put my hand up to knock, but it's pulled open immediately by Delilah.

She smiles richly at me, so full of joy that I feel as if I could reach out and touch it. I don't though, knowing my own feelings are just as contagious for someone like Delilah who practices medicine of the body and mind using her gifts. "Come in, come in. Everyone's waiting. Just straight down the hall," she says, pointing.

Alaric nods and walks through, and I follow closely, trying not to accidentally brush our host as I do so. She senses something, though, and she touches my arm.

I turn to look at her and see the recognition in her gaze.

"Later," she murmurs to me, leaving no room for me to get out of the conversation.

Reluctantly I nod, not really wanting to bring her into it when Kiah is her daughter.

At the end of the hall, a few women are sitting, waiting. I can see Zeke in the kitchen with his tablet, and I give him a little wave, which he returns. Octavia stands when I come into the room. "We need her awake for this, but we've left her in the magical sleep up until now. Are you ready?"

I nod back and move to sit down next to the woman. One of the other two witches with Octavia come over to us. She holds a hand above the woman's forehead and begins chanting some words, the rhythm soothing.

When the woman starts to awaken, I sit where she can see me, but not so close that I might scare her. Although, it is difficult to know how someone who has experienced trauma will respond.

She blinks a few times, then rubs her eyes and yawns. My own body responds instinctively, causing me to mirror her sign of sleepiness.

Once she seems more lucid, she looks around and sees the other women, but when I follow her gaze, I notice Alaric has placed himself out of view. I can't help but feel relieved at his sensitive and caring nature, showing me again just how thoughtful he is.

And I could be with him.

I pinch myself hard on the arm, determined not to drag myself down into the vault before I realize I've even opened it.

When the woman looks back to me, I stay still and smile softly. "Hello, my name is Everleigh. What's your name?"

She points to herself, and I nod.

"Naomi," she whispers hoarsely.

I point to the small table beside her. "Some water, if you want it."

Naomi picks up the glass and her hand immediately starts shaking. When the water sloshes over the sides of the glass, she begins to cry.

"Can I help you, Naomi?" I ask quietly.

She sobs as she nods, continuing to shake.

I reach forward and help her to hold the glass steady. She takes a few sips, only spilling a tiny amount.

Once she settles a little, I try to talk with her. "Naomi, these ladies here, they're my friends. They're here to help us, okay?"

She nods uncertainly, but doesn't speak, her eyes looking haunted.

"We know that you've been somewhere really terrible recently, and that it was so scary for you." When the shaking gets worse, I reach for a throw rug nearby and offer it to her. Her lips pull up in the corners—an attempt to smile—as she takes it and tries to spread it across her lap.

"Would you like some help?"

"P-P-Plea-s-se."

I spread the rug out for her, careful not to touch her because I have no idea what might be a trigger. Once it's out flat, she grabs a couple of handfuls and pulls it up to her chin. It's not cold in the room, but I think she's cold on the inside. Her aura is a fractured mess of deep blues, black, and dark reds—sadness, terror, anger, and confusion.

"Now, I know that time was really scary, but there are some other people who are still in danger, and we need your help to find them. Would you like to help save the others?"

The woman begins shaking erratically. I sit next to her, and just breathe, louder than I need to, in and out. Slowly. When her breaths start to mirror my own, I switch to a box breath—*in for four, hold for four, out for four, hold for four, repeat*—helping her body to slow her heart rate.

"Good, Naomi," I say quietly. "You're doing so well. Keep breathing, just like that."

After another minute, I try again. "To help the others, Naomi, I'll need you to do something for me. I understand that it's scary, but I'll be here with you. I can hold your hands to remind you we're in a safe place, to help you breathe, just like I did before. All you have to do is think about the first thing you remember once you were taken, okay. That's all, just the first thing." I reach out a hand to her, my eyes locked on hers, sincerity, care, and calm radiating from me and into her like my mother taught me when I was young.

I know it's working when she stops shivering. She takes my hand in hers, and just breathes, allowing herself to be unafraid for a moment.

I nod to Delilah, who is sitting on her other side, indicating she can begin.

I continue breathing with Naomi as Delilah chants her spell quietly. When she waves to me, I know she's ready.

"Okay, Naomi. It's time now, all right. Take a deep breath in. That's right, good. Now as you breathe out, I want you to close your eyes and think back to when that demon first took you."

She squeezes my hand incredibly hard for a human, driven by her intense fear. I keep her breathing by doing so myself in an exaggerated way.

I feel Delilah's magic begin to work, and then between one blink and the next, the entire room is overlaid by the scene in Naomi's head.

We're in a dank basement that looks as though it belongs in a prison. There are cells lining the walls and a cavernous space in the center. A space stained with blood.

I keep focusing my calming energy into Naomi, despite my tiredness, not wanting her to fall into this nightmare.

Delilah lifts a piece of paper above Naomi's head for me to read, and once I have, I nod.

"You're being so helpful, Naomi. You're really going to save the others. Just keep breathing." When I feel her hand squeeze my own softly, I continue, "What I need you to do now is to just picture anyone who was there with you, their faces, their clothes."

I begin to see others around her in the cells. "That's it, Naomi, well done. Remember, keep breathing with me as you think."

Slowly, the individuals inside the cells become clearer. When Octavia makes a small gasping noise, I can see she recognizes the witch. I try to alert her to not make noises as I feel Naomi begin to shake again.

"Shhh, it's okay, Naomi. You're safe. You are here in this room with me. You're holding my hand. It's safe here. Keep breathing. That's it. Well done."

I notice Zeke in the room, moving about silently with his tablet. Stopping for a minute near each of the beings in the cells, drawing them so quickly I'm surprised the tablet can keep up with his pen strokes.

I keep breathing with Naomi until Zeke is done with the drawings. Once he steps back out of view, Delilah holds another piece of paper up with a single word—*demon*.

I take a deep breath for myself and try to push the rising tiredness back.

"Okay, Naomi. You are doing so beautifully well. You're so helpful. We just have a single thing left to do. I know it's hard, but remember, you're safe. I'm here with you. This is a safe place. I need you to think about the demon who tortured you." Her shaking returns almost immediately.

I breathe deeply again, trying to build more calm within myself to push out to Naomi. It's a struggle. I'm so tired.

Come on, Everleigh. You can do this. Help the woman, so she can rest.

I feel when it's worked, both by the drain and the steadiness of Naomi's hands. "You can do this, Naomi. Last thing and you can be free of him. Picture the demon, or demons you saw."

An image begins to take shape in the center of the room. Black boots and jeans. A plain black shirt. A lean body, a neck of tattoos. A bald head. Finally, the demon's face.

I nearly drop Naomi's hand. I recognize the demon.

It's Blake's driver from the nightclub.

DISBELIEF

I MANAGE TO HOLD on and not scream out what I know. Instead, I allow Zeke to do his drawing since I definitely don't know the demon's name—and finding Blake to ask will likely be impossible at this point. Not to mention, revealing I know this demon won't help Naomi to trust me.

Zeke lets us know he's done by leaving the room, extra careful not to bump into anything. Once he's gone, Delilah releases the spell, looking a little tired herself.

I keep Naomi breathing with me while Octavia approaches us. She tips a small vial of clear liquid into Naomi's glass of water and then returns to her seat. The water in the glass ripples for a few moments, and then settles, as though nothing ever happened.

Relief rushes through me along with exhaustion and a small sense of victory at knowing more than we did about this case than before. Although, I don't allow the likely connection to Blake to throw me right now.

"Okay, Naomi. You can open your eyes now. We're all done."

She blinks a few times, letting go of my hand and covering her eyes against the brightness of the room. Once she can see again, she lowers her hands and looks at me with pleading eyes. "I don't have to think about it anymore? And I really helped someone else?"

I nod. "You don't, and you did help. I promise." I reach forward and pick up her water glass and pass it to her. "Here, drink up. It will help you feel better."

She takes the glass from me, and I feel a little surge of contentment that she isn't shaking nearly as much as before—that the grounding and exposure has helped her to breathe a little easier, even if just for now. It's certainly not a permanent fix, though I hope the potion will be.

It's not that likely. Trauma and memory draughts don't exactly go together.

They'll be keeping an eye on her, in case something more serious is needed. I can at least hope that something works out for someone besides me.

I feel the emotions in my vault rattle. The tiredness is making it harder to keep them locked down.

Naomi downs her water and falls asleep in a matter of minutes.

Octavia stands. "Elspeth, Mordred, can you please take Naomi back to her home now and place her in her bed? She will hopefully wake up and remember nothing. Make sure the scouts are in place to keep an eye on her as well, though."

The two witches nod their assent, and collect Naomi, taking her from the room.

Zeke and Alaric join us back in the sitting room, everyone taking a seat. Alaric slides in next to me, close enough for me to lean on, which I do immediately, the exhaustion dragging me down.

"You were amazing, Everleigh," Zeke says quietly, spinning one of the copper beads on his bracelet around. "I wish I'd had someone like you around when I went through my change."

I lock eyes with him. "I'm so sorry you didn't have someone, Zeke. That must have been such a hard time for you."

His sad smile tells me I'm right, but since we aren't alone and he doesn't say anything else, I let it go.

Octavia pulls our attention by saying, "Dorothea was definitely being held in those cells. I'm assuming the others we could see were the other missing supernaturals."

I feel Alaric nod and realize I've closed my eyes, so I force them open again.

"Yes," he says. "I'd say you're right. And the sketches Zeke did will help to confirm the identities. Did anyone recognize the demon by chance?"

"Oh, yes. Me." I hear my words slur a little and I try to be clearer. "It was Blake's driver. I saw him recently while working a case."

Alaric freezes. "Do you think Blake is involved in this too then?"

I yawn widely. "Honestly, I can't say. I don't know him well enough. He seems to have been pretty hell-bent on avenging Clara... but then he's also been killing off anyone who could tell us anything. I just—" I yawn again. "—don't know."

"Is she all right? Angels don't usually tire this much," I hear Octavia ask, although it sounds far away.

"It's the stasis she has on Clara," Delilah answers. "She's running out of time."

I feel the warmth of Alaric's hand stroking my hair, then nothing.

I jolt upright in a bed.

"Hey, it's all right, Ev," Alaric says from beside me.

My heart is racing. "What day is it? How much time have I lost? Is Clara okay?"

"Hey, breathe. Just like you told Naomi to do earlier. It's still the same day, or night anyway. Raine texted; she's with Clara. Nothing has changed. It's all okay."

I flop back onto the bed with a harrumph, and he chuckles, the sound making my stomach knot up in delight. I turn my head and smile at him, more relaxed knowing that nothing has changed yet—that I haven't lost much time.

"You're beautiful when you smile, you know," he says as he looks down at me.

He cups my cheek with his warm palm, and I lean into it, allowing myself to enjoy the moment. Soaking in the warmth of his compliment.

When I start to become more aware, I realize the bed I'm on feels unfamiliar. I look back up at my partner and ask, "Where are we?"

"Still at Delilah's. This is one of her spare bedrooms. Once we're ready, we can head into work. The twins managed to track down that driver of Blake's. He's in the holding cells. He won't answer any questions. They're waiting for us." His smile turns grim as he remembers the part of the job he doesn't enjoy doing as much.

I try to squash my inner demon's thoughts about how sexy watching him work is. The thoughts crack through anyway—a combination of being too tired and the feelings too strong.

Alaric's stormy gray-blue eyes seem to twinkle, and I feel the connection there, transforming his negative thoughts into more positive ones.

It might make us a little psychotic, but we all have our kinks, right?

My inner demon snorts in derision, not at all agreeing with my assessment of us being turned on by the primitiveness of watching each other dominate in the torture room.

I stretch out, arching my back from the bed. I feel Alaric's heat the moment before he reaches down and kisses my lower stomach. I startle from the unexpected touch for a split second before my toes curl of their own accord, heat pulsing in my core. A moan slips from my lips as he kisses me again. This time dragging his tongue across my stomach before nipping me. I moan louder, the feeling more delectable than any I've experienced before in my long life.

"Are you two okay?" Delilah calls from outside the door.

I slap my hands over my mouth, feeling much like I imagine the teenagers on the television do when they are busted by a parent.

Alaric winks as he sits up, pulling my shirt down for me. "All good here. Ev has just woken up. We'll head off shortly."

"I have dinner ready in the kitchen before you go. See you down there shortly."

My partner's eyes are full of hunger and mirth, and all I want him to do is keep going.

If only that was on the table right now. Duty calls.

Duty can go fuck itself. There are more important things.

I cover my mouth again when I make some odd kind of a purr noise in my own chest. Heat fills my cheeks, completely embarrassed. Alaric's wolf rumbles back at me immediately, and I suddenly feel better. The heat bleeds from my cheeks, and I sit up.

He moves so I can get out of the bed, but his eyes stay glued to me the whole time. He watches every bend and stretch, and I fully accept my inner demon's advice to bite my lip before turning away to give him my back while I bend to pick up my boots.

Alaric pushes himself into me so hard from behind, I jolt forward and am forced to catch myself on the bed. I feel his hard length grind against me, and I push my face into the duvet to muffle my moan. I push myself back against him, grinding my arse into his cock, the buttons on his jeans making the sensation feel *more*.

His hands slide down and grab my arse, hard. He squeezes me, pulling me tighter against him. He takes his hands away, and I whimper. But they're back a moment later, moving my hair aside so that when he leans down against my back, he can also kiss my neck.

His wolf rumbles from deep in his chest while he groans my name, a prayer.

Oh, hells I want him so bad.

Need him. Inside. Now.

Hot, wet heat pools in my underwear, soaking them, getting me ready for him.

A bang on the door makes me want to growl and tell the witch to fuck off so I can get some. I only realize I've done exactly that when Alaric covers my mouth with his hand gently and whispers in my ear, "Shhh. Down girl."

"Dinner is getting cold, and someone named Tessa called looking for you both. They're having trouble with that demon."

It's like being doused in a bucket of cold bloody water. I sigh through my nose, which Alaric leaves uncovered.

He tips his face down beside me and kisses me gently. "Later," he whispers. "Besides, I want to be somewhere I can hear you scream for me."

A shiver runs through my entire body at the thought, making me want to pull him back to me, damning the circumstances to hell.

But he gets up, then lifts me from the waist to pull me back against him. "Come on, you sexy minx. Let's get moving before she breaks down the door to feed us."

When we walk into the dining room, a roast dinner is sitting on the table. One piece of meat is noticeably more bloody, so I leave it for my wolf and take the seat next to it.

"How are you doing, dear?" she asks me.

"I'm all right. Just tired. The sleep helped, though. Thank you for the food."

"Mmm, of course." In her no-nonsense way, Delilah decides to ask me straight up, "What do you know about the witchling from your vision? Have you found her yet? To help Clara."

I choke on the piece of beef in my mouth, and Alaric thuds my back a few times to help me clear it. "Sorry," I mutter.

Delilah looks between us both, then addresses him, hand on her hip. "What am I missing here?"

He looks at me, and I glare back at him.

"Oh, out with it. Now, girl. Or I'll do some hocus pocus and pull the thoughts from your brain."

I turn my glare to her for a moment before I can stop myself, the inner anger lighting my demon eyes up. "Yes, I know who it is. No, I don't particularly want to tell you," I grind out in a tone I usually reserve for people I don't like. I rub my temples, trying to get my emotions and tiredness to sort itself out.

She squints at me, clearly thinking through the options. I keep my mouth shut.

"It's Kiah," Alaric says, deadpan. "That's why she doesn't want to tell you."

Delilah opens her mouth, then closes it again. She repeats the process a couple of times until her features settle on confusion. "Why isn't this a good thing?"

I take a mouthful of potato, refusing to answer and upset the woman who's been so helpful.

She sighs, throwing her hands in the air in exasperation, then turns to Alaric since he's more responsive than me.

He shakes his head at me and snorts out a breath of air. "Because she's already said she won't help."

Delilah's mouth drops open, her eyes radiating hurt and disbelief.

I jump in quickly, not wanting to cause a rift between her and her daughter when they've just found each other. "She's just a child," I say. "It's not her responsibility. I'm not going to force her into anything. It's not my way. And Delilah"—I look into the woman's eyes, making sure she's hearing me—"you just got her back. The bond you two have is still building. Please don't damage such a gift because of someone else that neither of you particularly know."

She's frozen, unsure what to say, the thoughts a flurry in her head. I know she's thinking about the rules all witches follow, about helping the community. But my words have made an impact too.

I push my plate away, not hungry again—a familiar feeling of late. "We need to go and get the information from this demon. We'll check in later, okay?"

She nods, mutely.

Alaric stuff's more food in his mouth as he stands, his stomach grumbling in protest. I shake my head and walk to the door, needing to leave before the vault breaks open again, before I force a rupture in Delilah and Kiah's tenuous relationship.

DESPAIR

A TEXT FROM TESS tells us to head straight to the holding cells when we arrive—everyone in the office has gone home to rest since there's nothing further for them to do until we get something from the demon.

We arrive at the holding cell, and Alaric requests the demon, Foras, be moved back into the interrogation cell. The guards do their job while we both wait outside.

After several minutes, in which I assume they're securing the prisoner, they walk out and join us. "Several supes have already had a go. He hasn't cracked yet."

My eyes flash red. "I like a challenge."

The two vamp guards look me over curiously, coming to the usual assumption that I'm mostly harmless.

They'll see. Time to have some fun.

Alaric and I walk in, and I glance at him, the heat already in my eyes. "Me first?" I ask in a saccharine voice.

He laughs and gestures for me to take the reins.

Normally, my angelic self doesn't like this, but with my aura so absorbed in protecting my sister, my demonic side slips into control with ease.

Not to mention life is fucked right now. A little torture sounds delightful.

I look at Blake's belligerent friend, half beaten, and still not talking, and I let my father's power free—his parting gift in death.

My insides fill with the heat of the Hells, of rage, of revenge. I let it consume me, pull me in, my sole focus now on getting the information I need at any cost. A feral grin spreads across my face as I stalk forwards.

The demon starts to look concerned, and I laugh, loud and from my belly. I bend down in front of him, locking my gaze with his, letting it fill my expression, letting him see the death in my eyes.

"Are you sure you don't want to tell me who you're working for?" I whisper. "One last chance before you gift me the opportunity of hurting you?"

He looks less certain, but still, he shakes his head.

I release the full force of my power into my eyes, the glow drawing his own out. He seems to realize in this moment that he's fucked. He opens his mouth to speak, but I don't give him the chance, the rage riding me while my angelic aura is off saving my sister.

I place a hand on each of his temples and draw on the flames of the lowest level of the hellish realms, dragging them to the surface. I unleash the flames through my eyes and into his. His worst fears are drawn out from the deepest crevice of his charred soul, and I force them into his mind's eye.

The demon stands in the middle of a storm, young—just a child—lightning flickers in the distance. The boy begins to wail, looking for somewhere to run. I force the electric yellow streaks closer, blowing up objects, then the ground. He sprints, trying to escape, but there's no escaping me. The lightning strikes right in front of him, blasting a hole in the ground and throwing him off his feet. My wild laughter echoes through the stormy sky and five streaks hit down at once. He screams in his head.

He screams in the room.

The smell of piss assaults my senses.

"Stop! Make it stop!"

I try to draw myself out of the depravity of his mind, certain he's ready to talk.

Instead, I feel myself fall.

"You need to let me wake her up," Raine hisses from somewhere far away.

"You're not doing it," Alaric growls.

My brain feels like mush.

"You two fighting isn't going to help her," Tess says, voice strained.

What on Earth are they on about?

They both ignore Tess, who sighs. I can perfectly visualize her eye roll from wherever I'm lying.

"She needs to bloody know what's happening, Alaric. Stop being so damn overprotective."

"You didn't see her, Raine. She completely passed out. She was bleeding from her fucking ears," he growls back at her.

Bleeding out of my ears?

I really need to get up.

My eyes crack open a sliver, but I can't see anything.

My body feels so heavy. Too heavy.

"Ev?" Tess asks. "Are you awake, sweetie?"

I think that's what she's saying, but it fades away.

My body jolts back and forth, making my brain rattle in my head.

I try to say, "Stop," but it just comes out as a garbled groan.

"Ugh, thank goodness, Ev. You've been scaring the bejesus out of me."

"Huh?" I mumble, my throat completely dried out. I put a hand on the outside while I battle to reattach myself to the world, trying to tell Raine I need water.

"Here," she says. "I'm holding the straw."

Still half blind, I just open my mouth, hoping she gets the hint. Thankfully she does, and the next moment, cool water is moistening my parched throat. I take a few more gulps, until my esophagus no longer feels like sandpaper.

"Raine, what's going on?" I peel my eyes open to find I'm curled up in my bed. My best friend is sitting next to me, looking like she's ready to throw up. "What's wrong?" I demand, alarmed.

"What's the last thing you remember, Ev?"

I try to think, sure that she's looking for something in particular. "I remember something about... bleeding ears, but before that just working on the demon."

Alaric wanders in from outside the room having heard my voice. He looks just as worried as Raine. "Hi," he says, finding another spot in the room, leaving a noticeable distance from my friend.

I look between them. "What's going on with you two?" Dread forms a pit inside me, and I can feel the vault I'd built crack open, the hopelessness yawning and swallowing me whole.

Clara.

I jump out of the bed, sliding past both of them, and rushing to the door, a little unsteady.

"Ev, wait!" Alaric calls out to me but doesn't try to stop me.

Neither of them prevent me from leaving and somehow that makes it even worse. I'm stuck inside the yawning chasm of despair, not knowing if my sister is dead or alive.

Stop and think. You can tell the answer to this. She's in your aura.

But I can't stop. I can't think.

I rush into her room and see my twin. My heart freezes. The blackness has spread across her chest and is almost directly over her heart.

I shakily move closer, needing to touch her, but too scared to at the same time. Carefully I reach out. She's colder than she was, as though the poison is sucking away her heat. I force myself to breathe. To push out the panic.

I close my eyes and focus on my aura. The usual golden hue is stained black, so much worse than the touch of darkness I usually experience after using my father's power.

I turn to my sister and the last of the golden hue surrounding her, which is holding her locked in the stasis. But even that is tinged in black.

I truly am out of time.

I look up and see both Alaric and Raine standing in the doorway, and I can feel the desperation in my eyes. *Needing* them to help me. *Longing* for a solution.

"Kiah?" I beg Raine.

Pink tears are pouring down Raine's face. She shakes her head. "I'm sorry, Ev. She hasn't said anything." She looks to Clara. "Will you let me ask Kiah? Please?"

They both become fuzzy as tears flood my eyes.

This can't be happening.

I was so sure I could save her.

I feel Alaric sit and pull me into his lap, and I break. I'm consumed with hopelessness and despair, knowing I am out of time and out of options. He just holds me, his warmth the only anchor I have to the here and now, my soul feeling less and less connected, telling me it's ready to let go. A wave of panic makes me shiver. I'm not ready. I know Clara isn't either.

Alaric squeezes me into his chest.

Raine drops to her knees in front of me. She reaches out and takes my hands, desperation filling her. "Please, Ev," she whispers, voice breaking. "I know it isn't fair to ask, and I know it's not what you want, but *please*. Let her go." She sucks in a breath with her tears. "Clara wouldn't want this. She wouldn't want you to die alongside her. She'd want you to live. She's always wanted you to live. And I know it's selfish, but I need you. I really need you. Please. Stay."

I look at my best friend through my tears, wanting so badly to tell her I'll stay, to always be here for her. But I swore the same to my sister, my twin, after our parents died. I can't speak. I don't have the words she wants to hear.

It would be breaking one bond to keep another.

I can't. In this case, my promise to my sister outweighs all else. Her. Alaric. My own life. Clara told me to live a little more. I don't think she anticipated I would die for her.

I know Raine can see the answer in my eyes. The answer I don't want to say out loud.

She nods brokenly and stands. "Okay, Ev. Okay. I love you," she says and then blurs out of the room. Clearly not able to stay and watch me die.

I turn my face into Alaric. Into the only man I thought I could love, and I cry harder. I mourn, knowing all the possibilities I'm giving up with this life. Knowing that when I die, that's it. There is no afterlife for me. No place I'll find my parents and my sister, happy again and waiting. There's just nothing. We all just cease to exist.

Even knowing all of that. Even with the possibility of love with the man who's embracing me. Even knowing I have best friends who want me here. Need me here. I still can't let go of Clara.

My future just holds me patiently. Not asking me to stay, already knowing I can't. I breathe in Alaric's warmth and drown in my exhaustion, feeling the pull of my stasis, feeling my aura weaken with each passing moment.

I don't know how long I sit unmoving, but the ache in my muscles tells me it's too long. I ignore it. I deserve the punishment, the pain, knowing the heartache my dying will bring to all of my newfound friends when I leave this Earth and cease to exist.

"I'm so sorry, Alaric," I whisper into his ear.

"Shhh," he says. His voice sounds thicker than usual, like he's fighting back his own tears. "Don't apologize, Ev. Don't ever apologize for being you and doing what you believe is important. I'm here for you, okay."

I didn't think it was possible, but the brittle lines of my heart fracture more as I curl into Alaric and let the pain and despair wash over me.

REVELATIONS

I wake up in my bed again, and I can hear Tess and Alaric arguing outside the room.

"Guys, is everything all right?" I call.

They both rush in when they hear my voice. Tess comes straight to me. "Hey, sweetie, don't strain yourself, okay. I just came down here because I got some news about the case. You really don't need to worry, though. I just had to speak to Alaric about it."

I sit up, hollow on the inside.

Right, the case.

"Did the demon talk? Before I... before I had to come back here." I look up at Alaric, trying to raise my eyebrows to show him I'm asking him a question, but feeling sure they aren't really complying.

I sigh. A sliver of frustration coming over me at the weakness in my body.

Alaric comes closer, his face a stone mask. "Tell her, Tess, or I will. She deserves to know."

For once, he's on the other side of this argument.

I look at Tess, waiting, hopeful that the case at least came to a happier resolution. Or that it maybe stopped with the demon.

Tess is teary now, and shakes her head, refusing to answer.

I try to tell her with my eyes that it's all right. Whatever it is, it doesn't matter. That it's okay.

She just looks away.

Instead, I turn to Alaric, my rock, the one I know won't hide the truth from me, no matter how ugly.

He nods, resolute. "The demon is dead. Nicon went in after I pulled you out. I—I watched the video later. The demon kept chanting something under his breath. He was completely unintelligible after you finished with him. But it was the same word over and over. Nicon couldn't make sense of it. He obliterated the demon. Basically lit him on fire and burned him from the inside out before ripping his limbs off one at a time while he was still alive. Still screaming that one word until Nicon removed his head."

I try to be shocked at Nicon's madness, but I barely feel anything. The demon deserved it after all the torture inflicted on the girl and all his other victims.

"Did we manage to find the other supes? Or their location at least?" I ask emotionlessly.

"No. We're back to being at a dead end after not really getting anything from the demon."

The dead look in Alaric's eyes tells me there's more. That something else has happened. "What else aren't you telling me?

You promised you'd always tell me the truth," I implore. "Don't shut me out again. Not now."

"I—" He closes his eyes and takes a breath, then looks at me. "You're right. I just… don't want to make things worse right now."

What could be worse? Do I really want to know?
Of course.

I lay the remainder of my shattered heart on the table and nod to Alaric, telling him I want to know. That I *need* the answer.

"It's Naomi," he says without any further delay. "She—"

I feel my head shaking back and forth in denial.

No. Not her too.

"She hung herself, Ev. When no one had seen her come out of her house in too long, they sent someone in to check. There were pictures everywhere of the demon. Of his eyes. She was some kind of artist. We were too late. She died looking into the eyes of that monster she'd drawn."

My heart breaks apart, the pieces floating down to dust on the earth.

In the place of my heart, I feel heat. A raging, fiery heat. I stand up, causing both Alaric and Tess to move back. I feel like I'm made from a sliver of hell.

"The word," I say to Alaric, my voice as dead as my heart feels. "What was the word the demon kept saying?"

"No one could figure out what it meant, it wasn't really clear." He reaches out to me. "Ev, you should lay back down. Rest. You don't have enough energy left."

I stare hard at him with my raging eyes, the redness glowing and reflecting off the television on the chest of drawers. "The word. What was it?"

But I already know. Some part of me has already figured it out.

His face is filled with concern as he tells me. "Azrul, or Arzul, or—"

"Arzule," I hiss. "It's the surname Blake uses in the human world."

The fire inside me burns away the last vestiges of hurt. No space left beside the fury. "What?" Tess says, her voice showing her complete shock. "Why would he be capturing and killing all those humans and framing other species? Why would he banish all those demons? His own kind."

I turn my flaming eyes to her, and she flinches. I don't have the space left to care. The only thing that matters right now is killing that fucker. "I intend to find out."

Tess holds her position by the door despite the waves of pure fury radiating from me. "How can we find him, though?" she asks. "No one, not even Nicon, has been able to actually locate him."

"There's no need," I grind out. "I'll simply invite him in. He's been dying to see Clara."

In that moment, it clicks. His desperation to see her, the way he killed any demon who might have a shred of information. How angry he was about the two men in the bar who genuinely cared about Clara. He's responsible for all the deaths.

The vision drags me in, a sheen of fire over it.

Blake resting above me.
Stroking my cheek.
He jumps up and I watch the defined muscles in his back.
Ready for round two.
He brings my drink.
Biting his lip, he tips it up to my mouth.
Sex and pain in his eyes like always.
An elixir.
It tastes wrong.
"Blake, what—"
I cough and splutter.
"Why?" I ask. Confused.
The only man I've ever cared for.
His eyes turn orange in their fury.
"Because your father killed mine. Their death battle stole the only family I had. Now I'm going to watch you die. And then I'm going to kill your worthless sister."
Pain ricochets down my throat.
Can't breathe.
"Leave... Everleigh..."
"Oh no, there's no saving her. Your family will be wiped from existence."
Silk sheets. Too soft. Can't hold on.
Can't breathe.
Need to warn Everleigh.

Need help.
Blackness calls.
Can't hold on.
Need.
Air.
Need—

A scream tears from my throat as I float out of the vision. The rage feels like it will swallow me whole. I'm on fire. I need to let some of it out. I can't give it the last of my control.

I pick up the closest thing in reach, unable to stop the flaming fury. The lamp in my hands explodes. Shards fly everywhere. The electricity from the cord and explosion zaps me.

The lights short out. And still I'm full of rage.

"Everleigh!" Alaric yells at me. "Stop. You're going to kill us all, including Clara. What in the hells did you just see? Tell us, so we can help."

"You're not in this alone, Ev. You have us, remember," Tess calls from her new spot in the doorway.

Safer to be away from me right now.

Save it. For Blake.

He's going to pay.

If we're going out, he's coming with us.

Blake is going to pay.

I snatch my phone off the bedside table, surprised it's still in one piece. I force my volatile emotions into a place of calm. They're no use if they burn out too soon.

We're not leaving this Earth without that piece-of-shit demon.

I unlock my phone and send a text.

Me: I've changed my mind. Clara is getting worse. I don't think she's going to make it. Come quickly.

Blake: She better not die before I get there. I'm coming.

"Oh, of course not," I mutter darkly, the rage simmering beneath the surface now. "You want to *watch* her die."

"Uh, Ev?" Tess mutters. "What is happening?"

"He did this to Clara, too, didn't he?" Alaric asks with a growl, his eyes becoming the silver of his wolf.

I look at him, my grin as feral and angry as I feel. "Yes. His true family name is Azrilarthius. Our fathers killed each other. He did this for revenge. And he's going to pay for it with this life."

A full growl rips free of Alaric, and my inner demon responds in kind. The call for vengeance now radiating from us both.

I turn my flaming gaze in the direction of my sister. "He'll be here shortly. And I'll be ready."

"He's coming here?" Tess demands. "Now?"

"Yes." I march past her and down the hall to my twin.

I lean down and kiss her cheek, trying to ignore the massive black mess that is her chest and the golden black aura surrounding her, now more darkness than light.

"I'll kill him for this, Sister. I love you."

I kiss her other cheek, then stand and turn to face my friends.

"Where's Raine?" I demand.

"I'm not sure, Ev," Tess says too gently for the inferno raging inside me. "I think she was finding it too hard to be here now."

I nod.

Fine. It's better this way.

I try to ignore the pain in my hollow chest that was once a fully functioning, if somewhat bruised, heart.

"Tess, can you guard my sister?"

She looks as though she wants to object, not wanting to be down here while I stand off against Blake. I walk to her and clasp her arms, letting some of the pain bleed into my eyes. The pain of loss and mourning. The grief I'm denying to finish this. To avenge us both.

"Please. I need someone to be with her."

She pulls me into a tight hug. "Okay," she says, voice cracking. "I'll stay with her. But please, Ev, don't die. We all need you here with us."

I smile at my friend. The one who could have become another sister, like Raine has. I watch the tears stream down her face. Knowing my smile is a goodbye, I kiss each of her cheeks. "Blessed be, Tessa. It's been an honor."

Unable to witness her pain any longer, I turn and walk out the door. I make my way past Alaric, and up the stairs, knowing he'll follow me. To the ends of the Earth, not just up some stairs.

Maybe even to his own death.

The thought stirs more anger. I won't let Alaric get hurt. Clara and I will be Blake's final victims.

And Blake will be mine.

When I reach the top of the stairs, I turn and grab Alaric. I pull him to me and kiss him fiercely. All the anger, all the pain, all the heat pours into the man who could have been my love.

The passion in the kiss feels like a promise and a farewell.

It feels like acceptance of my fate.

My acceptance.

And his.

I release him, my senses telling me Blake is coming. The wards buckle, trying to keep him and his bad intentions out. I forcefully override them.

"It's time," I state. And move to a better vantage point with a more open space—the living room.

What a waste.

I look at Alaric. "Make sure he can't leave once he enters," I demand.

He nods. Firm. Resolute. Stoic.

My rock.

Blake's arrival is marked by the thumps on the door. One bang after another. I release the swirling fury inside me.

Ready.

Death is his fate.

I look at Alaric, my could-have-been love. I take one last second to drink him in—a second I wish would last an eternity. Then I turn my fiery red gaze to the door.

It's time.

"Open it."

FURY

Blake storms into the room, and Alaric slams the door shut behind him. He locks it, then leans against it.

Blake sneers at him, then turns back to me. "So you know then."

No preamble. No fucking around.

The truth.

Finally.

"Oh yes. I know it was all you. The human victims. Framing the other supernaturals. Banishing all those demons. My *sister*." My anger swirls over. "How much you must have hated it. Pretending with Clara. Just so you could kill her later."

"She deserved it. You both do," he spits out at me. "Your father killed mine. I had to live my life with no one. I have no twin to call home. Why should you have each other?"

"Your filthy excuse for a demon father killed both our parents. What do you have to say to that?"

"They. Deserved. It."

I hiss, flames blazing behind my eyes. "And what about the humans? Framing the other supernaturals? Banishing the demons?"

He snorts in derision. "Power. Of course. Once I get rid of you both, I'll be able to reveal my connection to my father and regain his legacy. My biggest competition has been banished. The humans will hate most supernaturals." His nose scrunches, pulling his face into a sneer. "But not the poor, misunderstood demons. They didn't hurt anyone. Then I will have my seat at the top of the Council. All will bow down before me, and the Azrilarthius demons will rule once more."

He pulls fire to his hands.

I release my wings and unsheathe my blades.

My inner demon fills my voice, and I let her take control.

"Time to die."

He launches the first fireballs, and I blast them back with my wings, and move to the side. He roars at me in rage. I force my wings into the ether, running at Blake, and slash out with one blade, then the next.

He ducks and I growl.

Blake comes for me, punching with the heat of his flame. It sears my skin. I laugh, feral, at one with my inner demon and the fires of the hells. I push that heat down the length of my blades. The fire engraving words around them—black and red. Pain and death.

I rush Blake, slicing out with the blade in my right hand. He dodges, turning his back to me. I laugh as the blade in my left hand draws fire across his Achilles tendon. He turns back. Pain and fury in his eyes.

"Yes. Demon. Feel my wrath. Feel the fires of hell you so love."

"You fucking hybrid bitch." He launches off his one good leg, his punch connecting with my stomach. The fire lights up my insides, and I force what's left of my angelic light into the heat, extinguishing it completely.

It's no longer enough to simply slice him. I flip the blades in my hands into position to stab him.

I brave his flame, feeling it burn into me again. Knowing I have no angelic warmth left to burn out. It doesn't matter. I'm dying anyway. All that matters is taking this bastard with me.

I stab one blade into his stomach. The other into his ribs. The black and red flames begin to consume him from the inside.

I take a half-step back, moving out of his reach. His hands drop to his sides.

The heat burns within me.

It burns within him.

Flames and fury. Years of hatred.

It's not enough.

I stumble closer to him again and pull the blade from his ribs. I jam it into the other side of his stomach, relishing the scream that follows the movement.

His body jerks. Blood pours from his mouth.

It's still not enough.

I rip the other blade from his stomach.

"For the pain you caused my sister."

I lift the blade with two hands above my head. The fire of all the hellish realms is within my grasp, and I plunge it into his cold, angry heart.

I watch as the hellish flames consume him. This will be no mere banishment, but a final death.

The ebony and crimson flames move within him, and I watch them shine through from beneath the surface. Watch the hate and flames consume him from the inside out.

Hatred fills his face as he loses the battle with the deathly flames. One moment he's looking at me. The next, he's ash.

A distant nightmare.

My blades clatter to the ground in a heap. I drop to the ground and my own hellish flames desert me. I feel myself falling, and Alaric catches me, but it doesn't matter.

Blake's fire is inside me, eating away the last of my power reserves. Each moment they move through my body, my aura thins.

My hold on Clara is slipping. Reality is slipping.

"Alaric," I murmur. "Take me to Clara, please."

I feel him lift me. The world feels strange.

I feel light.

Too light.

Like I'm empty.

I hear Alaric talk to Tess as we enter the room, but I don't know what they say.

The flames burn inside me.

All I want is Clara.

After too long, he lays me beside her on the bed. I turn my head. "He's gone now, Clara. You're safe," I whisper. "I'm here." I reach out a hand, feebly trying to find my twin's. To hold it in mine.

Someone understands.

They move my sister's hand to mine.

I look at her, watching as my power drains away. I feel it, the moment the stasis fades. My sister's eyes flash open. Her other hand flies to her throat.

I squeeze her hand, pulling her attention to me.

Her head turns. Her eyes are panicked, and I feel myself fading.

I use what little energy I have left to push out, "He's gone, Sister. I killed him for us. We're safe."

Her panic fades, and so does the light from her eyes. I feel my own follow. My sister is the last thing I see.

LIGHT
ALARIC

I watch the light in Everleigh's eyes begin to fade, and I crash to my knees, barely able to feel it when they connect with the floor. All I can do is stare. Eyes wide. Not wanting to miss the last seconds of her life. I want to stop it from happening, but I can't. I don't have the magic Everleigh did. I would have given her everything I had if it would keep her alive.

But I can't. I'm stuck watching her fade. It's the worst experience of my life.

My ears pick up noise upstairs, and my senses force me to pay attention. A flurry of feet are rushing down the stairs. My body stills, ready for the attack. To protect my dying angel. But I register the voices.

Tess, leading people down. I didn't even know she had left the room.

I look back at the first real light in my life, watching her slowly peter out.

"Oh, God. We're too late," I hear Raine call from the doorway.

Then I see her, moving close. Hesitant. Not knowing what to do.

"Not a stasis, Raphael," Delilah demands. "Just keep their hearts beating."

He moves around me, swift and soundless. Light.

The Archangel goes to the head of the bed and places a hand on each twin. A golden light radiates from him, surrounding them both. He closes his eyes. Focusing. The golden light begins to pulse in a steady rhythm.

Delilah draws my attention by crouching down in front of me. "What has she been hit with?" she asks urgently.

"Demon flames," I say quietly, unable to look away from Everleigh.

The witch tsks. "Raphael, can you take care of that?"

The archangel nods, his eyes still closed. A slight frown mars his features while he works on ridding her body of the flames while ensuring their hearts continue to beat.

"Come on, Kiah. I'll do this with you. Come closer."

I turn, my eyes immediately finding the girl with the copper hair. Rage burns in my gut at the girl who could have saved them both but chose not to. I'm on my feet in an instant, but Raine blocks my way before I can take a step.

I growl low in my throat, my wolf trying to tear its way free.

The usually joyful vampire looks into my soul. "Wait, please. Give them a chance," she pleads.

I stand, frozen. Needing to do something. Anything.

The pain building to intolerable levels as Everleigh lies there. The only thread keeping her here, Raphael's holy light. I force myself to step back. To let them work. It goes against every instinct to allow them so close to Everleigh when she's so weak.

Raine stares a moment longer, assessing me. Making sure I'm not going to go for the girl's throat.

To the newly emerged young witch's credit, she manages to ignore me.

Delilah coaches her with a soothing voice. "That's it, Kiah. Place your hands over the darkest of the poison."

Kiah places both hands on Clara's chest, a slight shake to them.

"Breathe. Remember. Visualize the obsidian. Find it through the sensation. The body feels *right*. It's all as it should be. You'll know the poison when you feel it."

"I've got it," she murmurs, voice strained.

"Good, Kiah, good. Now focus. Send your flames into the obsidian. *Only* the obsidian. Find every trace. Burn it all away."

I move closer silently.

A quick glance at Everleigh tells me Raphael has removed the demonic flames. The pulsing light continues to keep her tethered.

I glance back at Clara and my eyes widen in shock. Beneath her skin, a golden flame emerges. It starts at the darkest, densest point of the poison, and slowly spreads. A carefully controlled blaze inside her body, burning away the blackness, and leaving her skin untouched.

I watch, mesmerized, as the last of Kiah's golden fire peters out.

She takes her hands off Clara's chest and stands tall. The young witch turns to me, her chin lifted, defiance and pride lining her features.

I nod in recognition and respect for the power she wields. She nods back, looking somewhat awkward now that her part is finished. Delilah ushers her away, whispering in her ear as she does. "You were brilliant my love. You are going to change the world."

Right now, I couldn't give a shit if she'll change the world. All I want is Everleigh.

The look Kiah gives her mother is full of a love that long since passed from my life. I turn back to Everleigh and move closer again. Raine comes to my side. We both watch the two women's almost lifeless bodies.

I use my wolf senses to listen to their forced heartbeats.

The room is silent for the longest time. I take up vigil beside Everleigh and wait. Listening, and praying, and hoping for a miracle. Knowing if anyone could grant such a thing, it's the archangel in this room.

I know we're not like humans. Once we go beyond the veil, there is no way to bring us back. But I hold onto my last shred of hope and just listen.

I kneel and rest the top of my head against the side of her stomach.

Waiting.

Breathing.

Hoping.

Listening.

Then I hear it. A change in her heartbeat. I lift my head and look at her. At her sister. At the Archangel. He nods to me once, and his golden light withdraws from the twins.

Their hearts are beating on their own.

In sync.

Strong.

Raphael ushers the witches from the room, leaving Raine and I alone with Everleigh and Clara. I don't spare Raine a glance right now, though. My world lies on the bed in front of me.

I listen to her strong heart, and I wait.

Nothing else matters.

A minute passes.

An hour.

An eternity.

She opens her golden eyes, a soft smile pulling up her lips, and joy explodes through me. Tears fill my eyes.

My light has returned.

DO YOU WANT TO FIND OUT HOW EVERLEIGH GOT STUCK WITH HER ROLE AS AN ENFORCER FOR FIFTY YEARS?

Head over to www.shaylaurent.com and when you sign up to my monthly newsletter, you get Haunted By Legacy, the prequel novella, for free!

DID YOU ENJOY THIS STORY?

If you did, please consider leaving a review on your favourite platform, it makes all the difference in helping other readers to discover my worlds.

Meet The Author

SHAY LAURENT

Shay is a fantasy author who lives in south-western Sydney with her partner, three young princesses, and three pretty kitties. Aside from getting all the cuddles, her life mostly involves psychology, writing, and photography—not necessarily in that order.

Long before Shay started writing, she fell in love with all things fantasy. She thrives on escaping into the magic and mayhem of other authors, and spinning the tales that run wild in her mind in her own books.

You can join Shay's reader group and connect with her on socials by visiting https://linktr.ee/slauthor03.

ACKNOWLEDGEMENTS

THANK YOU

My dear reader, thank you for taking the time to escape into *Burned By Fury*. I know each moment in our lives is precious and I'm grateful you decided to spend some of yours here. I hope you enjoyed reading this novel as much as I enjoyed crafting it.

Burned By Fury would not have come together without the support of some wonderful people, and I would love to take the time to thank them here.

Shannon, Kelsey & Jen—you made the dream real! Thank you all for the countless hours on reading and editing. For the enthusiasm on my good days, but especially on the bad ones. This book wouldn't have made it to *'The End'* without each of you. All of the late night chats, troubleshooting ideas, and making exciting marketing plans made this process a joy, and I'm eternally grateful.

To the team at Hot Tree Editing—you are all amazing! Donna, thank you for the speedy replies and for all your patience when making the arrangements. Mandy, many thanks for your wonderful final eyes read. I thoroughly enjoyed your insightful comments! Becky, once again, you are amazing. I love your thoughtful, constructive feedback, and your play-by-play impressions. I always have reason to smile when I get your edits. Most importantly, I felt I improved my writing craft with your support. I look forward to working together on the next story!

My cover designer—Julie, your amazing cover art was the inspiration behind this series, so without a doubt, this world wouldn't exist without you! You are brilliant to work with—your creativity, flexibility, and willingness to rise to a challenge make this part of the process one of my favourites. I'm excited for our next creative adventure.

Finally, thank you to my partner, princesses, and kitties. You all give me the joy in life to *want* to write and share the stories in my mind. I love you all, always.

www.ingramcontent.com/pod-product-compliance
Lightning Source LLC
Chambersburg PA
CBHW020253120726
47904CB00001B/183